Samuel J. (Samuel John) Bayard

The Life of George Dashiell Bayard

Late Captain, U.S.A., and Brigadier-General of Volunteers, Killed in the...

Samuel J. (Samuel John) Bayard

The Life of George Dashiell Bayard
Late Captain, U.S.A., and Brigadier-General of Volunteers, Killed in the...

ISBN/EAN: 9783337091194

Printed in Europe, USA, Canada, Australia, Japan

Cover: Foto ©Raphael Reischuk / pixelio.de

More available books at **www.hansebooks.com**

THE LIFE

OF

GEORGE DASHIELL BAYARD,

LATE CAPTAIN, U. S. A.,
AND
BRIGADIER-GENERAL OF VOLUNTEERS,

KILLED IN THE BATTLE OF FREDERICKSBURG, DEC. 1862.

BY

SAMUEL J. BAYARD.

NEW YORK:
G. P PUTNAM'S SONS,
FOURTH AVENUE AND TWENTY-THIRD STREET.
1874

INTRODUCTION.

FOR a number of years I have been frequently solic-
ited by my family, and by many friends of my son,
the late General Bayard, to prepare and publish a *Memoir*
of his brief career. Though such a tribute was due to
his memory, nevertheless the effort to render it, was felt
by me to be so painful, that I have too long shrunk from
making it.

But my advancing years admonish me, not to postpone any longer the execution of what I consider a
sacred duty.

The ample correspondence of General Bayard has
enabled me to give a correct narrative of his life, in a
great measure written by himself.

From his letters the reader will obtain a better
knowledge of his character, principles, and motives of
action, than any more elaborate biography could furnish.

The record of his life needs neither apology nor
defence. He was as faultless as a son, a brother, and
a gentleman, as the most fastidious and exacting could

wish. The motto of the great Captain, who made illustrious his name, was ever the inspiration of his life—
"*Sans peur et sans reproche.*"

To my grandchildren, the nephews and nieces of
General Bayard, and to the young military aspirant, I
commend the study of his history. Let them emulate
his noble character and his ardent patriotism, his generosity, his affection for his family, his dauntless courage, and his exemplary performance of every duty
devolved upon him.

SAMUEL J. BAYARD.

CONTENTS.

CHAPTER VI.

CHAPTER VII.

CHAPTER VIII.

CHAPTER IX.

CHAPTER X.

CHAPTER XI.

CHAPTER XII.

CHAPTER XIII.

CHAPTER XIV.

CHAPTER XV.

CHAPTER XVI.

LIFE OF

GEORGE DASHIELL BAYARD.

CHAPTER I.

Nativity—At school in St. Louis Mo.,—Boyhood on the Prairie.

GREAT Revolutions are distinguished by the appearance of new men emerging from obscurity. Opportunity invites the development of talents, and the field of strife and danger is soon crowded with aspirants to fortune and fame, who were before unknown.

The English Revolution in the seventeenth century, and the French Revolution in the succeeding century, each furnished a brilliant array of statesmen and soldiers, who then first became historical—arbiters of peace and war, and architects of empire.

The American Revolution, by which the independence of the United States was established, was no less fertile in the production of distinguished characters. A host of statesmen and soldiers whose names were previously known only in limited circles, then soon became illustrious throughout the civilized world.

Our recent civil war, and the social and constitutional changes which it produced, may well be said to constitute a second American Revolution. In its progress, as in other Revolutions, there suddenly sprang from comparative obscurity, many, both in civil and in military life, whose names will be remembered in history.

Lieutenants, Captains, and Colonels in the regular army, and not a few politicians in civil life, became on one side and the other Brigadier, Major and Lieutenant-Generals. Some of these sudden elevations only developed incapacity, while others revealed abilities of the highest order. Thanks to the admirable training of West Point, there were few conspicuous failures among the new-made generals, of those who were graduates of the U. S. Military Academy.

We propose in the following pages giving a sketch of the brief career of one of the soldiers of the Union Army, who though unknown previously, out of military circles, rose rapidly to distinction, and in fifteen months gained a reputation familiar to the whole country.

George Dashiell Bayard was born at Seneca Falls, Seneca County, New York, December 18th, 1835. His father having relinquished the profession of law, had in 1833, purchased some real estate at Seneca Falls, Seneca County, New York, and taken up his residence there.

In the appendix will be found some account of the ancestry of Bayard—interesting to his relatives and family friends : though it may be thought of little value by the general reader.*

No intelligent estimate can be formed of the future man, from the first eight or ten years of boyhood. Precocity is a promise seldom verified by manhood.

Young Bayard was a docile, affectionate and intelli gent child. He was healthy, but not robust,—generous

* See Appendix A and D.

in disposition, and easily controlled by an appeal to his good sense or his affections.

After learning at home to read, he commenced when five or six years of age, going to school, where he soon made good progress in the first elements of knowledge.

In 1843, his father removed with his family to Iowa, then recently organized as a territory.

On the way to Iowa, while at St. Louis, his father formed the acquaintance of Major A. J. Dorn, who had established a school for boys, which was to a limited extent military in discipline and organization. The pupils were dressed in uniform, taught the manual exercise and drilled regularly. Bayard was placed in charge of Major Dorn, and continued at his school for two years. At the St. Louis school the subject of this narrative formed, probably, his predilection for the career of a soldier. His teacher became much attached to him, and gave the most favorable report of his deportment and progress. He seemed to have the faculty of inspiring with affection all who became intimate with him.

His fencing master was the celebrated Col. Korponay, the Hungarian exile. Korponay, pleased with the intelligence and manly bearing of his pupil, became very fond of him, and always saluted him with the title of the Little General.

About six years afterwards, it appeared from the papers that a revolution had commenced in Hungary in resistance to Austrian tyranny; and it was announced that Korponay was about to return to his country to help achieve her liberty. Bayard, without consulting his parents, immediately addressed a letter to Korponay asking permission to go with him as his *aide.* The letter probably never reached the gallant patriot, as he had already sailed, and no response to it was ever received.

The school of Major Dorn was given up by him, about a couple of years after Bayard was placed there, and he returned to his parents at Fairfield, Iowa, where he attended the village school. About this time a Camanche pony was presented to him by a relative. Though probably thirty years old, he still had the spirit and vigor of a colt—and was capable of great endurance. No fence was an impediment to him, and when out of his stable he went where he pleased. He was so docile that he would come whenever called by his young master, and would eat anything from his hand. As soon as the prairie chickens were grown, Bayard and his pony roved the prairie in pursuit of them, and always came home loaded with game.

But hunting and chasing the prairie wolves at other seasons was the favorite sport of Bayard.

Some of his friends among the young men of the neighborhood would accompany him with their hounds ; and often from sunrise to sundown, over the large prairies in the vicinity, pursued their game.

His parents preferred that he should thus spend his holidays and leisure time, rather than with other boys lounge around the village and fields. The exercise tended to develop his strength, while in his rough experience there was enough of risk and danger to excite his courage and influence his character.

Though his health was uniformly good, he was by no means athletic, but rather delicate in appearance, owing to his rapid growth. His habits and prairie life at this time probably exerted a happy effect on his constitution, and were doubtless the cause of his ultimate physical strength and capacity for endurance.

On one occasion when in his tenth year, with the permission of his parents, he started off alone on his pony, to pay a visit to his cousins who had recently settled sixty miles off, on the Des Moines river. After he had overstaid the time prescribed for his absence, his father began to be anxious respecting his safety. But as he was about setting out to go for him, the young gentleman rode up enveloped in the plumage of turkeys, wild geese, prairie grouse and other game with which his pony was covered.

He had no intimates among boys of his own age, and seemed to prefer the companionship of his father to other associates. He was fond of reading and never required urging in the prosecution of his studies.

At his earnest solicitation—though not by two years of the proper age for admission to West Point as a cadet, his father made application for him, for the vacancy which would occur in 1851, for the first Congressional District of Iowa. Both the Senators from that State and the Member of Congress for the district, supported the application, and filed in the engineers' department recommendations in his favor, and had he remained in that State, he would probably have received his cadet appointment for that district.

CHAPTER II.

Removes to Trenton, New Jersey—At School in New York—In Morristown, New Jersey—Appointed a Cadet by Mr. Fillmore— Preparation for Examination—Admission.

IN the spring of 1849, his father having returned to New Jersey, Bayard was sent to school at the Academy in Trenton. After a year's residence there his parents removed to New York city, and their son was placed at one of the excellent free schools there.

Again his family changed their residence, and Morristown became his home in 1851. Notwithstanding these changes, Bayard's studies were prosecuted with diligence and improvement. He had made good progress with his Latin, and was pretty well grounded in the common branches of an English education. He wrote with facility, and occasionally would write for the newspapers articles of considerable merit. But being intent on going to West Point, his studies were pursued with reference to his admission to the Military Academy.

Under a very competent instructor, Mr. Crane, of Morristown, he devoted considerable time to mathematics, and under Mr. Luna, a Spanish teacher, commenced the study of Spanish.

At the commencement of the session of Congress of 1851-52, the father of Bayard applied to Mr. Brown, the Member of Congress for the district to which Morristown belonged, for the cadetship in his gift, there being a vacancy for that district.

Mr. Brown and Bayard's father had been friends from boyhood, as were *their* fathers before them, and Mr. Brown it was thought would not refuse to appoint him. But he deemed it his duty to be governed in his selection by political considerations, and expressed his sincere regret that he could not with proper regard to his political friends appoint young Bayard.

He appointed in succession two young gentlemen, sons of his political friends, neither of whom remained at West Point more than a few months.

Commodore Stockton, then a Senator from New Jersey, in the winter of 1852, asked from Mr. Fillmore, then President, the appointment of Bayard as cadet *at large*.

It so happened that Mr. Fillmore had then sixteen cadets to be appointed at large. For these appointments there were several hundred applicants. Mr. Miller, the colleague in the Senate of Commodore Stockton, was an applicant in behalf of his son. The President however complied with the recommendation of Senator Stockton, and appointed Bayard a cadet at large.

In August 1856, the father of Bayard having sent to Mr. Fillmore a copy of his *Life of Commodore Stockton*, received from him a reply, from which we give the following extract:

"I am gratified to hear that your son has graduated with so much distinction at West Point. I hope and trust that this is but the bud of promise, which will soon unfold its full blown honors to himself and country. I congratulate you upon being the father of such a son.

"Truly yours,   MILLARD FILLMORE."

Mr. Fillmore was censured acrimoniously by the Whig papers in New Jersey for his preference of Com. Stockton's nominee, while his action was highly commended by the political friends of the Commodore. The son, whose appointment as a cadet Senator Miller desired, was a young gentleman of merit ; he offered his services to the government early in the war, and was distinguished for gallantry and good conduct, rising rapidly in the service, but when a Lieutenant Colonel was prematurely cut off by disease, and died universally lamented.

Stimulated by the notoriety which the papers had given to his appointment, and determined to vindicate the preference of Senator Stockton and Mr Fillmore, Bayard applied himself vigorously, under his friend and teacher Mr. Crane, in preparation for his examination at West Point in June. He was pretty well grounded in the rudiments of a common school education and felt little apprehension as to his ability to stand a satisfactory examination—but this confidence did not induce him to relax his industry, and he continued his preparatory studies to the last. His chief solicitude was, respecting his being able to satisfy the surgeon's inspection as to his physique.

Every candidate for admission to the Military Academy, besides the examination to which he is subjected as to his proficiency in the common branches of reading, writing and arithmetic, must submit to an examination by the resident surgeon of the Academy, of his freedom from disease, and any defect of limb, lungs, or constitution. Bayard, now sixteen years of age, having grown very rapidly in the previous two or three years—

was tall and slender; and though strong and vigorous, had the appearance of a youth of rather delicate organization. Dr. Cuyler, the surgeon at West Point, informed some of the friends of Bayard, that owing to these appearances, he felt great solicitude respecting his capacity to endure the rigorous discipline of the Academy—but that his great regard for his family—with many of whom he was intimate—induced him to overlook the indications of want of strength which his examination revealed, and trust to that development of youthful health which West Point life so often realized, in justification of his favorable report. He manifested the soundness of his judgment and his sagacity by this conclusion.

Thanks to the previous active life of Bayard, exercise in the open air only served to develop his strength and improve his health. He gained in flesh and weight from the time of his admission to the Academy, and graduated a strong though not robust man, with a sound constitution, capable of enduring all the hardships of the camp and the severe cavalry duty on the Western Plains.

The West Point life of Cadet Bayard will be better told in his own language than by the narrative of another. His letters give in detail, a pretty accurate account of the training, discipline and management of the Military Academy. They are likewise interesting, as indicative of his habits, tastes, and character. They will show, that while zealous to perform his duty, he was inspired with generous aims and a lofty ambition. His correspondence therefore will be given in full, omitting only those portions of it which relate to his family.

To his Mother.

" WEST POINT, *June* 3*d*, 1852.

" I suppose you will expect a letter from me, to learn how I like this place. Know then, that a harder, or more severe workhouse is not to be found anywhere : I hate it. We are treated by the cadets of the other classes with such indignity that I feel like shooting every villain of them : If I could leave with honor I would do so at once.

" I am threatened with a return of my old complaint, the quinsy, and I fear may have to take a turn in the hospital. I have not the heart to write further, for I feel decidedly bad."

To the same.

"WEST POINT, *June* 4*th*.

" I feel better to-day and am in better spirits. As I learn the rules better, I get along pleasantly.

" I fear I have been reported three times, in which case I will have the exquisite pleasure of walking sentry this evening. But all arises from ignorance of the rules, as they are neither written nor printed. An officer came up last night and told us different regulations and duties, but as there were so many of them, we could not recollect the half of them. But experience will soon give me command of them, so that by the time of the examination I will perhaps be pretty well versed in them.

" We are drilled morning and night, about an hour and a half, on the stretch, besides several other times during the day."

To his Sister.

" WEST POINT, *June* 9*th*, 1852.

" Upon going to parade ground for drill, I received the intelligence, welcome or unwelcome, that I was upon the sick list, and must go to my quarters. I have therefore a good hour and a half to indite some more of my experience of cadet life.

"There is one thing pretty certain about it, and that is, that it is not the exceedingly moral, the extraordinarily polite, or the surpassingly superior thing it is thought to be, by aspiring young men, seeking fame at the cannon's mouth.

"Mother is entirely mistaken if she supposes that I do not make allowance for the *peculiar* character of the school or its objects, or that I did not expect to experience rigor and severity of discipline. I did expect all this; I did anticipate weary work and hardship; but never anything like the dog's life and slaving toil to which we are subjected. Had I foreseen anything of the kind Master Miller might have had his appointment and welcome.

"But as mother and father wish me to succeed in passing through here with honor, I shall not flinch, but use my best endeavor to gratify them. I will not relinquish my efforts while my health permits.

"Last Saturday I was promoted at drill above six or eight of the "chaps" into the third squad, and would undoubtedly have been promoted at the next drill, if I had not been ordered to the hospital.

"We are marched by our officers to and from meals, which, for one thing, are better than I expected. Upon entering the mess-room we take our places and remain standing until the officer cries in a loud sonorous voice, 'Take seats' when we all sit down. The '*plebs*' have separate tables from the cadets at one end of the room, and the cadets are marched to the mess-room and take their seats before we enter.

" When done, they (the cadets) rise at the word "cadets rise" and are marched to their quarters. When we are done, we rise at the cry "candidates rise," and then we are marched to our quarters. You must know that we are not recognized as cadets, by the other cadet classes, and are always addressed and spoken of by them, as *plebs*. As we pass along they hoot and shout contemptuously *Plebs ! Plebs ! !* They play a good many tricks on those who they think will stand it, but are rather shy of those who they think would resent their insults."

To his sister.

"WEST POINT, *June* 14*th.*

" I received your letter the same day I returned from the Hospital, and you may be sure it was opened with the greatest pleasure. I am daily improving in strength. I hope soon to enjoy even better health than I did previous to leaving home.

" The drill is quite easy now, and I like it : in fact, had rather drill than not. At first it was harder, as I had to learn the rudiments before I could march : but now that I know them and keep moving, it has become quite easy. Oh ! it was *very* hard at first, and I fainted once in the ranks.

" The parade, (as it is called) continues in all its severity. In consequence of my illness, I have had leave of absence until to-day. I must now return to it after this, and if I do have to fall out, I hope there will be nothing worse. If that parade was to last after examination, I would hardly be able to stay : but I am thankful it ceases as soon as we are admitted."

To his sister.

"WEST POINT, *June 16th*, 1852.

" I had intended to answer your letter which I received yesterday evening, but deferred doing so, to go and see the fireworks on the plains which the graduates displayed in celebration of the last night of their stay in these classic walks. Most of them leave to-day ; and judging by my own feelings, they must do so without the least emotion of regret.

" The examination will take place some time during this week : but what particular days, it is impossible to say. The mental examination will probably be on Saturday, the day we go into camp. The medical examination however, will, it is believed, take place a day or two before, perhaps to-morrow. I do not feel much anxiety on the subject as I expect to pass, and it does not trouble me much, therefore, what day we get examined. As soon as it is over I will drop you a line and let you know the result.

" There is one boy here, a nephew of Mr. Venable, of the House of Representatives, (who was at Princeton College with father), under five feet in height, and also under sixteen years of age, who it is said has an order from the Secretary of War * that he shall be admitted. I do not think this fair ; if they do it for one, they ought to do it for others. The reason assigned for this departure from rule is, that young Venable is believed to be a great mathematical prodigy and genius.

" There will be, I think, between six and ten of the candidates for admission rejected. There will be about twenty or thirty more rejected at or before the January

* George W. Crawford.

examination, and about fifteen afterwards, making about fifty discharged in all. In the present graduating class, there were only forty-four who went "clear through," out of near ninety with which it commenced. I doubt if more will get through in my class, four years hence.

"I have seen Loder and Nevius, of New Jersey. Nevius is a clever fellow. To Loder I have taken quite a fancy. Nevius was, you know, appointed by Congressman Brown, in preference to me. I hope he will be able to stay here. I like Loder very much, for he seems to have the instinct of a gentleman. The two young plebs who are to occupy the same tent with me in camp are Loder and Taylor, son of the late Lieutenant Colonel Taylor of the army.

"For the last two days the heat has been intense, and in the afternoon during drill almost enough to kill a dog. In the evening yesterday one of the plebs fainted during parade and was carried off the ground. Almost every afternoon one or more of them become so sick as to compel them to fall out of the ranks. I have fallen out of the ranks three times altogether.

"The change in the classes, by the absence of two of them, one on furlough, and the other graduating, has completely changed our officers. The absence of some I deplore ; but for that of others I rejoice. All along, the head officer on parade (who stood by, but seldom said anything) was Rose, and the next, who, in fact, gave all the commands, was Hood of Kentucky. Then come Messrs. Villipigue of South Carolina, and Turnbull of Maryland.

"As Rose never gave any commands, but merely received the reports of Mr. Hood, I don't miss him much :

come on and try again on the 1st of next September.
Unless he exerts himself very industriously he will fail
again. I regret his failure, as I know you and his father
have been friends all your lives. Mr. Brown, too, will
regret the failure of his appointee.*

"I am also sorry to say that Dickinson, of Iowa, is
also rejected. I felt an interest in him because he was
from the Congressional District from which, if we had
remained in Iowa, I expected to come as a cadet.

"One named C., of Michigan ; another B., from Connec-
ticut ; J., from Alabama ; T., from Ohio ; G., from Pennsylvania ; H., from Virginia ; complete the unfortunate
eight. G. was appointed at large. Parents or guardians,
before they send their boys here, ought to be assured
that they are capable. All that is required is, what
every boy of ten years of age can acquire at any common
school—provided they have any capacity for learning.
If they have it not, it is cruel to subject them to the
mortification of rejection, which if they have any sensi-
bility, must cloud all their future lives.

"As to Campbell, of Texas, of whom you spoke in one
of your letters, he assumes so many nativities that,
though he has been here a week, to-day is the first day
that I was aware of it. Instead of being from Texas, he
was never there, though his father lives in that State.

"When I asked him where he was from, he replied

* Mr. Nevius, though he returned to West Point, did not continue there. He subsequently became a Civil Engineer, and in that
capacity was in the service of the Camden and Amboy R. R. Company for many years, and highly esteemed. He died while in the
employ of that Company. He was a son of Judge Nevius, one of
the Judges of the Supreme Court of New Jersey.

from South Carolina. I made no further inquiry, and did not see him again until this morning. I find that he has generally lived in South Carolina, though he resided three years in Cuba. He is appointed from Alabama, and his father now lives in Texas. In consequence of all this, it was entirely owing to accident that I found him out—which I was desirous of doing, as his father is a friend of Uncle Dashiell.

"Campbell belongs to Company D., while I belong to Company A., so that our rooming together is out of the question. Gaston is a fine-looking fellow, but has engaged his room-mates.

"To-morrow, I will receive my musket, and after that will have to learn the musket drill. I expect I will receive an order in a few days to obtain my uniform. The whole of Company D. received orders for their uniforms to-day."

but Hood * (of late 2d, from 1st class), who takes his place, I do miss, as he was a fine gentlemanly and obliging commander. In his place we have a new man whose name I have not yet learned. Both Villipigue and Turnbull go upon furlough to-day. Villipigue is one of the most clever persons I have met here, and I regret his absence exceedingly. He is a gentleman in every sense of the word, an order of beings very scarce here.

"But Turnbull's absence delights all the *plebs*, who had from him the most rigorous treatment, though no doubt intended for their benefit. He was the crossest and sharpest of all others to whose commands we were subjected. His absence is some compensation for the loss of Villipigue."

To his Father.

"*June* 23*d*, 1852.

"I think I may now consider myself a Cadet, without much danger of being deceived.

"Those boys (eight in number) who were from various causes unable to pass, were called up to-day and were informed of that fact; but they have the privilege of coming on and trying again in September, which a number of them will probably do.

"The proof of my passing which I take for granted, is, my not being called before the Superintendent to be informed of the contrary.

"There is no doubt about it, and you must therefore not fail to come up on Friday and stay till Monday, if no longer.

"I am sorry to say that Nevius was among the distin guished eight, who could not pass. But he says he will

* General Hood, of the Confederate army.

2

CHAPTER III.

Cadet Life at West Point.—From June Examination 1852 to January, 1853.—Letters.

IT will be seen from his letters that Cadet Bayard, after his admission, complained no more of the hardships of West Point, but satisfied with his situation adapted himself to his duties and was animated with an ardent desire to excel, and graduate with credit.

His transgressions of the rules of the Academy were never of a flagrant character, and seemed to be the result merely, of the audacity of youth, which delights in encountering risks, rather than a reckless insensibility to the dictates of duty. He complained and indeed resented the treatment to which as one of the *plebs* he was subjected, but no longer considered *that* so intolerable as to make him willing to leave the Academy.

To his Father.

"WEST POINT, *July 23d,* 1852.

"I read your letter a few days ago, and will now answer it if I can find time.

"As I said before, I will write as often as I can, but as we cannot call a minute our own, it will be impossible to write as often as I desire. Walking guard is a great absorption of time as well as a decided bore and nuisance. It sometimes nearly wears me out, but generally I stand it pretty well—better than the average cadet. The drills have again been changed, very materially. Instead of drilling an hour in the morning, we drill but forty minutes. The artillery drill continues the same as before, but the evening drill has also been changed in its length. Instead of an hour as before, we are now out *an hour and a half.* Instead of little squad drills as before, the whole battalion is drilled, and I think the old cadets do much worse than the new ones. There are three or four sent either to their own tents or to the guard tent every day for inattention or not going through the manual fast enough, or something of the kind. My turn has not come yet, though it undoubtedly will come. I was, however, sent to the guard tent the other day for being late: but upon explaining the circumstances to Alden the next day I was immediately released. This was my first sojourn there, and I hope will long be the last ; although the guard tent is quite as agreeable as the camp.

"In camp, it is almost impossible to study, for we are constantly interrupted ; and after coming in from one of those long drills, I feel very little like study.

"I correspond with Mr. Luna * in Spanish—and he sends my letters back corrected. By thus corresponding I will not forget what Spanish I have learned. We have now little more than a month of encampment remaining—and then to the barracks and our books. I start in the first section, as they are arranged alphabetically ; and to *stay* in that section requires earnestness and indefatigable industry and exertion. I shall stay there as long as possible, though I rather think I will

* His Spanish teacher at Morristown.

soon fall to the second or third, either of which are
good sections.   There are seven sections, so that even
the third or fourth will carry a cadet through with honor,
and without the least chance of failing at the final examination, though he should not answer half the questions
asked him.   If I stand anywhere above thirty, I will be
doing well, for that would be above the middle of the
class.   I am well at present, though even old cadets have
often to fall out at the long drill in the evening."

To his Sister.

"WEST POINT, *July 25th*, 1852.

" Perhaps you think from my long delay in writing, and
particularly in answering your letter, that I am forgetful
of my duty.   But if you do, you are entirely mistaken,
for had I the time I should certainly write much more
frequently, but as leisure hours are a gratification not
among the delights of West Point, I am obliged to suit
myself and my inclinations to the necessity of the case,
and write when I can, and not when I would.   When
cousin E.'s letter arrived, I was upon guard, and had not
been arrested or put' in the guard tent.   But the day
after I had the exquisite pleasure of being sent there for
being late at dinner roll-call.   But on being taken
before Captain Alden the next morning and explaining
the matter, I was released.   Were it not for the name
of the thing, I had as lief be in the guard tent as in
camp.   There were three other new cadets, and four old
ones in confinement at the same time that I was.   You
must not confound *confinement in the guard tent* with
arrest, for there is a wide difference.   We are sent to the
guard tent to await a hearing before sentence by Cap-

tain Alden. If we give a sufficient and satisfactory excuse, we are released, if not, we are placed under arrest or otherwise punished according to the nature of the offence.

"Early next month a *report* of my conduct for this month, will be sent to father—and as soon as he receives it I wish he would send it to me.

" We have pretty tough work and they seem to be growing more strict and rigorous every day, much to the tribulation of our class. But I shall do my best to stand it. We are worked severely : our class is said to be more intractable and to get more reports than any other class of *plebs* for several years. Dickinson of Iowa received his reappointment some time ago and has been going to school at Cold Spring. I hope he will pass as well as the others that come back.

" Schofield* has been dismissed for allowing the cadets to fool with and play tricks upon the new cadets in the section room. Some new cadets, when asked about what took place in the room, told the truth, and he was consequently dismissed for breach of trust. Alden however could not get the cadets of any other section to "*peach*," so that Schofield alone is punished when others were as guilty as he, and many more so. Schofield's cadets were principally young and "green," which accounts for their telling. I believe he expects to get reappointed, and indeed I think he ought to be. He was a first class man and stood No. 6 in his class last June and was much liked by both new and old cadets.

"One of my tent-mates, by the name of Van Alstyne from this State, has resigned at the request of his father.

* Since Major-General Schofield.

I am very sorry for it, as he is a very gentlemanly young man."

To his Father.

" *August 1st,* 1852.

" You misunderstood what I said about my standing next year in my class. I merely wished to put you on your guard against expecting too much of me. There are not a few in the class who have been over, and know thoroughly the course of the first two years, besides being known as possessing a genius for mathematics. I will of course study hard, and do my best in every respect, but hope you will consider all things, and not be disappointed if I should be thrown lower than you expect. Regard for you, my dear father, would of itself lead me to do as well as I can, and to be studious. Demerit marks for other causes than deficiency in a cadet's studies, impair his standing. So I again hope you will not count too confidently on the highest standing : satisfy yourself with my good standing, not below the middle, and I hope you will not be disappointed. If I stand higher, so much the better.

" I have made a small bet that General Pierce will be elected President by a two-thirds majority. If Commodore Stockton had not thrown away his chances, I might now have bet on him."

To his Father.

"WEST POINT, *August 14th,* 1852.

" I hear that it is proposed in Congress to pass an act, adding another year to the academic course in this Institution. If this is the case, cannot the Commodore contrive to have Latin and Spanish introduced among the studies ? Unless both these languages are introduced, I would not, if I had a seat in Congress, vote for the Bill.

Latin should be taught as the foundation of all the languages of the civilized world. I think an institution renowned as this, should send forth its graduates prepared to make themselves conspicuous among the graduates of other literary seminaries. Spanish especially, should be taught here on account of our close relations with many nations using that tongue. I think if these considerations were submitted to Congress by one so able as the Commodore, there would be no difficulty in the matter.

"Unless studies as important as these are added, I think the bill would be unjust and uncalled for. Were they added, I would have it include this year's class. Four years is plenty long enough to stay here, unless we get a good equivalent for the additional year.

"If convenient, come up here before the 28th, as after that I would be unable to see you but a short time in the day. We have battalion drill every afternoon with music, and now is the time to come up. After the first, when we shall be in barracks, it would interrupt my studies—so I hope you will come up and stay a few days, and see the battalion march out of camp. Cautioning me against eating too freely, fruit, corn and melons, was quite superfluous, as these are luxuries of which I have not had even a glimpse since I have been here.

"I have but two demerit marks as yet. These I could get off if I wished it ; but I prefer they should remain, as a person with no demerit is a very unpopular being here."

To his Mother.

"WEST POINT, *August* 31*st*, 1852.

' Now that I am once more in barracks, I hasten to

2*

write to you, although it be only to tell you that my health continues excellent, and how much I was disappointed that you were not here yesterday to see the battalion march out of camp.

"The furlough class returned upon the 28th and their addition makes the battalion much larger, and appear much better than when you were here.

"Our lessons will probably be given out some time to-day and I will then have to commence a series of hard study such as I never had before. I will do as well as I can, and I hope that is all that will be expected of me.

"I have room No. 15, which is up in the 4th story and it is very tiresome, sometimes, to get up. Our room is what they call a tower room, and I am told that it is a very good one. My room-mates are Gentry and Taylor, and as none of us use tobacco, I think we will manage to get along pretty well.

"You will be glad to learn that among the "*Septs*" (as they are called) who were examined day before yesterday, Willetts, Nevius and Dickinson, and in fact all but one or two rejected in June, *passed* very readily."

To his Sister.

"WEST POINT, *Sept. 24th*, 1852.

"I employ my first spare moments since we have returned to barracks to answer your letters, which I have too long neglected.

"I am getting along pretty well in section room with my studies, though there is no telling where we stand for some time yet.

"The sections are arranged in alphabetical order, which of course places me in the First section. I have therefore to endeavor to remain where I am, and will be well satisfied if I can do so. Alexander's name coming first on the list, he is squad-marcher of our section. The person whose name comes next, after our section is taken out—is squad-marcher of the second section—and so on through the class. After the first two weeks the transfers are made and we are then arranged according to merit. The duty of the squad-marcher, is to form the section, call the roll, and march it to and from recitation, etc. The man who stands first (after transfer made) in the section is always squad-marcher.

"At present we study algebra and grammar, but before long we will commence rhetoric and geography. The geography consists principally, I believe, in drawing maps, and I am sorry I did not pay more attention to it when I had an opportunity.

"I have a copy of the cadet camp Polka, which I will send to you girls as soon as mother comes up. But you shall not have it until some of you do come up.

"General Scott is now here and it is said that he will soon review the cadets. I believe he was to have reviewed us last Friday, but he was prevented by the rain—not much to our disappointment.

"Captain Brewerton was relieved from the command of this post upon the first of September, by Lieutenant Colonel Robert E. Lee. I do not know how the change will affect us—whether it will better our condition or not. Colonel Lee is of a good Virginia family, and is doubtless a gentleman."

To his Mother.

"WEST POINT, 16*th Sept.*, 1851.

"Major Garnett* will relieve Captain Alden as commandant of cadets on the 1st of November. Who he is I do not know. He is said to be a severe disciplinarian. So much the better.

"As to the things I want you to bring when you come up, I will mention them all to you. Cadets are proverbially the greatest beggars imaginable. Shut out as they are from the surrounding world, they naturally turn to their friends for needful supplies—often thoughtlessly and without being aware of the unreasonable frequency of their demands. Excuse me then, dear mother, if I am or have been extravagant in my requests. I know you would give me anything in your power that was proper; but I would a hundred times prefer to do without all, than to put you to the slightest care or vexation. All that I care for now, is a gold pen and a supply of good letter paper, as they charge most extravagantly for everything of the sort at the Commissary Department.

"I am waiting for the transfers with some impatience, as I want to know where I stand. When they *are* made, there will be a vast deal of travelling done by some fourth-class men. It will however depend considerably upon the recitations this week, and those who do well will go up, and those who do not succeed so well will go down. I missed one day last week while in the hospital; but luckily I did not lose anything. I think I will be in the first section at any rate; as my health improves, I shall study harder."

* The Confederate General.

To his Father.

"WEST POINT, *Oct. 9th,* 1852.

" Now that Saturday once more gives me an afternoon to myself, I can write home more leisurely than I could any other day. The fact is, on recitation days our time is so broken up into parts and parcels, that before I have fairly commenced a letter some duty compels me to lay aside my writing materials abruptly.

" You tell me to give you the West Point news. Here we are never disturbed with news ; but enjoy a uniform routine of duty and everything else, from going down to our meals and recitations, is nothing but recurring drills —marching—parade, etc., etc.

" A member of our class leaves on Monday ; G—l, the nephew of the illustrious candidate for the Presidency. Not finding West Point suited to his taste, he has resigned, and I think it about the best thing he could have done, for this place is exceedingly conservative and abolitionists are not favored. But politics here, are eschewed, and the politician is in no esteem.

" When you were here I spoke of going home on Christmas, if I could get leave. But on consideration I have concluded not to apply for leave, as I doubt whether Garnett, who takes command of the battalion on the 1st of November, would grant it, and I should dislike to be refused. Garnett has the reputation of being the strictest man that has ever been here. When he was here as Instructor of Infantry tactics he was, I am told, court-martialled for some act of exceeding and undue severity. There is little doubt but that he will put through the battalion a regular course of arrests and punishments for trifles hitherto treated as venial. We are now studying Blair's Rhetoric and I intend to do better in it hereafter than I have done hitherto. I am still in the first section and I think it will not be a very difficult thing for me to stay there, in Mathematics. But I am not so sure as to Ethics, for I confess, though I can recite and speak tolerably well, I do not know much about English Grammar—and do not find it an easy matter to discuss ethical questions.

" There are in the class quite a number of very smart and talented men who have been over and in fact, know the course so well, that they do not have to study to understand it but merely to learn the lesson for recitation. In this, many of them have a great advantage over others and I may say over me. But although there are many possessed of fine talents and perseverance, yet the half of the class is composed of about the hardest set you can possibly imagine.

" About twenty-five or thirty of them will I fear have the pleasure of visiting home in January. It is said that this is the most reckless and jolly class that has been here for a long time, and I think, taking it all in all, the assertion is not very wide of the mark. There are indeed some noble fellows among them, and I regret to say that many fine-hearted, generous companions will leave us in January—not at all for want of capacity, but merely because they will not take the trouble to study."

To his Father.

" WEST POINT, *Dec.* 12*th*, 1852.

" Our January examination is rapidly approaching; it is now but a few weeks of the eventful time. I shall be glad when it is over, principally because we will then be done with Algebra, which I like less than any other branch of Mathematics. After January examination, we finish our present ethical studies and begin French, and study plain and descriptive Geometry, which before June are also completed. After we pass the January examination we receive our cadet commissions, when we are at last full members of the Military Academy. But we shall still be snubbed by the other classes as "*plebs*," and as such, will continue until the next class comes, in June, 1853.

" The eighteenth of December, my birthday, is now near—when I shall enter my eighteenth year. If I live to graduate I will be in my twenty-first year, and free from this prison once more and forever.

" Judge Nevius was here the other day to see his son, and I saw him and found him very pleasant. He has no idea that his son will be unable to pass the examination and I pity him more than I do his son, for he appears a kind-hearted old gentleman and very fond of his son. It makes me sad when I think of the many clever fellows we shall probably lose soon. How much their parents will be mortified by their reckless disregard of the advantages of an education here. Their parents know its value, if *they* do not.

" I hope our valuable legislators at Washington, amidst the battle for the spoils and Galphin* speculations, will for a little while turn their attention to this out of the way place, and give us a new riding-hall and other things which we need very much. This Academy has been most shamefully neglected by Congress, and everything

* A claim paid by Government, and said to be fraudulent.

it ever did for it was only after it had been begged humbly and repeatedly for years.

"I sincerely hope Congress will have magnanimity enough to give General Scott his Lieut.-Generalship, which most certainly he richly deserves.

CHAPTER IV.

To his Mother.

"WEST POINT, *Jan. 9th,* 1853.

"I WAS examined in Mathematics last Monday, and in Ethics yesterday. The Board finishes the examination of our class to-morrow, and in a day or two our standing will be read out. I had intended to delay writing until I knew exactly how I stand ; but as you appear so anxious, I feel it a duty to let you know the result.

"I did very well in Mathematics, and will, I think, come out eighth or ninth in the class. In Ethics, however, I did badly, which will throw me a few files, and I will not stand in that branch as well as I expected. Nevertheless, I think I shall stand above twentieth in the class. This will probably appear bad work to you, but I hope you will remember that there are *ninety* in the class. It is my own fault that I don't stand above twelve instead of twenty, for if I had studied as I should have done, I would have stood higher. But hereafter, I intend to study Ethics more severely, and I hope you will hear a better tale in June. My *general standing* in each branch of my studies will be about fourteen this January, and if I neither fall nor rise before next June, it will be about eleven or twelve, since Mathematics then counts more than Ethics, which it now does not. But this is mere conjecture. I may come out in June worse, or I may come out better than I expect. I merely write now to relieve your anxiety. In a day or two all will be certainty and I shall let you know at once. General Campbell, (Consul at Havana formerly) was up here a few days since and young Campbell brought him up to see me. He said he was well acquainted with Major Dashiell."

To his Mother.

"WEST POINT, *Jan.* 10*th*, 1853.

"The standing of the fourth class in Mathematics and English studies was read before the battalion this evening. I came out ninth in mathematics as I expected—but better than I dared to hope in Ethics—that is thirteenth. Below is the list of the first section in mathematics: 1st Houston, 2d McAllister, 3d Bailey, 4th Riggs, 5th Webster, 6th Lee, 7th Taylor, 8th Hascall, 9th Bayard, 10th Lomax, 11th Snyder, 12th Gaston."

To his Father.

"WEST POINT, *Jan.* 22*d*, 1853.

"I am sorry to inform you that I have received a considerable number of demerits this month, although I have taken much care to avoid them. I shall be careful hereafter.

"I believe I did not tell you my *general standing*—that is my standing, taking everything into consideration. This is the standing with respect to which our names are arranged in the catalogue. I stand eighth, which you will perceive is better than I stand in any single branch of our studies.

"Willetts—Nevius—and a majority of those found deficient leave to-morrow. I should like to know who will be appointed in place of Willetts and Nevius. Your friend Mr. Vail will probably appoint some Morristown friend—but not Miller, I think. It is rather singular that both my competitors have been found deficient—Nevius whom your *friend* Brown preferred to me for the District, and Willetts* my competitor for the appointment at large. Those who sympathized with Senator Miller's disappointment would no doubt have been delighted, if I had been compelled to leave West Point for deficiency. I don't think they will have that gratification."

To his Mother.

"WEST POINT, *Jan. 28th*, 1853.

"I am much obliged to you for the skates you propose sending. I borrowed a pair the other day and was on the river during the afternoon. You need not hesitate to send them, for there will be no more danger on them, than if I go on the ice without them or on borrowed ones.

"The weather lately has been very cold, and to go down to reveille before day, is not the pleasantest duty in the world, although I suppose it is exceedingly healthful—for I never before enjoyed such good health as I do now.

"I am at present studying French. This, my dear mother, is going to spoil my general standing, I fear,

---

* Colonel Willetts, of the Twelfth Regiment of Volunteers of New Jersey, distinguished for gallantry in the late civil war.

next June. There are many in the class who already know French well, and of course excel the beginners—and will do so, no matter how hard we study ; I therefore forewarn you that French in June will affect injuriously my general standing ; but I will study it hard and do my best."

To his Sister.

"WEST POINT, *March 6th,* 1853.

" I have not done my duty of late, as a home correspondent. But I have had a fit of hard study, and I presume that will be an acceptable excuse.

" There was considerable excitement throughout the corps this morning ; and for a Sunday morning the incident which produced it was not very appropriate.

" Just as the battalion was entering the mess hall this morning a cadet named Grattan, the first sergeant of his company (from Illinois, and first class man) behaved in an insulting manner to Steuart of Virginia, a second class man. Steuart—who is called *Beauty* Steuart, from his ugliness—told him to move off as he did not wish to have a fuss with a dog like him ; and thereupon Grattan very gracefully kicked him, whereupon they both went to work to try their pugilistic abilities. They were separated by those who were near them ; but it did not end here. No sooner had the battalion broken ranks, than Steuart pitched into Grattan, who however was prepared for him, and knocked him down. Steuart jumped up and tried it again ; but just at this moment, the officer of the day came up and ordered them to their quarters under arrest. And so the matter rests at present, but it will not end here. There is no telling what will be done with them, as fighting with one another is a flagrant offence. But one thing is certain that *this* and the Gay affair have produced a deep bitterness between the two classes.

"On the twenty-second of February our class took the oath of allegiance to the United States, and we received our warrants. As I stood eighth in general standing, I received the eighth warrant. But the bugle sounds for church, and I must away."

To his Mother.

"WEST POINT, *March 24th,* 1853.

"If I neglect every one else, I will not neglect to write to you.

"For the last few weeks, our lessons have been such as to render necessary the devotion of hours generally given to relaxation. Drills have commenced again and I have *had,* and have long extra tours of guard duty to walk. I have been on post so much for the last week that I am completely worn out.

"Major Garnett is going to have the battalion one of the best drilled corps in the United States. If you come up next summer, you will discover an astounding difference in its discipline.

"I have got some sixteen more demerit marks this month. I will explain some other time. I got them all in one day. I am straining every nerve to get as few as possible between this and June.

"We now have drills and dress parades daily. We will commence descriptive geometry in about a week, as by that time we will have finished reviewing trigonometry. Thus in nine months do we complete a course in mathematics, which away from here, occupies generally about two years.

"I am tired of hard study and shall be glad when camp comes again. The third class encampment is infinitely easier than the *plebs'* encampment.

"I believe the list of new plebs has not yet been published, and I suppose therefore, you do not know who are appointed. From New Jersey, they are Canfield (in place of Nevius) Thurston, (at large), Wildrich and Harris. Mr. Quattlebum of South Carolina, one of the new plebs, will curse his stars for having such a name. As will Mr. Dresback of Ohio, who will be ordered by the corporals to *dress-back* oftener than will be agreeable. Among those from Missouri, is Manning M. Kimmel, whom I knew in St. Louis. Poor devils, these plebs!! They little know what a *hell* upon earth they will have to endure for the first few months of probation here."

To his Father.
"WEST POINT, *May 31st,* 1853.

"I have not indulged much of late in letter-writing, as I have been in studious preparation for examination, and I have felt some resentment on account of the falling off on the part of my correspondents, who are becoming very remiss.

"To-morrow will be the first of June. On that day last year, I bid you all good-bye, and took my departure from the "heights of Morristown" to enter upon my "Plebeship"—of the horrors of which I had no adequate conception. Well! many changes have taken place since then, in everything and every body, some for the better and some for worse. I am a little wiser for my experience. When I look back upon the year which ends to-day it appears literally to have *fled* away. It seems but a few weeks, since I bid farewell to " home sweet home." I was buoyant with hope, and proud that my boyhood's dream of a soldier's life was to be realized. I confess that the *starch* of my spirit was somewhat limbered by my experience as a *pleb.* But we are no longer *plebs* after the June examination.

" To-morrow we are reviewed before the Board of Visitors, which then begins its work of inspection and examination. Garnett has the corps under better discipline than it ever was before, and it will doubtless show itself to advantage. At *Review* we wear our white pants for the first time this year, and I fear we shall have rather a cool time of it. For the first time the corps will fire before the Board. This firing is the most disagreeable part of the drill, as it dirties our guns so that it requires about an hour's work before we get them clean again.

" Visitors are beginning to show themselves here already, and this morning there was quite a troop of ladies at guard-mounting, and among them some bright ones, exhilarating to behold."

" *P. S. June 2d.*—I have been so occupied for the last two days, that I was unable to fill this sheet until the present moment.

Yesterday we passed in review before the Board, and the battalion covered itself with honor. Never was the cadence of the step better preserved, or the Manual better performed. We had a fine day for it, and the white trousers were not so cold as I anticipated.

" About twenty " *plebs* " have arrived, and it is enough to make one burst with laughter to see them marching to meals. Such stumbling, treading of heels, etc., etc., accidents incident to flank movements among recruits, I never before saw equalled. Alas! for the *miserables*, I pity them. But it is the traditional prerogative of the other classes to treat the *plebs* with contempt. It would be more honorable and magnanimous to welcome them with kindness and brotherly affection.

"The examination of the first class began to-day. *We* are examined in Mathematics, before we are examined in anything else. But that will not take place before to-morrow week at least. I must begin to study very hard. I am in hopes of doing well, but there is no telling, as a person cannot form any idea what he is going to get: so that he has to know the whole course if he would be safe. I flatter myself that I know the course pretty well.

"Mr. Canfield has not yet arrived, nor any of the other Jerseymen. For the honor of the State I hope they will be able to stay here."

To his Mother.

"Camp Jefferson Davis,
West Point, *June 25th*, 1853.

"I received your kind letter some time since, but owing to the hurry and bustle always attending the Examination, I have been prevented answering it before. If, my dear mother, you only knew how busy we have been kept since the first of this month, I am sure you would not reproach me with neglect. Since we have been in camp I have walked post nearly every other day, while before we left the barracks all things were in such confusion and in such an unsettled condition that no one could compose himself to write without constant interruption. Such, dearest mother, have been some of the causes why your letters have not been answered. Pray, mother, excuse, but I will do better hereafter.

"I did very well throughout my whole examination.

"Our standing was read out a day or two ago. I am well enough satisfied, although I should have preferred coming out better in French. I hope that my standing, dear mother, will not disappoint you. I came out eleventh in Mathematics, which you will perceive is two files lower than my standing in it in January. In Ethics my standing is ninth, which is a rise of four files, as I came out in those studies thirteenth, in January. My *general standing* for *the year* is ninth, a fall of one file. Had it not been for my demerit, I should have come out seventh, which would have been a rise of one file since January. They brought me out twenty-second in French ; somewhat low —leaving more room for improvement next year. I wish the new "*plebs*" were in the battalion. I cannot stand this way very long of going on guard every other day.

"I just marched off this morning and am almost as tired as I can well be, and my feet are blistered from walking, and yet I am detailed for guard to-morrow.

"They played the mischief with the corps generally, this year at the examination. They found eight men deficient in the second class, four men in the third class, and *fifteen* in ours."

To his Father.

"CAMP JEFFERSON DAVIS,
WEST POINT, *July* 18*th*, 1853. }

"For the last week or two I have been quite favored with the visits of friends, acquaintances and kin. T— of Newark, introduced me to his mother and sister, and he being a "*pleb*," I offered to escort them in exploring the surroundings here. As they were from Jersey, and therefore my constituents, I paid them all proper attention.

"The other night while, about nine o'clock, I was walking post, the corporal came to me to relieve me for a few minutes as he said a gentleman wished to see me. It was Major David Hunter (a cousin of yours) and he told me to come up the next day, as he had a flock of cousins of mine with him, who all wanted to see me. Accordingly I got leave the next day in the afternoon and went to the hotel. I was introduced by the Major to the Misses, and found them very agreeable, and enjoyed myself very much in their society for the two or three days they were here. Miss D. was from Mississippi and the Misses K—s from Michigan, sisters of Mrs. Hunter.

"Mr. and Mrs. Dalrymple, of Morristown, were also here. I am expecting Aunt Mary and my four Kentucky cousins daily, as you say they will soon leave Camden.

"You cannot imagine to what a state Garnett has brought us. Never was there such an encampment here before, and I sincerely trust there never will be such another. I believe that if there were any good reason to justify it, there would be a mutiny. He has taken our liberty from us by such imperceptible degrees, that before we were quite aware of it, we awoke and found ourselves prisoners.

"We may hereafter when in active service possibly realize the benefit of all this tyrannical rigor.

"Saturday morning, one of the officers found a cadet

drunk out of camp before reveille.   Garnett after breakfast ordered the Instructors of Infantry Tactics to inspect
the tents for liquor.   Lts. Nelson and Cogswell each
inspected the tents in their companies, by taking each
piece of clothing separately out of the lockers, tearing
all the bedding apart and shaking it, and also shaking
everything out of the clothes-bags.   Clitz and Wilcox
merely came to the tents and asked the cadets if they
had any liquor in their tents.   Nelson found a box of
cigars, and ordered the owner to turn them in to the
Quartermaster; but before he had left the tent five
minutes, some cadet (the owner fortunately not knowing
who) went in the tent and ran off with them, and that
was the last Nelson heard of them.

"Clitz was very indignant at being required to perform
such a duty.   He said to us—" You will excuse me, gentlemen—this is unpleasant work.   Do not be afraid of
your tobacco.   I am inspecting for nothing but liquor,
and prefer your word to any search."   Wilcox said
about the same thing.

" After Cogswell had ransacked all the tents in his
company without finding anything, somebody took a
whiskey bottle and set it up before his tent.   In a few
minutes he came along to go into his tent and at once all
the cadets set up a loud laugh.   All this you will say no
doubt was very foolish.   But these little incidents and
pranks help break the monotony of cadet life.   The
cadet found drunk had just returned to the academy having been suspended last spring for using threatening language to a cadet.   He will now certainly be dismissed.

" We received the new catalogues last Saturday.   One
will be sent you at Camden from the War Department.

" You speak in your last letter about the cadets petitioning the President to allow the corps to visit the Crystal Palace. I suppose you are not aware that any cadet guilty of such an awfully heinous offence, such as that, would be immediately dismissed. Major Garnett has, I understand, permission to take the corps to the city if he wishes to do so. But he says the *plebs* are too gross and unmilitary—which by-the-by, I am sorry to say is the truth—and without them (one class being absent on furlough) we scarcely have a corporal's guard—much less a battalion."

To his Father.

" CAMP JEFFERSON DAVIS,
WEST POINT, *Aug.* 21*st*, 1853.

" I hope to see you here on Thursday afternoon, and if so, I shall expect you to stay at least until Saturday afternoon. If, however, the girls do not wish to attend the party on Friday (which being the last of the season, will be kept up till twelve o'clock) then you had better come up Saturday and stay till Monday, as I do not think tents will be struck until Monday, which they would like to see.

" The regulation concerning this matter is generally to strike tents on the 28th. The furlough class does not get back until the 28th, and hitherto they have always got back whilst the corps was in camp. I think it certain therefore, we will not go to the barracks until Monday. I hope however, the girls will be up in time for the party."

To his Mother.

" WEST POINT, *Sept.* 25*th*, 1853.

" Having some spare time this evening, I shall devote

it to answering your letter which I received a few days since. Although you were unable to come up with father this month, I hope you will come some time during the fall. Only think! it is nine months since I have seen you or any of the girls, and if you don't come during the fall, I shall not see you probably before I go home on furlough.

"I am getting along in my studies about as usual. French is as dull and as great a bore as ever. In Mathematics and Analytical Geometry, they are so easy that it is almost impossible to study them. Drawing I do not know whether to like or dislike, though at present I incline to the former.

"Those cadets who were "*hived*" (as they say here when an offender is caught) in that grog-shop were not even put in arrest. Their punishment is to walk four Saturdays from two to four P. M., equipped as sentinels, in front of the barracks. The reason of this light punishment is, I believe, that the officers find that they had no right to send the *officer of the day* off limits to "*hive*" them, and therefore fear to stand a court-martial. *Tattoo* beats—farewell."

To his Mother.

"WEST POINT, *Nov. 2d*, 1853.

" You have all, I suppose, been at a loss to account for my long silence upon any other grounds than those of laziness and indifference.

" Neither of these unworthy causes however, have kept me silent. The truth is that one day last month I was disappointed in getting a letter from any of you, when I felt confident of receiving one, and in the bitterness of my grief, I made a vow that I would not write to any of you that month. This vow, although I often regretted having made, I religiously kept. October has now gone. November with its bleak winds and frosts, is about to introduce us to another winter, and with these changes come also the expiration of my vow.

"Everything always continues the same here, so that if I were not to write to you till next June, I should have no more to tell you than I have at present. We all "fess," * drink and smoke, get reported, and when we *can*,

> ' Toast the lovely flower that blooms
> At Benny Havens, oh !'

as often as usual. All of which is sometimes enlivened by a private fight, which comes off by appointment. And this sums up the whole programme of performances here from one month to another.

"Don Señor Jose Yres Perea, of New Mexico, having received over his hundred *demerits*, resigned the other day to prevent being dismissed next January.

"I am much obliged to father for the Ledger, which I now receive daily. The only objection to it is its lack of interest, only about a column of news in it of readable matter, and that I generally read the day before in the *Times* and *Herald*.

"Day after to-morrow we finish reviewing Analytical Geometry and will then study the remainder of Descriptive, which we did not learn last year.

"You must bear in mind, that my standing in *drawing*

* That is *confess*, they don't know a lesson, and accept the demerit mark as the penalty.

before January, is merely my standing in my section, and not in the class. The reason of this is, that they do not *transfer* any until then, and that some of the best *drawers* in the class, stand low in studies and are therefore in the second section. In January the transfers will be made and there will not be more than half a dozen above me. Besides, our present drawing consists of mere Topography and we do not commence pencilling until after January."

To his Father.

" WEST POINT, *Nov.* 13*th*, 1853.

" I received your letter a few days since and thank you for the information it contains, and also for the good advice.

" As to *drinking*, when I spoke as I did in that letter to mother, I had no reference to myself, but merely to some of my friends.

" What you say about French being easy, is very true, and that is one objection I have to it. I always need something difficult to arouse me to exertion. We have been through " Warped Surfaces " once and we finish the Review day after to-morrow, and the next day take up " Shades and Shadows and Perspective."

" I am studying hard so as by January examination to make up for the time lost while in the hospital.

" I much fear that I will not do as well in January as in last June. But I hope to recover lost ground—by next June."

CHAPTER V.

*Life at West Point in 1854—Oration before Dialectic Society—Goes
on Furlough—Verses by Mrs. General M. G. Scott.*

VERY few letters of Cadet Bayard for 1854 appear
to have been preserved. What have been found
are given in this chapter. None contain any reference
to the January examination of 1854. His standing was
not materially changed, although he lost much time while
confined in the hospital.

To his Father.

"WEST POINT, *Feb. 12th*, 1854.

" I have been requested to declaim at a public exhibition of the Dialectic Society (of cadets) next week.
The audience will consist of the two hundred cadets, with
the gentlemen and ladies on the Point. I have not yet
chosen my subject. It will tax me considerably to compose and memorize my oration and do my duty as a
student.

"We have just commenced a new branch of Mathematics, so entirely different from any I have heretofore
studied that it will require the utmost assiduity to do
well. But I like to encounter difficulty, as it concen-
trates my mental activity and stimulates me to extraor-
dinary exertion."

To his Father.

"WEST POINT, *Feb. 26th*, 1854.

"I should have written before this had I not been so engaged that it was not possible to do so.

"The exhibition came off well, there being a large attendance. I succeeded, according to all accounts, very well, and it is said, particularly in my delivery. A lady said she thought the views expressed were very " sound!" I was surprised to feel myself so much at ease. But as soon as I got through my first sentence and looked the audience squarely in the face, all my terror and trepidation vanished. I will give you the speech when you come up. And if I ever leave the army, and become a great lawyer, it may be amusing to see my first effort as an orator. But I had rather fight than talk.*

"There are but two more days before the winter months will have passed away, but I fear Winter himself will not be so complacent as to leave so soon and with so little to remember him by. Furlough appears a great deal nearer now that I can say nothing but spring intervenes. I must be careful that I do not get in any scrape which would cut me off from my *furlough*.

" A member of my class, Ferguson, of South Carolina, who was lately tried for absence after " taps," and who escaped so easily with a few extra tours of guard duty, has got himself in another difficulty, from which I fear he will not get off with such comparative impunity. He attempted to give a second-class man a caning, for some provocation or other, and was, I am told, doing it in fine

* He did not send the oration, as it is not found among any of his papers.

3*

style, when unfortunately for him an officer came up and sent both him and a friend who was with him, to their quarters in arrest.   I am afraid it will go very hard with him.

" The list of plebs for this year will soon be out, and we are all looking for it impatiently.   When we see that, we shall begin to feel as if we were second-class men.   Is it not likewise almost time for the appearance of the names of members of the Board of Visitors?   I hope for, and do not much doubt of your appointment.

" Major Garnett is still absent on leave.   It is rumored that he does not intend to return; but this news is too good, I fear, to be true.   Garnett is a good officer—but unnecessarily severe ; he means well, no doubt, but is too much of a *martinet.*

" It is now in the small hours of the morning.   Being restless and unable to sleep, I left my iron bed and have pleasantly passed an hour or two in devotion to my correspondents.   As I have now nearly exhausted my paper as well as my stock of West Point gossip, I shall once more invoke the drowsy god—and I trust with success."

To his Mother.

" WEST POINT, *March* 14*th,* 1854.

" I have just returned from riding, and having an hour to myself I shall employ it the best way I possibly can—in writing to you.

" We rode *out* of the Riding hall this afternoon for the first time this spring.   We went past Cozzens' Hotel, and being a beautiful evening we had a very pleasant ride. We have had charming weather this whole month,—all the snow has disappeared and with it all the ice, which has so long locked up and spanned our noble river. The robins have reappeared, and the buds begin to swell. As I am writing both door and window are open. We have dress parades every evening and guard mounting on the plain every morning. I wish when father comes up in June to attend the Board, some of the girls would come up with him. When they were here last, it rained, so that there were only *undress* parades. I hope this will not shock you as much as it did Mrs. Partington. This good old dame, upon hearing that in rainy weather the cadets had *undress* parades, dropped her spectacles in holy horror at such barefaced barbarism. She thought that if they must parade naked it would be best to do so in fine weather ; but she hinted that she did not believe it. She thought the cadets too modest to do such a thing, and she finally wound up by declaring that the next stormy weather she would come up and see for herself whether it was so. Her remarkable, interesting and highly instructive adventures while here would, if published, make a volume quite as unique as that left us of the founders of New Amsterdam by Knickerbocker.

"The names of the members of the Board of Visitors are now published. I am glad that father is one of them. Does he know any of the others? I hope you will come up with father in June. Three months yet !—I shall then finish Mathematics *proper*, the study of my remaining years being chiefly the application of the principles which we have deduced and learned the first two years. Day after to-morrow we will commence *Integral Calculus*—I trust it is as easy and pretty as *differential*.

"On guard this evening ! What tiresome work this

walking post is? Walk, walk, walk, up and down and down and up.

> ' With my musket on my shoulder **and**
> My bayonet at my side,
> But alas ! hard fate prevents,
> Taking some fair lady and
> Making her my bride.'

"When I am on post I always, (or to make it general as Professor Church would say) a cadet always does an immense amount of thinking. Some may doubt this,-- thinking that a cadet does not *always* have the *material* to think with. But having had considerable experience on the subject, and having experienced it in all its lights and bearings, I have come to the conclusion that it may be truthfully, without one jot of abatement, said that a cadet always does an immense deal of thinking while serving his country as sentry. In those hours I lay out innumerable plans of spending furlough, each one as I proceed growing more and more visionary, and therefore more charming. Having spent and enjoyed my furlough in divers different ways, I skip over two years, (being very short, I may do so without affecting the result, see *diff. calculus*,) graduate,—enter the army in a cavalry regiment, distinguish myself highly, etc., etc., etc., ad infinitum. These are the day-dreams which console us for all present sufferings."

To his Sister.

"WEST POINT, *May* 1st, 1854.

"In one month from to day, father will be here with the Board of Visitors, in performance of what he will find to be a tiresome duty. In twenty days after, I will be probably home ; and then with what pleasure will the few fleeting weeks of furlough pass away.   As for my not anticipating pleasure with you all in your quiet country home, the idea is perfectly absurd !   How could you have thought of such a thing ?   E. says I am changed.   I do not deny it. I am changed greatly in some respects, but in fond remembrance and love for the dear ones at home, I am the same as ever, with the exception that my affection for you all has increased tenfold with absence.   And good reasons there are for that unchanged and increased love.

" Two years in the world (for West Point is a little world in miniature,) is enough to satisfy any one of the hollowness of all professions of friendship, and the utter heartlessness of *all*, men or women.   No matter how warm may have been their protestations of regard, no matter how intimate your acquaintance, there are none but would desert you in trouble, and find something to please them in your misfortune.   You disappear and you are forgotten by all but the dear tenants of " sweet, sweet home."   Never until I left it, did I appreciate how matchless is the love lavished on one by the inmates of *home*.   There alone one is certain that the smiling face does not belong to the insidious and crafty foe."

To his Father.

"West Point, *May 24th*, 1854.

"I received your letter last week, and should have answered it sooner, but my time is so occupied in preparing for examination that you must excuse me.

" I cannot tell the best day for the girls to come up until I know how long they propose staying.   You had better come up the last day of this month, if not before.

There is always some intrigue going on in the Board of Visitors, as to who shall be President of it, and who shall deliver the address to the cadets.

"Lewis Coryell, of N. J., your friend, has been here, and I got well acquainted with him. He is a great politician, a great Calhoun man and a great friend of Com. Stockton. He says you will certainly be chosen to address the cadets.

"Garnett drills us now every evening, in order to bring back the corps to the state of discipline it was in before winter set in, so that we may display to advantage in presence of the Board of Visitors. It is very strange that the list of *plebs* does not come out. It has always hitherto been published long before this. Two or three of the poor devils have been here already. West Point doubtless appears to them now a charming place, all very fair and beautiful, and the prospect of becoming cadets very alluring now. But before another month has elapsed they will experience very different feelings ; then there will be cursing and gnashing of teeth, and they will say with Van Buren, " Our sufferings *is* intolerable."

"You will be up, I conclude, on Wednesday week, at furthest, but as we will probably have to hand in our applications for leaves (for furlough) this week, I wish you would sign the enclosed and forward it *immediately*, or I may not get it in time, and consequently be reported for not handing it in on the proper day."

After the June examination the class of cadet Bayard was entitled to a furlough of sixty days. He maintained his previous standing, but as his father was pres

ent at his examination and as he returned home on the
1st of July, no letters were received from him in relation
to it.

His furlough was spent chiefly at home, varied by
visits to his relatives in Princeton, New Brunswick, Brooklyn, and elsewhere. He left his home, (then in Morristown) in June, 1852, a stripling, tall, slender and at that
period of life when the constitution assumes its peculiar
character, of sound health or predisposition to delicacy
or disease. But the hardy exercise and regular habits
of West Point developed the natural vigor of his frame,
and in July, 1854, he had every appearance of becoming
a strong, active and athletic man.

The members of the furlough class had agreed to
rendezvous at New York on their way back to West
Point, and return together to the Academy. The following letter, after Bayard's return, will indicate the
reluctance with which he relinquished the pleasures of
his furlough:

To his Mother.

" WEST POINT, *Aug.* 30*th*, 1854.

" Here I am, landed once more for two years, and a
terrible landing it is too. I am just recovering from the
worst fit of the *blues* I ever before experienced. As I
have but little to do this morning, I shall let you know
that I am about as well as could be expected under the
very trying circumstances.

" We came up here from New York in the cars, and
arrived a little after two P. M. At four o'clock we reported our return to the commandant, and at five we
were formed for the purpose of *sizing* the battalion. As

fortune would have it, I got in company A, so I am no longer able to room with Bennett. My new room-mate is named Lomax.* He is a first rate fellow, and I am therefore resigned to circumstances.

"*Sept.* 1*st.*—I was interrupted the other day before I had finished this letter. We are now at our studies, and having something to do. My mind is diverted, and I feel a great deal better. One cannot appreciate home until he is away from it. I suppose I shall not leave this place for two years, which is a pretty long time to look ahead to. But I thank my stars that when that time comes, there will be no return to this place such as I have just experienced. But I shall soon find out that every place and condition of life has something with which to find fault and create disgust.

"I send you some verses by Mrs. Gen. Scott, written to welcome the return of the furlough class of 1850."

'THE RETURN OF THE FURLOUGH CLASS OF 1850.

"BY MRS. GENERAL SCOTT.

" There's a stir in Camp Gaines—all observers may see
  'Tis a moment of interest—a moment of glee ;
  Each Cadet has turned out—every tent is unmanned,
  Cadets pace to and fro—or in gay groups they stand ;
  Some object their welcome—they seem to await
  While all eyes are turned towards the ' South Gate.'

' The forbidden ' South Gate,' where Cadets are denied
  Their exits and entrances—where on one side,
  In frowning black characters, always are seen
  The words ' Shut the Gate,' (but none saying come in).
  On the other in ghastly white letters appear,
  The four horrid syllables, ' No smoking here.'

* General Lomax, of Confederate Army.

Oh ! answer ye classes, what may ye await ?
What pleasure approaches you thro' the 'South Gate?'

" The Furloughs are coming—and now must be near,
There is dust—there's shouting—' The Furloughs are here ! '
They are here—how they cheer ! as their brothers they hail ;
At the sight what delight and affection prevail.
Now rush they—now blush with arms intertwined
To be pressed to each heart—that's so brave, true, and kind.
Oh ! well might ye, fellows ! with rapture await
Their coming to-day and gaze towards the ' South Gate.'

" Ye privileged men ! (alas ! furlough's no more),
Whom that portal admits which opes not for the corps,
And who deem this the happiest day of your lives ;
Alexander, bright Bonaparte, musical Ives,
Rose, Casey, Smith, Sheridan, Morgan, Van Voast,
Each new second class man, all hail ! to your post !
May your duties be followed with ardor as great
As you felt when so wildly you passed the forbidden ' South Gate.'

" We welcome you back to the camp and the plain
Where your favorite Clitz will soon drill you again ;
Oh ! blest among students, ye now may renounce
All fears of being worsted by much ' cherry bounce,'
Late hours, cigars, or unwholesome rich food,
While your minds with fresh love shall be daily imbued ;
May you be happy at each turn of fate,
As when your blithe Furlough Class passed the ' South Gate.'

" The girls will have got home, and will give you all
the West Point news. We are now at Philosophy and
Chemistry, and I assure you we have our hands full.
This is by far the hardest course of the four. I am on
guard to-night, and while walking my post, I shall do
nothing but think of the 'loved ones at home,' and my

late furlough which I passed so deliciously with you all. While on post, is the only time we have for reflection, and I suppose it is well for us that it is so, for otherwise we should be too sad and downcast to bear with this place."

CHAPTER VI.

*Life at West Point, 1855.—Delegate Convention of Cadets—Proposes
to go to Nicaragua—Goes to Hospital with Sprained Ankle—
His preference for a Cavalry Regiment.*

To his Sister.

"WEST POINT, *Jan.* 14*th*, 1855.

"ON Saturday (yesterday), we were examined in
chemistry, and our examination is therefore over ;
I mean for our class. I am happy to say that I did very
well in chemistry, which is much more than I can say
with regard to philosophy. I did not like to tell you all
how I had done in ' Phil.' before I knew my standing,
as I was afraid mother would feel uneasy, notwithstanding all I have said on this point. I will now tell you the
facts of the case. Lieutenant Reynolds called me up at
the examination and gave me a mean contemptible little
demonstration, which I never dreamed would have been
given out. I was completely taken by surprise. I wrote
my name on the middle of the board and turned round,
and said I could not do it, in other words I '*fessed cold
with a clean board*,' as the saying is here under such circumstances. I had the sixth mark in the section for the
whole time from September to January, and if I had done
as well as I expected, should have come out fifth. As it is
I have come out ninth, so you see they only *threw* me three
on my files on my '*fess*' in Phil. Our standing having

not yet been read out, I do not know exactly what it will be, but I have no fear that it will be materially worse. Only one of our class will probably be found deficient at this examination.

"I was not aware until a short time ago that Mr. Stratton had appointed any one in place of Harris from his congressional district. It seems that he has appointed a young gentleman named Harker,* who came on in September, and I think he will *stay*."

To his Sister.

"WEST POINT, *March* 19*th*, 1855.

"We had a drill to-day for the first time this spring, and a great drill it was, the mud being ankle deep.

"They are rapidly clearing the ground for the new Riding hall, (which Mr. Benton could not defeat), and will probably finish it next year, so that we will ride in it before we graduate.

"There were twelve cadets put in arrest Saturday evening for going to Cold Spring ; first and third-class men.

"I did remember your birthday, and I wished very much to write to you on that day, but could not get time. But I will say now, what I then intended to say.   I hope you and your sisters will all pay more attention to your writing.   A lady should write a good hand if she possesses no other accomplishment.   It is for your sex an ndispensable accomplishment, and being entirely within your power, should by all means be attained.   Unless you make it a *practice* always to write with care, while you are forming your handwriting, it will always remain im-

* General Harker, killed in the battle of Kenesaw, Ga. A noble and gallant officer. He was a native of Gloucester county, New Jersey

perfect. A lady is supposed to have more time to devote to her letters, and besides writing a good hand, she should be able to write a good letter.

"A lady's letters are considered indicative of her mind and character, more so even than a gentleman's; for the reason that they generally are more sentimental, and express emotions and feelings with more intensity. To write a good letter requires care, attention, and practice. Practice makes perfect, but it must be the *practice* which improves, not that which degenerates. Please do not think hard of what I have said. It has been said not in a petty spirit of fault-finding, but from my anxiety for your improvement."

To his Sister.

"WEST POINT, *April 12th*, 1855.

"I can write you but a few lines, as I positively have nothing of interest to say, cooped up as I am still in this hospital. When I shall get out is impossible to say, as you know these attacks of quinsy are sometimes tedious. I think I shall be released from confinement in a few days. I am glad that father did not come up, for I want to be well when any of you visit me. Doctor Barnes is attending surgeon, Doctor Cuyler having been ordered to Fort Leavenworth. In my next I hope to be able to announce my departure hence, for the sumptuous hash and molasses of mess hall.

"Did you see among the names of the members of the Board of Visitors, that of our old friend Charles Negus, Esq., of Iowa Territory. He is to be here. I shall be very glad to see him, as I remember him as a kind neighbor and worthy citizen. I am reading Thiers' History of the

French Revolution. He is not equal to Alison as an historian. And has not as just an appreciation of the bad features in the character of Napoleon. He is not as philosophical as Alison, though I suppose his work suffers in translation."

To his Mother.

"WEST POINT, *April 20th,* 1855.

" I have been so incessantly occupied lately that I have been unable to write letters.

" It is now less than a year and two months to the day destined to celebrate my adieu ! to West Point and cadet life. When examination commences I shall have no time to think about time, and it will consequently gallop away unheeded.

" We have finished the review of permanent works, and to-morrow begin to review Civil Engineering. We are through with artillery, and the next recitation in it will be at examination. In ethics we are done, with moral science, and are reviewing *law.* So you see we are gradually drawing our studies to a close: and after three years almost continuous work, ' it is a consummation devoutly to be wished for.'

" I hope father has not failed to attend to the appointment of Mr. Kirkpatrick as visitor, as I would like to see our New Brunswick cousins here.

" Mr. Vail I see has not appointed McKensie, but some one named Kirkpatrick, * from Sussex county. Is he a relative of the New Brunswick K.'s ?

* Kilpatrick was the cadet referred to, since General Kilpatrick. The newspapers had it Kirkpatrick.

" Several of our class talk of going to Nicaragua. If I do not get in a mounted corps, what think you of my getting leave of absence for a year or so, and going with them ? Walker is in want of scientific soldiers for organizing his artillery and ordnance. Of course he would give me at least a captain's commission. One or two campaigns there would be more pleasant than Indian fighting in New Mexico. I should gain distinction and experience ; which might serve me in case the United States goes to war—as in the ordinary course of events she may."

To his Sister.

" WEST POINT, *May* 3*d*, 1855.

" You must not expect as many letters from me as usual. June and examination are now near. June is the most eventful month of the year at West Point. All look forward to it with impatience. Third-class men can talk or think of nothing else but furlough ; first-class men of graduating ; second-class men rejoice that they are about to reach the top round of the ladder here, while the fourth class exult in the prospect of ceasing to be *plebs*, and discuss the merits of the new plebs, as they occasionally put in their appearance. None look back on the past ; they are all too busy peering ahead. Nothing bright or pleasant can be discovered in the past or present. Imagination is employed in decking with gay colors and fascination the future, beauties and joys it may never possess."

To his Mother.

" WEST POINT, *May* 11*th*, 1855.

" I regret that father could not come up last week : and now I do not want him to come until my confinement is over.　The punishment is for visiting after taps.　Carroll bought half a dozen shad and we cooked them after taps in Van Horn's room.　We were all busy feasting, when Wilcox with his dark lantern appeared to disturb our festivity.　It was a ludicrous sight, and we all could not help laughing, Wilcox himself indulging in a grimace howl! You gentlemen (he said), appear to have a fine time of it. Spite of the interruption, I never saw provisions disappear so rapidly.　Some tried at first to hide behind the bookcase and under the bed.　Van Horn and all were reported. Van Horn was reported for seven different offences : First, light in room after *taps*, second, trying to hide light with bedquilt at window, third, provisions in quarters, fourth, cooking in quarters, fifth, allowing noise in quarters after *taps*, sixth, not putting out light when directed, seventh, out of bed after taps.　Those reports of Van Horn will give him near forty demerits and he will be lucky if he is not cut off of furlough.

"What I said about going to Nicaragua was rather an experiment, to ascertain what you would say on the subject.　I have no great opinion of those South American States.　Their people are a miserable mixed race. And I think we inherit from our English ancestors an antipathy to the Spaniards.　They have degenerated from the days of Gonsalvo de Cordova, whose fame and valor rivals the Chevalier Bayard's.　I think Mr. Walker has no business in Nicaragua.

"A report has just reached us that *Crampton* * has been dismissed. Such shouting and hurrahing greeted the news, you would have thought, had you heard it, that we were to take the field to-morrow.　It has produced the

* British Minister.

greatest excitement throughout the barracks. Visions of *Brevets* for gallant and meritorious conduct dance through the brains of many a first-class man. The only drawback which the war would compel some of us to submit to, would be the loss of the furlough and a few weeks of happiness at home, which all so ardently long for. But the demands of duty cannot be disregarded. An English war for Americans is esteemed preferable to a war with any other country. England's hate for us is heartily reciprocated. Nothing but dollars and cents keep us at peace so long. As it was with Carthage and Rome, one or the other some of these days, will have to succumb ; and of course it will be Great Britain."

To his Mother.

"WEST POINT, *May* 16*th*, 1855.

" As I have but a short lesson in chemistry and philosophy for to-morrow, I will devote my spare time this evening in writing to you, and paying my debts to other correspondents.

" I was very sorry to hear of the accident which frightened you all. If I was only home, I could soon take the devil out of the ponies. Jeannie made a narrow escape, which she would not have done with less presence of mind. Those Canadian ponies are often very vicious.

" I shall be unable to attend the marriage of cousin *Ess.* The marriage of a cousin is not an affair which entitles a cadet to leave of absence. A sister's marriage only enables him to enjoy that privilege. If they were to give every one *leave* to attend a *cousin's* marriage, there would be no end to it. Cousins are generally more numerous than sisters, *mine* immeasurably so.

4

" Infantry drills commenced on the fifteenth inst., and they will continue the remainder of this month, and on the first we will give our distinguished friend Negus a review. I regret that truth compels me to say that I fear it will be but an indifferent one. *Billy Walker* is a good hearted, easy old fellow, but not a man to have here. He cannot put a battalion through like Bob Garnett. He has got a crotchet in his head at present, however, and is occupying himself with putting men in arrest for *wearing un-uniform gloves.*"

To his Sister.

" WEST POINT, *May 21st*, 1855.

" Yours has been received. Mr. Negus has not yet arrived. I am glad he paid you a visit at Woodbury. He will arrive probably this evening. I have been so busy lately, that I have been unable to write to any of you. You must all excuse and have patience with me till after examination.

" The weather is pleasant, but slightly cool, rather too much so indeed for white pants, which we will probably don to-morrow.

" The plebs are beginning to straggle along, three or four having been here for several days."

To his Mother.

" WEST POINT, *June 5th*, 1855.

" I was examined in philosophy this morning and did very well.

" Yesterday we rode out with the first class at squadron drill. The day before that we had battalion drill, and to-day a skirmish drill.

" Mr. Negus handed me the box and bundle, for which I am thankful.

" I am going to work, and studying my chemistry faithfully as I did my philosophy, and by so doing shall be prepared in that diffuse and extended study. If I do as well in that as I did in 'phil,' my general standing will be much better than I feared it would be.

" The *Furloughs* leave within ten days or thereabouts. I wish that I could go with them, always provided that I did not have to go over second class course again. Soon I shall now be to all intents and purposes a first class man, God willing. When I thought of such an event three years ago, it seemed an age before it would happen, and was considered rather a probability than anything else. But now it is here at last, and we find that there was more pleasure in the anticipation than there is in the possession.

" We will probably go into camp next week."

To his Father.

"WEST POINT, *June 16th,* 1855.

" Our friend Negus still moves about here as majes-tically as he did on the prairie. I have frequent talks with him, and he seems much pleased with all he sees here.

"There is no one going to address the Dialectic Society this year. The committee appointed to attend to the matter put it off until it was too late. I was elected president of the society last month for the ensuing year. I shall need a copy of Jefferson's Manual, in order to perfect myself in parliamentary rules.

" Our camp will probably be called Camp Lee, in

compliment to the Colonel.   A first class encampment ranks next to a *plebe* encampment in the duties to be performed.   Besides camp duties, we have to recite in both artillery and infantry tactics."

To his Sister.

" Camp Calhoun, West Piont,
        June 19th, 1855.

" Here we are at last in our last encampment.   The tents were pitched this morning between eight and ten, A.M., and at twelve, M., the battalion marched into camp. You will perceive by the date of my letter, that Colonel Lee was not complimented as rumor said he was to be.

" Camp is but a poor place for letter-writing, not that time is wanted, but the accommodations for it are not convenient.

" I now begin to realize the fact that this is my last year of cadet life, that I am a first-class man, and if I look forward with dread to studying infantry and artillery tactics during the cruel heat of July and August, I bear in mind that it will soon be over.   So far our encampment has been quite easy, as drills for the first class do not commence until after the first of July.

" I am now living in my old company B, though I expect to go back to company A, when we return to barracks.   I am tenting with McAllister.

" The third of July would be a good day for you to come up.   On the morning of the fourth, there will be a salute, the battalion will be formed under arms and marched to the chapel, where Bailey will deliver the oration, and if he does himself justice, it will be a good one.   At night, the first hop of the season will take place, and like the last one on the twenty-eighth of August, will extend until twelve o'clock. The next day the drills commence."

To his Mother.

"Camp Calhoun, West Point,
July 1st, 1855.

"This day we become first-class men, *de jure* as well as *de facto,* and it is pleasant as we look back over the trials and vexations of our past course at the Academy, to remember that at this time next year we will be enjoying the delights of home, God willing. Camp life, far more than that of the barracks, induces thoughts of our past lives, and conjures up visions of the future.

"The order of the procession on the fourth, will be, first, band, second, orator of the day Bailey, third, chaplain and reader of Declaration of Independence on his right, and the president of the society, (your humble servant), fourth, the escort under arms, fifth, the rest of the corps without arms, sixth the Academic Board and staff, seventh, citizens who may desire to join the procession and enjoy the benefit of the dust raised by the others.

"All those men who were suspended last spring on account of demerit have returned. Vinton and Reno again swell the ranks of our class to fifty ; forty less than when we commenced in 1852. I painted four pieces last year, and shall obtain possession of them and give them to you when you come up. Their artistic merit, I must confess, has not been discovered, but still I know you will value them as much as if they displayed the finish of a more masterly and elegant brush."

To his Sister.

" CAMP CALHOUN, WEST POINT, *July 24th,* 1855.

" In my last I gave you an account of the drowning of Cadet Wonderly, whose parents live in Philadelphia. His body was found, and buried this afternoon with military honors. I was lieutenant of the escort, because I was lieutenant in his company; and although I felt very unwell, I did not like to decline, since it would then fall to some one else, and it was not a pleasant duty.

"General Totten is here, and is testing the strength of different materials for fortifications.

" The *plebe* squad drills were discontinued to-day, and to-morrow company drills commence. We will finish working in the laboratory to-morrow, and will then begin Practical Engineering.

" Cogswell, Clitz, and all the old officers will have to leave the coming fall, and then I think I shall be in Wilcox's company.

" P. S. *August 4th,* 1855.—I have not been able to finish the above letter, and owe you all apologies for not writing oftener ; so I will heap them altogether, and say to one and all that I have positively had no time for letter-writing. We have to go to drill (infantry) in the morning before breakfast. Then immediately after breakfast comes morning parade and guard-mounting. Half an hour after that, artillery drill, which lasts an hour and twenty minutes ; after this is over we have to go to practical engineering out by the cemetery, where we remain two hours, and get back just in time for dinner. After dinner we have to study our artillery tactics, which we recite in, and get back half an hour before evening drill, which last takes us until within half an hour of parade. By which you will perceive that by the time evening comes I must be pretty well exhausted, and in no condition or mood for any epistolary work.

"Last week, when I was on guard, the officer of the day was reported for allowing citizens at the reception tent after taps, and I for permitting members of the guard to visit them, for which each of us are confined in camp for a week."

To his Mother.

"CAMP CALHOUN, WEST POINT, }
August 15*th*, 1855. }

"I have so little time now, that I cannot answer half the letters I receive.

"This encampment, I am most happy to say, is now approaching its close. Our time is much more occupied than when we are in barracks. We have to pursue our studies, thus having the duties of barracks with none of the conveniences. But though this work is hard and constant, yet it is lightened by the joyous reflection that ten months more will close forever our tedious cadet life—a time, the pleasure of which is about half, I expect, in anticipation. 'Man never *is*, but always to *be* blest.'

"I am now enjoying my liberty after the recent confinement. I went to the hop last night; the evening was quite cool, and we had a pleasant time. I hope to see you here the last of this month. This is my last encampment, and you must not fail to come."

To his Mother.

"WEST POINT, *Sept. 5th,* 1855.

"I write to you again from my old residence, the hospital. Monday I was trying to mount my horse for some time, but he being rather wild, would not let me even put my foot in the stirrup ; at last I made a spring, got my foot in the stirrup, and endeavored to throw myself into the saddle. But in this I failed ; the horse started off at a run, and down I came, but could not extricate my foot from the stirrup until it was badly sprained. It is very painful, but the consequence I most regret is that it will throw me behind in my studies. The doctor says I will not be able to ride again for a month. Yesterday I worked my way up to barracks, but it was so painful that I shall not try it again until my foot is better."

To his Father.

"WEST POINT, *Sept. 17th,* 1855.

"My foot was getting better until day before yesterday, when I hurt it accidentally. I have been now nearly two weeks in this infernal hospital, and 1 am getting terribly tired of it. I am gradually falling behindhand in my studies, especially logic. I attended engineering for several days, but found that I was hurting my ankle by moving about so much and I stopped it. I have not recited in either mineralogy or logic, but have kept up with the section in the former. I intend next week to attend all. Hard study will soon bring me up.

"When we graduate there will be a terrible rush for the mounted regiments. Indeed many will have their friends at work before, to secure appointments in the dragoons or cavalry. You must do what you can for me at

Washington. With the aid of Thomson and the Iowa senators, and others you can induce to back me, I ought not to fail. If I do not get in a mounted regiment, I will leave the army when the four years have expired ; and in the meantime study law. I am not so sure but I have mistaken my profession. The law is the great avenue to fame, fortune, and power in this country, unless war should intervene. In that case I should prefer the army."

To his Sister.

"WEST POINT, *Nov.* 27*th,* 1855.

"You surely cannot complain this time of my tardiness in replying to your letter, for I received it this morning.

"Saturday we expect to ride in the new hall.

"It is now just a month to Christmas. I foster the hope of being able to meet some of you in Brooklyn, but it is not probable.

"We still have dress parades on the brain, although it has become pretty cool and winter-like.

"We have had some quite exciting times here lately, in consequence of a censure of the corps by General Totten, in Orders, with regard to the testimony of cadets on courts-martial, and what he terms our 'Code of Morals.' He substantially charges us *indiscriminately* with want of regard for truth, and ungentlemanly conduct.

"Last Saturday night, after the corps had assembled in the Dialectic Hall, (I have stated in a previous letter that we were to have a public meeting) and while awaiting the arrival of officers and ladies, I proposed that we should resolve ourselves into a meeting, to protest

4*

against the groundless and false charges of Gen. T., which rested on the testimony of men, who, when in the corps last year, were notorious as possessing no character, and unworthy of belief.

"This being done, I offered a resolution to the effect, that the several classes of the corps should hold meetings immediately after dinner the next day, and appoint five delegates, each to meet in convention, and agree upon some form of protest.

"This, after a little discussion was unanimously adopted. The five elected by our class were Gaston, Snyder, McAlister, Poe, and Bayard.

"The delegates assembled to-night in Gaston's room and proceeded to business. We hope to be able to do everything in a becoming and lawful manner. But if the Superintendent refuses to forward the protest, it will be sent to the War Department. The committee men will run no extra danger as we propose having it signed by every man in the corps. By this means they will be able to pitch on no one as ringleader."

To his Sister.

"WEST POINT, *Dec.* 17*th*, 1855.

"Preparation for examination next month now makes engrossing demands on my time. I have no fear of the result, as I have got into pretty good habits of application. As it is now little more than six months when our final examination takes place, I am anxious so to stand that I shall not disappoint you all then.

"To-morrow will be my twentieth birthday, and this will make the fifth one spent away from home. I wonder if I shall ever pass another with you at home? That is a question it is difficult to answer.   Next year, I shall, at that time, (if in the country as I expect) be in all probability in the far west, in winter quarters, at some interior fort, with faint hopes of ever enjoying the pleasures of home, for years to come.

"I will not waste my life in the inglorious pursuit of Indian thieves and robbers on the plains.   In four years after I graduate, if I don't resign and take to the law, I will offer my sword to the Sultan or the Pasha of Egypt. The east of Europe and the west of Asia are the true theatres of military glory.

"I don't think I will be able to get leave to visit home, or even Brooklyn, on Christmas.   Instead of which, I shall be hammering away at Engineering, the Britannia Tubular Bridge, and determining the breaking weight of timber of multifarious sizes and kinds."

CHAPTER VII.

To his Sister.

"WEST POINT, *Jan.* 13*th*, 1856.

"AGREEABLY to my promise I write, though this is the first opportunity I have had for some time. You must be well aware that my time is wholly occupied preparing for examination in my different studies as they successively come on the stage. Thursday I was up in engineering, and did not do as well as I expected, coming out lower (twenty) than I ever came out in any study yet, at any previous examination. But I still remain in second section, and I will certainly rise in it between now and June, so that my *general standing* will be as good as it was last year. If I can do this, I will certainly be able to get in a mounted corps, which is now the extent of my ambitious aspirations.

"In five months more I shall be at 'home, sweet home;' and what pleasant times I anticipate! But alas! I shall soon have to leave it for some distant post, unless by good luck that post should be Carlisle ; although, if it was not for the pleasure of being near you all, I should prefer immediate employment against the Indians. But before I leave you we will have some jolly times. We will have some pleasant rides among the pine glades of

Gloucester and the sands of West Jersey   I will assist you in breaking Starlight and his mate* of some of their naughty tricks.   If I am stationed at Carlisle I shall furnish myself with a first-rate horse.   What color shall he be ? "

To his Sister.

"WEST POINT, *Feb. 27th*, 1856.

"We are getting a class-ring made.   What kind of stone would you advise me to have put in it ?   Don't you think sardonyx looks best ?   The chasing adopted I think very handsome.   The device will be a gun firing from an embrasure at a vessel ; a *chain shot* has just been fired from the gun.   The motto is 'SEPARATED YET UNITED.'   The chain shot which was formerly used in sea-coast defences, consisted of two shot corresponding to the calibre of the piece, united by a chain.   This is conceived to be symbolical of our class, the individuals of which, like the two shot, will be separated ; yet whether mountains or oceans divide us, we will always be *enchained* by the remembrance of the many happy days of fellowship we have enjoyed here together.   'Tell me what you think of it.

"Less than four months to graduation !   What a pleasant sentence to write.   But as the time grows shorter my joy becomes less ecstatic, and I look at things more coolly.   When I remember how many responsibilities and troubles I will then encounter, I almost doubt whether our present comparatively easy life, to the routine of which we have adapted ourselves, be not more agreeable."

* Ponies.

To his Sister.

" *March* 2d, 1856.

" A cadet is to be pardoned, I think, for any failure in the character of a correspondent, as he always writes under great disadvantage.

" To rake out anything from our daily routine of duty must require a very commendable spirit of perseverance and an enormous amount of ingenuity. Now as I possess neither of these qualities in a remarkable degree, I hold myself excusable for all my derelictions in this line. Just consider a day's duty, for instance.

" First comes *réveillé*—as unwelcome as the blasts of winter—arousing us from dreams of home and happiness and ushering in the toils of the day. Jumping up half asleep one mechanically slips into some clothes and slip-shod hastens down shivering to infernal roll call. The next half hour should be spent in fixing up your room; but a first class man generally puts that off until the half hour release from quarters between return from breakfast and eight o'clock. Half an hour after *réveillé* the inspection drum beats, at which I have to inspect the rooms in my subdivision, comprising the two upper floors in the 2d division of barracks estimating from the east. Of course I do not have to inspect my own room, so Lomax lies in the quiet enjoyment of his morning nap while I go round freezing and inspecting. I see that the floors are swept clean, the beds made up, the wash basins inverted on stand, and lamps in their proper places on mantel, and am now, after some months' experience, fully qualified for instruction in all matters pertaining to such housekeeping details. From this time to breakfast, there is an hour spent either in sleep or study. From eight o'clock until eleven we are drawing at our problems. We recite now in cavalry tactics which we recite from twelve to one, P. M., Mondays, Wednesdays, and Fridays. At two in the afternoon artillery and moral science require our presence. These studies alternate weekly—recitation three times in one week and twice in the other one week, *vice versa* the next. These of course have to be studied the remaining study hours between three and four o'clock P. M., and the evening of the preceding day and in the hours between eleven and one P. M. on those days that we do not recite in cavalry tactics. After four o'clock comes parade and supper, and half an hour after the latter comes evening call to quarters, and the studies for the succeeding day are commenced. At ten P. M., when *taps* beat, I have to inspect my subdivision for *all present* and report at the guard room to the officer in charge ; and this closes the day's work. Now although I cannot complain that we have not plenty of time to learn everything and besides have spare time, yet one is so tired and exhausted when that spare time comes that letter-writing or indeed almost anything else besides sleep is entirely out of the question. I read, to be sure, but it does not amount to any thing, for with my continual study, my mind becomes so tired and harassed that it is only the lighter kind of reading I can attempt.

"The first migratory birds which the arrival of spring (spring indeed ! with snow piled up all around us) has brought, is announced in the arrival at the hotel of Mrs. — and Miss —. They were both here last summer for some time. The former has a relative in the corps, and is quite pretty and agreeable. The latter was here last summer with a younger sister.

"Some of the class to graduate in June, talk of having a ball at Cozzens' the night we are relieved. I myself am opposed to it ; and shall try and prevent it. Should they have one, will you girls come up to it ? Mrs. G—will give us one in the city ; there is no doubt of it. I did not intend to go to it, but now that she is determined to give it, after her son has been unable to remain here, that is kindness which I think we all should appreciate. I shall therefore attend."

To his Mother.

"WEST POINT, *April* 21*st*, 1856.

"Spring has at last come, and we are once more on the plain at duty. Drills, dress parades guard mounting etc. This delightful recreation invigorates and raises the spirits of every one. A bright shining spring morning is the most lovely of the year. Such days remind me of my last spring in Morristown. I know not whether the pleasure of receiving my long hoped for cadet appointment made me look joyously on everything, or whether my faculty of discrimination then first began to be developed ; but I certainly never passed a spring which I look back upon with so much pleasure. I shall always remember it as one of the most delightful periods of my life. We had such magnificent grounds around our house ; then there were the neighboring orchards, in which we used to shoot robins—Carlo, my pretty setter who used to go walking with us every day ; Speedwell pond, on which George and I rowed so often. Then, too I used to walk with father every evening in the valley beneath Mount Washington, where the General marched his few troops round and round, deceiving the British as to the force he had. Ah! those were precious days, never to return again, and I come down to thoughts of my present situation.

"The advent of spring makes graduation appear very close at hand. Soon June and the renewed splendors of summer will come.

> ' Hurrah for the merry bright month of June,
>   Which opens a life so new,
>   When we doff the cadet and don the brevet
>   And change the grey for the blue,'

as an old cadet song runs. You recollect the *Siege Battery* up near the hotel. Our class were there at drill two days engaged in mounting the guns and howitzers belonging to it, which we dismounted last summer. This finished the drills for our class proper.

Four first class men are now detailed each day to superintend the fifth class, making cartridges in the laboratory. Three of us to superintend a portion of the second class at the siege battery, and five are placed over the rest of that class at the *Mortar Battery* near the flagstaff. Then there are three chiefs of section, one chief of line of caissons, and six chiefs of pieces for Mounted Battery, at which Captain Clark is now exercising the soldiers as drivers; and finally there are six detailed to superintend the third and fourth classes at the Battery of field howitzers now on the plain near the encampment ground. This last, however, is merely temporary, for as soon as the drivers are efficiently drilled at the mounted battery, these two classes will be attached to it as cannoniers. Thus a total of twenty-eight first-class men are on duty every evening."

To his Father.

"WEST POINT, *June* 3*d*, 1856.

"The 1st of June so long wished-for has come and passed, and graduation is now not far off.

I have been hard at work with my engineering ; we will be examined in a day or two on that subject. How I shall do on it is uncertain. On other subjects I expect to do well. Several members of the Board of Visitors have arrived, and among them Mr. Kirkpatrick.* He sent for me, and I obtained a permit to go to the hotel. I spent a pleasant evening with him and his family, and with his sister, Mrs. How, had much conversation about our family and all its branches. I hope to be home by the twentieth."

To his Father.

"WEST POINT, *June* 8*th*, 1856.

"I was up in Ethics day before yesterday and did very well. The Engineering standing has been read out and I am nineteen in it, one file higher than in January. I think my *general standing*—that which finally appears on the catalogue—will be ten, eleven, or twelve ; certainly not lower: and I shall then have a right to expect a mounted regiment.

"I shall go to Washington immediately after graduating and urge my claims to a lieutenant's brevet either in the Dragoons or Cavalry.

"I wish, father, in the meantime, you would ask your friends in Congress—the senators with whom you are on the proper terms, and the members of Congress from New Jersey, to back my application.

* Hon. Littleton Kirkpatrick, a cousin of cadet Bayard's father

" Four years ago the goal beyond which my ambition did not venture to stretch, was to graduate with credit to myself and with such a standing as would be gratifying to my family. In a few days more that *ultima thule* of my hopes four years ago will be attained ; and now burying the past, and looking forward to the future, the horizon, though dark and doubtful, is vastly enlarged. I have not submitted to the drudgery, anxiety, and privations of the last four years, merely for the privilege of chasing Indian thieves, or rotting in some remote and isolated post of the interior. I am a soldier. Alexander, Cæsar and Bonaparte were only soldiers, so far as it respected their ascent to fame and power.

" If there should be no war in which the United States should be involved, I shall seek some other field after a few years—time must determine *where* that field will be. It may be Asia or Africa ; or if nothing else offers, there is the *law*. That profession is allied by nature to the military profession. It is perpetual war on rascality. The bar and the bench are always engaged in that sort of war."

According to the *Regulations* of the Military Academy, each cadet of the first class, who, at the annual examination in June, is found qualified for a commission, receives a diploma signed by the Superintendent and members of the Academic Board, and his name is presented to the Secretary of War with a recommendation for a commission.

The final standing of Bayard in his class was eleven. A standing quite equal to his expectations. But considering how much ill health he had while at West Point, his social disposition, and indifference to receiving demerit marks, to a moderate extent, his standing was satisfactory to himself and his friends, and such as justified his being assigned to one of the mounted regiments.

CHAPTER VIII.

*Appointed Second Lieutenant in First Cavalry—Fort Leavenworth—
Difficulties in Kansas—Service on the Plains.*

TO be appointed a cavalry officer, was one of the most cherished hopes of Bayard, even in boyhood. His preference for that branch of the service is frequently explained in his correspondence: During the few years he spent on the prairies of Iowa, he was much in the saddle, and became an expert and bold rider ; and fond of horses, which no doubt had its influence in producing his preference for the cavalry.

He was familiar with the family tradition, that the Bayards in America were descended from a branch of the family of the Chevalier Bayard.* He was aware that the title of Chevalier was given him from his great skill as a horseman, and his exploits as a cavalry leader.

All the historical memoirs of the Chevalier which young Bayard could obtain, he perused with avidity. There can be no doubt that the heroic character of the Chevalier, his generosity, magnanimity, affection for his friends, and his dauntless bravery, had a great influence in moulding the character, and inspiring the ambition of the subject of these pages.

He was also familiar with the history of his great-

* Appendix B.

grandfather, Colonel John Bayard, who in the war of the Revolution, commanded the first troop of Philadelphia cavalry. *

In the course of his instruction at West Point, he came to know the duties of a cavalry officer, and that they were more severe and fatiguing than those of officers of the infantry. But his experience there, seemed to increase his preference for the cavalry service. In conversation, he often adverted to the fact, (as justifying his preference for the cavalry), that all the great battles, ancient as well as modern, were won by cavalry charges.

Soon after graduating he went to Washington, where he met his friends and classmates, Fitzhugh Lee, and Lomax, who likewise preferred the cavalry. Together they made personal application to the Secretary of War, to be assigned to mounted corps, and with the aid of their friends, they all succeeded in obtaining the wished-for assignments.

Bayard was appointed second lieutenant in the First Cavalry, his commission bearing date August 1st, 1856.

This regiment was commanded by Col. E. V Sumner, whose headquarters were at Fort Leavenworth, Kansas Territory. Including cavalry and infantry, there were several thousand troops in Kansas at this time. The duties of this cavalry force were particularly onerous. They were charged with the defence of a vast extent of territory, from Indian tribes—who, unless checked by the military, were disposed to rob and murder the settlers. They were subject also to the requisition of the Governor of Kansas, then the seat of incipient war between the Free-State, and the Pro-slavery parties.

* See Appendix C.

The Territory had been recently organized, and the population was scant and scattered. Settlers were intruding on lands to which the Indian title had not been extinguished, and squatting on public lands not yet surveyed. The defeat of the Missouri Restriction—the "Compact of Peace" of 1820, opened at once the fertile and inviting lands of Kansas to those desirous of extending the area of slavery. Mr. Douglas, aspiring to please both north and south, expected to propitiate the south by this repeal ; while he doubtless foresaw that the Kansas Nebraska Bill insured success to the populous north—the strongest in numbers, wealth, and enterprise. Practically, it was an invitation to civil war, and the border elements of discord rushed impetuously to the conflict.

Southern and northern colonists in organized companies, came armed and equipped to assert, by force, their right to introduce or exclude slavery. The people of the State of Missouri, anxious that their neighbors should adopt institutions similar to their own, and stimulated by local and other demagogues, entered Kansas in troops, armed and accompanied with artillery, determined to vote down the resident population—a majority of which was opposed to the introduction of slavery.

Of course collisions soon took place, and the presence of a part of the regular army, to act as a *posse comitatus* in aid of the civil authorities, became necessary for the preservation of the peace.

On the cavalry the most active and important duties were devolved, and they were alternately ordered by the War Department to chastise Indian marauders, and by the Governor of Kansas to preserve the peace and defend the lives of the inhabitants of the Territory. The letters of Lieutenant Bayard, during his four years ·service on the Plains and in Kansas, will enable the reader to trace his career during that time, and will show something of the various and arduous duties, of the frontier service of the cavalry officer. They will likewise give some graphic sketches of encounters with the Indians, whose hostile disposition nothing but the fear of chastisement restrains.

West Point officers previous to the war, were very reticent on the subject of politics, and habitually declined to converse on it. When at home in his furlough year— and after graduating, Lieutenant Bayard would leave the room whenever political discussions commenced. It was doubtless this aversion to talk on political subjects, which will account for his saying so little in his letters from Kansas, about the border war then waged with ferocity on that battle-field—the prologue of the rebellion of 1861. Having been ordered to report at Fort Leavenworth on the expiration of his furlough, October 1st, Lieutenant Bayard arrived there within the time appointed, as appears from the following letter.

To his Father.

"Fort Leavenworth, K. T., *Sept. 24th,* 1856.

"At last I am here after a tedious journey—the particulars of which I gave you in a letter from St. Louis, and one from Jefferson City.

"I shall have to furnish myself with a horse, saddle and some other accoutrements. A good horse cannot be got here for less than one hundred and forty dollars. I must have a good one. How long I remain here depends on my health, which just now is not such as will warrant joining my company when they return to Lecompton.

"Leavenworth is beautifully situated on a high bluff, and is now a busy place, and crowded with troops. I called on General Smith this morning. He is quite an old man, judging from his appearance, and his health is not good. He appears much broken, but is still a fine-looking man.

"A train leaves here on Friday, October second, for Lecompton, and I will go up with it if well enough. My company is now on an expedition north, towards Nebraska, and it may be some weeks before its return to Lecompton.

"Lieutenant Steuart* with his company, had a very pretty fight with the Cheyenne Indians the other day, and the talk is now, of a Cheyenne expedition.

"Things are in a very unsettled state politically, in this Territory. I can as yet say nothing from my own knowledge, and can only repeat what I hear from others.

"The troops have now in custody about a hundred and twenty prisoners, most of them Free-State men. Just about half the fights you read of in the papers as having occurred here, have no foundation in fact. They tell me Captain Walker, captain of my company, is a fine fellow, and will be most glad to see me, as he has no lieutenant with him at present.

"Major Porter was kind enough to invite me to stay with him while I remain at the fort. If I had staid with the lieutenants at their quarters, I should not have liked it so well, as their room is drenched with whiskey from morning till night. The temptation to a young officer to

* J. E. B. Steuart, the Confederate General.

5

drink is hard to resist.   But I am determined that I will not contract the habit.

" *Oct. 1st,* 1856.—I was interrupted last night and could not finish this letter. News has just come that Lane has entered the Territory with some four hundred armed men, in violation of the Governor's proclamation, and that all the troops have left Lecompton to go in pursuit of him.

" There is a very pleasant society here, composed in part of many ladies whom I knew at West Point, officers' wives, etc.

" About Kansas matters, I am still at a loss for reliable information.   The Territory is invaded by large bodies of Missourians, the largest portion of whom do not design becoming residents, they come avowedly to make Kansas a Slave-State.   On the other hand, northern emigrants are pouring in, the most of whom come as permanent residents and settlers, though their leaders propose to stay no longer than is required to defeat the pro-slavery men.   My opinion is, that it is impossible to make Kansas a Slave-State.   The administration, backed by the army, are not strong enough for that. Of course no officer expresses any opinion in favor of one side or the other. What is most wanting here, is a Governor of commanding talents and weight of character. Governor Geary is a good man and desires to do right; but he is not a great man. The people generally have no confidence in the fairness and justice of the administration. They believe that for party purposes, the Democrats want to bring in Kansas as a Slave-State. If this be so, it is the worst move the Democracy ever made, and will in the end break the party into fragments."

" FORT LEAVENWORTH, *Dec. 7th,* 1856.

" I was much gratified to receive your letter last evening. It is a great treat to receive a letter from home
when one is so far away as I am now. You will, I trust,
all of you write frequently without reference to my an-
swers. I will write when I can, but when in the field, it
will be impossible for me to write often. We shall have
neither tables nor chairs in our tents, and but very imperfect means of carrying along with us any supply of writing
materials. I therefore fear that when in the field, weeks
may elapse without my being able to get off a letter.

" Bennett, with his light artillery, who came up on a boat,
left yesterday with a train, to join Colonel Cooke's command on the Nebraska line. I had hoped to go with him
but could not. I am afraid I will be detained here
several weeks. Sawtelle, Plummer, Thompson, Bell and
Crittenden, are all fine fellows, and I pass my time very
pleasantly. My duties are not arduous, I attend roll call
and am officer of the day in my turn. The news last
night was, that Vinton had resigned ; if true, it promotes
Lomax into my regiment.

" They say here that our regiment is now pretty well
weeded out, so that promotion in it will be slow. Bennett is I think about the luckiest man in the class.
There are four or five " lieuts." who have this summer been
put in the 4th Artillery—some of whom, if not all, will
resign before long. Besides that, the regiment has been
ordered to Florida, and that will cause resignations, if
not deaths. Bennett, however, being on duty with the
light battery, will not have to go to Florida.

" In my letter to mother from St. Louis I endeavored

to give you a tolerable idea of my performances there.
The society there is delightful. I certainly did pass my
time very agreeably.

"The election on Monday passed off very quietly. It
was entirely a one-sided affair. The Free-State men
took no part in it. The Missourians all along the border crossed over, took the necessary oaths and voted.
They were passing through here, backward and forward,
all day long on the day of election, and there were more
votes polled in Leavenworth city, as well as at other
places, than there were residents.

"Col. Cooke was sent north to the Nebraska line to stop
any armed bodies of men invading the Territory from that
direction. But no impediment was offered to the inva-
ders from Missouri. Col. Cooke captured two hundred
and twenty-five men, in whose wagons he found boxes of
muskets, pistols, sabres, etc., while they brought no agri-
cultural implements, nor did the Missourians have any of
the latter. The prisoners were sent to Lecompton, where
they were released by the Governor—which he would not
have done probably had the election not been over.

"The army has been made the scapegoat throughout
this whole *imbroglio*. The pro-slavery men denounce it,
because it don't do all they require of it ; and the
Free-State men complain that it is merely here to help
Kansas to become a Slave-State. I think neither party
has any cause of complaint against the army. The officers obey orders, and keep the people from murdering
and violence—and in my opinion act with great prudence
and discretion. If it were not for the interposition of the
army here, there would be a civil war which would soon
spread and involve the North and South in deadly conflict.

"Captain Walker, of Free-State notoriety, was here a day or two ago, and from him I learned a good many things respecting the contest now going on in this Territory. He appears to be a plain, unpretending, and well-intentioned man, and quite different from the renowned Col. Titus, who, from the best accounts I can obtain, is a braggart and a coward. Walker admits candidly that many outrages have been committed by Free-State men since the sacking and burning of Lawrence, but he says their provocation was great, and that their lawless acts have always been condemned by the most reputable and influential men. He gives a terrible account of the outrages committed by Missourians, which, if true, they are worse than savage barbarians.

"I should have joined my company before this, but the doctor would not consent to it. I am now however, better, and hope to leave this soon."

To his Father.

"CAMP NEAR LECOMPTON, *Nov. 9th,* 1856.

"As this will probably be the last opportunity I shall have of writing to you for some time, I embrace it to give you some account of my movements.

"We left the fort on Tuesday the fourth, in the midst of a severe storm of wind and rain and passed through Leavenworth city, where we picked up Clark, the Indian agent. Crittenden and I proceeded twelve miles from the fort, and camped on the banks of a small creek known as the Little Stranger. Halted and pitched our tents and picketed our horses before dark, shortly after which, Sturgis, who had remained at the fort awhile, rode into camp. I brought out with me my servant, a negro boy, who does our cooking for us. It appeared a good deal like old times in Iowa when we were out turkey-hunting.

"We were late getting off next day, but Sturgis sent a detachment ahead to halt Clark, who had gone on further, and as we were responsible for the safety of the public money he had with him, Sturgis determined he should not go off alone so far. Six miles from the *Little Stranger* we crossed *Big Stranger*, and four miles beyond that we found Clark. Leaving Crittenden and myself with about a dozen men to accompany the wagons, Sturgis and the remainder of the company pushed on with Clark, who having an ambulance and a good team of horses was able to get along at a more rapid rate than our mule teams. We reached Lawrence where we crossed the Kansas or Kaw river about three in the afternoon, and rode over to Major Wood's camp, until the wagons which we left about a mile behind came up. Finding that it was getting late, I rode down to the river to see about them, and found that one of them had stuck just as it was getting off the boat. This mishap detained us till sundown, and Sturgis had given us orders to join him at Lecompton or he would have no forage for his horses. We accordingly had to push on twelve miles to Lecompton, where we arrived after a cold ride about half-past nine o'clock. The next day being stormy, Sturgis did not move, but left the next morning in a worse storm of sleet, rain and snow. Having taken a bad cold and being threatened with an attack of my old complaint quinsy, I remained with Captain De Saussure, who is camped here with his company. He leaves to-morrow morning for *Paoli*, thirty miles from Westport, and thence he goes to old Fort Scott for the purpose of capturing a gang of horse thieves and marauders that infest that part of the Territory. Colonel Cooke has for the present attached me to his company. At Paoli I will see assembled the Peoria, Piankeshaw, Shawnee and Kaskaskia Indians, and at Fort Scott the Osages. They say it is a fine country. We take rations for twenty-one days, but we may have to be there longer, and may possibly have to winter there. I like De Saussure very much, and I shall be the only lieutenant with him."

To his Mother.

"FORT LEAVENWORTH, K. T., *Nov. 17th*, 1856.

"You will be surprised by the date of my letter. When I wrote to father from Lecompton, I did not expect to get back here so soon.

"We left Lecompton the next morning as we had purposed, favored with excellent weather. Left Lawrence with its famous fortifications on our left, and crossed the Waukansas at Blonton's Bridge, and some seven miles further struck the Santa Fe road, where we encamped for the night. Next day, after marching some twenty miles, camped near the house of Black-wolf, the Shawnee chief. We arrived at Paoli about noon the next day, passing through the Shawnee reservation and into the country of the Mecos, Peoria, Piankeshaw, and Kaskaskia Indians. They are all pretty well civilized, owning large farms, and having considerable improvements. The greater portion of them are about half white. Friday, Captain Walker, of my company, arrived with the company, having gone as escort to the agent of the tribes above mentioned. " De Saussure presented Walker Col. Cooke's order to join De Saussure. We had learned by this time that the band of freebooters we proposed arresting, ranged over a wide tract of country, from the Pottawattamie Creek to the Neosho, and had even crossed the Missouri border, and drove off all the cattle and horses of a farmer, and plundered his house.

" Neither the Commissioner nor the marshal had arrived, and nothing could be done until they came. Every thing conspired to make us believe that we would be detained in that region so late that we would be compelled to winter at Fort Scott.

" Under these circumstances De Saussure determined to send me in to the Fort to secure supplies and clothing. I left Saturday morning, and, leaving my wagon with a corporal and guard to come on at leisure, I pushed on thirty-eight miles, and stopped about three o'clock at the house of a half breed Shawnee, *Blue Jacket*. I had a cold ride, but got in by three o'clock P. M., a distance of twenty-six miles.

" Here I find all the cavalry and infantry except two companies of the first and one of the latter. The selection of the two cavalry companies is left to Major Sedgwick, and his detail is not yet known.

" Bennett, with his company, has been ordered to Old Point Comfort, and he will be in here in a few days. He's a lucky fellow ! "

To his Mother.

" FORT LEAVENWORTH, K. T., *December 1st,* 1856.

" My last letter was written under the impression that I would pass the winter at old Fort Scott, situated in the southeastern part of the Territory—a post far more agreeable than this, in climate, comfort, and everything. The orders given us by Col. Cooke were issued with

such an arrangement in view, and De Saussure, Walker
and I, were in high glee at the prospect of having a carte
blanche to make ourselves comfortable there for the winter. Having made up our minds to this, I came in here
to obtain the necessary supplies, rations and clothing.

"On my arrival the Adjutant-general, Major Deas, informed me that he was convinced we would be ordered
in here.

"The Governor of Kansas, who, by the way, has a
great idea of adding to his importance by keeping troops
dangling at his heels, it appears, has asked for two companies of cavalry and one of infantry to remain at
Lecompton, and he would then dispense with the remainder and allow them to return to Fort Leavenworth.

"At this time Major Sedgwick is in camp near the
Nebraska line with four companies of cavalry, and the
light artillery, while Colonel Cooke was at Lecompton
with a squadron of dragoons, and a portion of the sixth
infantry under Colonel Andrews. An order was accordingly issued from headquarters instructing Major Sedgwick to detail the two companies of cavalry to go to Lecompton, and ordering all other companies in to this post.
It was after the issue of this order, and before Major
Sedgwick's detail was known, that I arrived. Nothing
could therefore be done until that was known, and from
Sunday until Thursday, I had to wait, although De Saussure expected me back that day.

"On Tuesday Bennett arrived with his company *en
route* for Old Point Comfort, and I was thus enabled to
spend several days with him. A friend and classmate is
only properly appreciated when among comparative
strangers.

5*

"On Thursday I received orders to take De Saussure rations for ten days, and the order for his and Walker's return. I started my wagon under charge of a corporal early Friday morning, with orders to proceed to Paoli, where I would overtake him. I left the fort Saturday afternoon about three o'clock, and stopped a little after dark at the house of Johnny-cake a Delaware, seventeen miles from Leavenworth. The next day I rode into Paoli, a distance of forty-four miles, by sundown, some three hours after my wagon had arrived. Paoli last summer was crowded with families driven from their farms on the Pottawattamie creek, and the country in the neighborhood of Ossawattamie, by the freebooting bands (real or pretended,) of Free-State men. Ossawattamie is situated at the confluence of the Marais de Cygnes and Pottawattamie creek, beyond which the stream is called the Osage river. Here that prince of cut-throats and marauders (Brown) made his headquarters last summer, and carried on the war against Missourians and pro-slavery settlers. Captain De Saussure was stationed near the town all last summer, but his orders were positive, not to interfere unless the civil authority deemed it necessary. The consequence was, that as all the civil officers had fled before his arrival, Brown ruled and ravaged the country adjacent with impunity. The Missourians finally mustered in force, marched on the town and burned it. It was a portion of Brown's party that we were ordered to arrest.

"*Baptiste* Peoria, chief of the Wacos and Peorias, and who has the Indian title to the land on which Paoli is situated, gave me a letter from De Saussure, directing me to join him on Sugar creek. On my way there I passed through Ossawattamie, and saw the remains left by the pro-slavery party. I reached camp on Sugar creek after a march of twenty-five miles. I was heartily welcomed by De Saussure and Walker, who had almost given me up, and considerably surprised them by the order for their return to Leavenworth. In my absence they had captured seven men, Bill Partridge, Townsley, the four Kilbourn boys, and one Vaughan. One of the Kilbourns escaped, Vaughan was discharged for lack of evidence against him ; the others were sent to Lecompton. They are a notorious gang of desperadoes, accomplices of Brown.

"The morning after my arrival, De Saussure, in obedience to the order I delivered, broke up camp and started for the fort, where we arrived on the twenty-eighth of November.

"*December 6th.*—I could not finish my letter begun on the first, and have had no time since for letter-writing. I am on guard to-morrow and also on a court-martial to try some of the prisoners, of which there are now more than fifty—some charged with desertion, one for murder, but the greater number for drunkenness.

"I have again met here Colonel Titus, on his way to Nicaragua with a hundred men. Walker has promised him a Brigadier Generalship. He will take with him some of the disturbing elements of Kansas.

"I received a letter from Fitzhugh Lee, dated Carlisle, Pa., Nov. 20th. He said he was going on a visit to Philadelphia, and would try and revisit Woodbury."

To his Sister.

"FORT LEAVENWORTH, *Dec.* 18*th*, 1856.

"This day I complete my twenty-first year. It is

about six o'clock in the morning, and I can make no more auspicious beginning of my new year than by writing to you, dear sister.

" Between courts-martial, boards of survey, guard, drill, and attendance at regular roll-calls, my time is so occupied that it leaves little of my working hours that I can call my own. On courts-martial and boards of survey, the junior officer is always recorder, and is compelled to write out the proceedings.

" What I said about B— does not, I hope, induce you to believe that I am at all dissatisfied with my regiment. So far from that, I am so well pleased, that if I had the choice of all regiments of the line, I would select this. There are a very agreeable set of fellows composing it, and nearly all are married or engaged to be married : which renders it much more sober and quiet than it otherwise would be. The hardest cases in the regiment are now away.

" The resignation of Captain McClelland, of this regiment, promotes Taylor, I think, to a second lieutenant, leaving Fitz. Lee the last of the cavalry brevets. I entertain strong hopes that he will yet be promoted into my regiment, in which case there will be four of our class in the same regiment. My promotion so far has been quite rapid, having risen *two files* in *three months* by the resignation of Vinton and McClelland.

" I consider our regiment one of the best officered regiments in the service. And should a war occur in which it could be tested, I think it would indicate fully the opinion I have expressed. The army within this generation will be called upon to perform great deeds, and in the shadowy mists of the future, (you know by birth I am a Seer), * I see the military, the chief of all the professions. I may not live to see it, but I see it now with my *mind's eye.*

"Whenever you repine at my being in a mounted corps, and therefore destined for frontier service, call to mind, that while others are loitering away their time in forts and garrisons, *I* am in the field, learning the prac tical parts of my profession, of which as yet, they can know little or nothing. As for the exposure and hard-ship incident to the service, they agree with me much better than a more quiet and lazy life. You know I never enjoyed at home, after we left the west, as good health as I did at West Point ; and since my service in the field, my health is far better than it was for months previously. Some four or five years hence, when I obtain leave to go home, I will have become such a complete border ruffian, that I fear you will hardly recognize me. I shall then, I hope, have gained a reputation which will do no discredit to my name. My captain expects to get leave for four months shortly, which will give me com-mand of the company. He is to be married to a daugh ter of General Hernandez, of Cuba.

"I don't know that it would not be a good thing for me to get married. I should then not be subjected to temptations and convivial company.

"There are some charming half breed ladies, who re-sort here from the interior. What do you girls say about it? The great Wyandot Beauty is now here, Miss D. The Misses E.'s, from St. Joseph, and other feminine celebrities also. I am puzzled and dazzled in the glare

* He was born with a *caul,* and the Irish nurse who snatched it from his head, predicted that he would be a " *big man.*"

of their charms to know at whose shrine I should bow.

" Things are all quiet in the Territory now. Our expedition appears to have struck those maurauding parties at the south with wholesome terror, and Governor Geary says that he apprehends no further disturbances at present. The land sales have been going on for some time past. The lands sell enormously high. After entry at the land office, the claims to the land entered sell for three or four times the government price. The land is good, but no better than hundreds of thousands of acres of Iowa lands, which are in market at one dollar and twenty-five cents per acre.

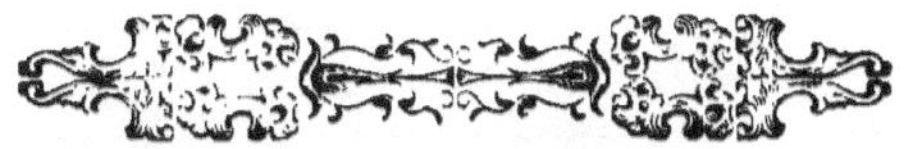

CHAPTER IX.

Life at Fort Leavenworth, 1857.—Expedition to the Arkansas.—Fight with Cheyennes.—Winter Quarters at Fort Riley.

To his Father.

" FORT LEAVENWORTH, *Jan.* 2*d*, 1857.

" YOUR letter came to hand some days ago, in the midst of Christmas festivities. I thank you for your good advice, and hope to profit by it. I agree with you as to the political views you present. The sectional strife, growing in fierceness, must in a few years lead to civil war. Then the military will be called on to perform an important part in the conflict the politicians will bring about. God only knows what the result will be. But while for my country I shall deplore such a horrid fate, I shall endeavor to carve out for myself a name honorable to my family. I am just in the proper position for doing so, come what may. The cavalry arm is the best of all in which to become thoroughly acquainted with the practical details of campaigning and a soldier's duties generally. In four years I shall be completely conversant with that branch of my profession. I should then like to study the theory and science of war more fully, and should then like to spend a few years at West Point as Instructor. Dragoons, on account of their horses, have so many more duties to attend to than officers of other corps, that they have much less time to themselves. While on duty, in camp or the field, all reading or study must be extremely desultory.

"The army will have to be increased in a few years. As the settlers and emigrants penetrate the country, collisions with Indian tribes will increase. When that takes place, I shall make a bold push for promotion into one of the new regiments. In the mean time opportunity will occur for distinguishing myself, and I don't think that a captaincy in four or five years is too much to expect.

"I have enjoyed myself during the holidays very well. There have been balls and parties without number, and many pretty ladies from Weston, St. Joseph's, and other places. In short, life in Kansas is not so barbarous, after all. There were two balls in Leavenworth city on New Year's eve. One at the Planters' House, and one at McCracken's Hotel ; the former Pro-Slavery, and the latter Free-State. Most of the officers went to both, but as all my lady acquaintances were at the Planters' House I remained there. We left at five o'clock in the morning in order to go to *reveille*. I am told that even at the Planters' House there were more Free-State ladies than there were Pro-Slavery ladies. All agree that the girls from Lawrence fully maintained their reputation for beauty. The fact is, the Free-State settlers outnumber all others about five to one, and there is about as little chance of this being a Slave State as there is of my flying in the air.

"As to Kansas politics, you can get fuller and more authentic intelligence from the New York *Herald* and *Times* than we have here. It is to the New York papers that *we* are indebted for Kansas news. To be sure, much of it is spurious, but that serves the purpose of the politicians as well as if it were true. The Lecompton Constitution is doomed. The people will never submit to it here. As submitted to the people, it is a nefarious swindle."

To his Father.

"FORT LEAVENWORTH, *Feb.* 14*th*, 1857.

"Our recruits will be up as soon as navigation opens, and we shall then have to go to work and drill them. Nor will we have much time for it, as it is proposed that the expedition to the Plains shall start the 1st of May. I, however, doubt whether we will get off before the middle of the month. We cannot start before the grass on the prairies affords food for our beasts.

"Lomax and McClernand, of my class, have arrived here. Captain Walker has been refused leave to go and commit matrimony.

"There is quite a fair prospect of more trouble in this Territory next summer and fall. The Missourians say they will have the State if they have to bring into it five thousand men. The Free-State men, confident in their numbers, which are constantly augmented by swarms of adventurers animated with fanatic zeal, have no fear of the ultimate result. The Missourians and Pro-slavery party are prompted by political motives principally, which are not of sufficient force to combat the moral and political impulses which stimulate the Anti-slavery men. Walker will be as powerless as Geary ' to ride the whirlwind and direct the storm.''

To his Mother.

"FORT LEAVENWORTH, *March 3d,* 1857.

"I have now nearly recovered, having had a tedious confinement. Some fears are entertained here that the proposed Cheyenne expedition will be given up. But there is no telling what the magnates at Washington may do from one day to another. They are often disposed to listen to illegitimate sources for information. In my opinion the Cheyennes require looking after.

"Captain Walker has at last got a two months' leave to go and get married. His intended is a lady of St. Augustine, Florida, not Cuba, as I think I said in one of my letters home. This will give me command of my company—pretty good for the first year of a second lieutenant. But it devolves on me at present a vast amount of duty; and therefore my correspondence will have to be curtailed.

"I am kept on the go, from morning until night. Started up at *reveille,* immediately afterwards comes stable call, when we have to go down to the stables and superintend the cleaning, watering, etc., of the horses. After returning to quarters, dressing, and breakfast-call sounds, and immediately after that comes dress parade, then guard-mounting, then drill in quick succession. At twelve M., the quarters and messes of the companies are to be inspected. From that time to drill at four P. M., ostensibly we have nothing to do, but half the time is occupied by some company duty, or in my case, bakehouse affairs. Drill at four P. M. an hour and a half, and then stable call again, and then *retreat.* So much for the way my time is spent, and when night comes, I am pretty well worn out. I have not yet entirely recovered my strength, and feel the fatigue more than I should otherwise.

"The Hon. R. J. Walker, I see, is now appointed Governor, as for some time past, it has been known here he would be. He is an able man, I have no doubt :—but he has no conception of the task he has undertaken to perform. No Governor, not even the archangel Michael, could give satisfaction to all parties here."

To his Father.

"FORT LEAVENWORTH, *April* 15*th*, 1857.

"You will, no doubt before you receive this, have seen in the papers the orders we have just received from head-quarters. It has stirred us up here, and all rejoice in the prospect of an active campaign on the Plains for the ensuing summer. I will state the substance of the orders lest you may not have noticed them particularly.

"1*st*. The 10th Infantry are to leave Minnesota and come here ; also six companies of dragoons now at Fort Riley.

"2*d*. Colonel Johnson, with two companies of infantry and two squadrons of cavalry, is to proceed South and run the southern boundary of this Territory.

"3*d*. Two squadrons of 1st cavalry are to proceed up the Arkansas river.

"4*th*. One squadron of cavalry, one of dragoons, and three companies of infantry, are to go up the Platte river.

"General Harney is to leave Florida and take command at Fort Leavenworth.

"The two columns on the Arkansas and Platte are to be subject to the direction of Colonel Sumner. Major

Sedgwick, by command of Colonel Sumner, will lead the two squadrons on the Arkansas. They will comprise Steuart's, Beall's, Walker's, and McIntosh's companies. If Walker does not return before we leave, I shall command the company.

" If we don't meet any Indians, we shall have at least some good buffalo hunting.

" Forage for ten days is to be sent forward from the fort on the routes, to supply us till the grass grows sufficiently. One or two howitzers will be taken with the Platte and Arkansas columns. Pack-mules not to exceed five hundred, are to be procured for the Quartermaster's Department, and we are to go "*fully equipped and prepared for distant service.*" That sounds very much like Utah.

" This is far better than staying in the Territory all summer, subject to the orders of Governor Walker. I presume we will not return here before late in the fall, if then.

" Should we go to Utah, we will not return for a year or more. There is but one consolation we should have in going to Utah ; it would cause some resignations in our regiment and make promotion more rapid.

" As for our getting a fight out of the Cheyennes the coming summer, it is doubtful. For while the War Department is sending out a hostile expedition against them, the Indian Department have invested thousands of dollars in presents, including, no doubt, rifles and ammunition. So much for official unity and consistency displayed by the mighty men of Washington. If they would turn over the whole management of Indian affairs to the army, millions would be saved, while the Indians would be kept in quiet subjection. The Indian Agents, and the Traders and Co. create all our Indian wars.

"Talking about going to Utah, Col. Sumner and most of the officers here think that we will go ; but I will not believe it until I see the order for the march.

"That troops will be sent there with the new Governor I have no doubt, but I think they will send infantry and not cavalry. If we were to go there, it would kill all our horses, and we would have to foot it until we got back to a civilized region.

"The troops which do go there will have to stay there for two or more years."

To his Sister.

"FORT LEAVENWORTH, *May 12th*, 1857.

"I have been in camp since the 1st of May, and during most of the time we have had pleasant weather. Just now, however, it is raw, wet, and disagreeable. It is a very backward season, and on that account there is no grass as yet on the Plains, and Col. Sumner finds it impossible to start by the 16th as he expected.

"I have been busy preparing myself, as well as my company, for the Plains. I now have plenty of good coarse clothing, the only kind suitable for such work as ours ; stout hickory shirts and soldiers' clothes are indispensable. A pillow and four or five blankets, buffalo robes, and an India-rubber cloth, to spread on the ground, constitute our bedding arrangements. You may imagine me starting for the Plains dressed out in gorgeous array, with a black felt hat with broad brim, coarse jacket and trowsers, hickory shirt and high-top boots, and you will have a pretty correct idea of a 'Border Ruffian,' alias, campaigner. I have a very good servant—he is an excellent cook, which is the great *desideratum* in an officer's servant. We anticipate a pleasant trip. How often shall I think of you all in your quiet home at Woodbury, while I am marching over the prairie so far away. Oh, when shall I see home and its dear inmates again? Major Deas, of the Adjutant-general's Department, and Lieut. Carr, of my regiment, have been appointed *aides-de camp* to the Governor, together with Lieut. Walker (his nephew) of the sixth cavalry.

"*May 16th.*—I could not finish the above the day I commenced it. We now expect to be off the day after to-morrow. Major Sedgwick's column, to which I belong, has been in camp a short distance from garrison, but sufficiently near to perform all duty in garrison—which is disagreeable. But my grievances of this sort will end with our departure. We now expect to get back by the first of November.

"I was relieved on the thirtieth of last month of the duty of Post treasurer, which was very harassing, onerous and responsible ; all my time being required to attend to my company's duties and prepare it for the Plains. I have effected a radical change for the better in my company.

"To use the words of Col. Sumner at inspection a few days ago, "from being one of the worst, it is fast getting to be one of the best in the regiment." He has repeatedly complimented me in the highest terms for the neatness and good condition of my company. Little good it will do me, though, if Walker returns soon, and relieves me of the command. If I could only keep command of my company during the campaign, it would be a marvellous piece of good fortune—a second lieutenant of less than a year's standing favored with a command, which few attain permanently in ten years ! and that in an expedition in the course of which fighting is expected. If we do have a fight, and I am in command, I will make " G" company win laurels. It will be very hard if Walker joins me before the campaign is over ; for I have had the whole trouble of fitting out the company, have worked like a galley-slave for weeks, have been accountable for an immense amount of property, it being necessary to draw for the company, supplies of all kinds, ordnance, clothing, camp and garrison equipage and quartermaster's stores. Nor can I turn them over to Walker until we get back. Walker is a nice gentleman and very clever but is inefficient, and lacks force.

" When we get off, we shall proceed by easy marches fifteen or twenty miles a day. Whlie out, we shall probably get a mail about once a month if we are not very unlucky, and you must therefore write, some of you, every week. I will write whenever an opportunity occurs for sending a letter."

To his Mother.

"CAMP NEAR INDIANOLA, K. T., }
May 20th, 1857. }

" I cannot allow an opportunity for writing to you without improving it. At last we are off, bound we know not where precisely, nor how far we shall go, nor when we shall return.

"The first night we camped twelve miles from the Fort, on Stranger creek. Yesterday we marched twenty-three miles and camped on the Grasshopper. To-day we made seventeen miles, and we are now camped three and a half miles from the historic town of Topeka—chronicled for fame as the place where the Free-State constitution was formed. To-morrow we cross the Kansas river, which will take all day probably. We have had delightful weather, and if the grass was only a little better for our horses, we should have nothing to complain of.

"Major Sedgwick says my company is the best in the regiment. We have a very pleasant set of officers. Sedgwick is a first-rate old fellow, and an universal favorite. He does all in his power to make everything on the march as agreeable as possible. Sturgis is overflowing with fun and good spirits. McIntosh, Stanley, Lomax, Doctor Corey, Long, McIntyre and Wheaton, are all pleasant gentlemen, and enliven the camp with social intercourse. Our men are all in fine spirits, and anticipate a fight with the Indians. Doctor Corey, who messes with me, and is a very agreeable gentleman, goes down with his ambulance to Topeka to-morrow to get some things, and we all avail ourselves of the chance to write.

"We have passed through some of the most beautiful prairies I ever saw. The country is quite thickly settled—a large portion of the lands being taken up and occupied."

To his Sister.

"CAMP NEAR COUNCIL GROVE, K. T.,
      May 24th, 1857.

"After a tramp of six days, we arrived this afternoon at Council Grove, a small town consisting of a few traders' houses, around which were lounging many dirty Indians. We will be here all to-morrow, loading our train with grain for our horses and mules. And it is a fortunate delay, for our horses need rest. Twenty miles a day, for a horse loaded down with the heavy equipments of a dragoon soldier, is pretty hard travelling, although in case of necessity they are sometimes made to go thirty, and even forty. This, however, is but seldom. The column never moves out of a walk; and we generally dismount and walk a mile or two during the day to relieve our horses. The longest march we have yet made was twenty-three miles. We generally get into camp, *i. e.*, select the ground and picket our horses, an hour before the wagons arrive.

"Each company, with its officers, has two wagons to carry their mess-kit, tents, etc., etc. Then there are three. or four ammunition wagons, and near fifty provision and forage wagons—of course, all six-mule teams.

"Having command of my company, my time is pretty much occupied and I often envy the Doctor his leisure and ease. He and I generally kill on our march during the day, sufficient game,—plover, curlew and ducks to supply our table, and we live like fighting cocks. Our route at present is through a beautiful country of undulating prairies and fertile valleys. In a few days·we shall reach the range of the buffalo.

"We had a severe thunder-storm to-day just after picketing our horses, and one of them was struck and killed by lightning. Do you know what is meant by *picketing* the horses? Each man has a picket-rope and pin for his horse. The pin is of iron and about fifteen inches long, which is driven in the ground. Through the top of it, there is a ring to which the rope eleven yards long, is fastened, the other end being tied to the headstall of the horse.   This allows each horse a circle of twenty-two yards in diameter, within which to crop the grass.

"Our camp was fairly overrun to-night with Indians of the Kaw tribe—a miserable worthless set of beggars, vagabonds and thieves.   The little papooses were running round and rolling in the dirt in all directions, with nothing on them but strips of ragged blankets.

"There is little prospect of Walker's being able to join us this summer, which leaves me in command of the company, a piece of good fortune quite remarkable.

"I am in excellent health.   Camp life always agrees with me."

To his Father.

"CAMP ON ARKANSAS RIVER, ⎱
June 2d, 1857.   ⎰

"As we approached this river, the soil rapidly deteriorated.   The country is sandy.   For the last few days we have passed numerous towns of prairie dogs, who, squatted in front of their domicils, keep up a ferocious barking, but as we come nearer, dart into their holes quick as a flash.

"Buffalo hunting is the only diversion we have to relieve the monotony of our march.   I shot one to-day after running him about four miles.   My horse was pretty well exhausted by the time my sport was ended.   I could have shot him at any moment during the whole chase, but wanted to crowd him over near the road.   The buffalo are in great numbers near our camp.   They move in herds of thousands, and we dash among them and single out a fat fellow, and when we get him where we want him, shoot him.   It is exciting sport, and I enjoyed it very much.

"To-morrow we will probably reach the neighborhood of the Camanches, Kiowas, and Arrapahoes, who are in camp near Pawnee Fork, and will then have to keep a sharp lookout for our horses at night.

"Four miles from here we passed, on Walnut creek, an Indian trading station, where we were told that the Cheyennes had taken their families up into the mountains, and with the assistance of some young Sioux warriors were preparing for war. But I have little faith in the reports of these Indian traders."

To his Mother.

"CAMP ON THE ARKANSAS,
June 22d, 1857.

"We are now between ninety and one hundred miles of Bent's Fort, which we left five days ago, and in a day or two we will leave the river and strike across the country to the south fork of the Platte, where we are to meet Col. Sumner. At Bent's Fort we found in camp some five or six hundred Arrapahoes. No sooner did they hear of our arrival, than they all mounted their ponies and came down to our camp, with their chief at their head, for the purpose of having a talk. The chief with eight or ten warriors, went up to the Major's tent, and smoked the pipe of peace, etc. They were nearly starved. Having been told by the lying traders that we would pitch into them as well as the Cheyennes, they were afraid to go into the buffalo country, and there being no game about Bent's Fort, they had been living on roots for some time. They begged hard for provisions, and the Major gave them a beef or two. After dark I rode through their camp with Lomax and the Doctor.

"Since leaving the fort we have traversed a country, almost barren, and with difficulty found grass for our horses.

"For the last three days we have been in sight of the Rocky Mountains, Greenhorn, Ratan Mountains, and Pike's Peak. The river, which below Bent's Fort is wide and shallow, has now become deep and narrow, the water clear and cool, and the banks precipitous. Although it is very hot on the march, in the afternoon we have a fine breeze on getting into camp.

"We have been living on venison chiefly, of late. The Doctor and I bought a cow from an emigrant train, so that we have plenty of milk, and altogether live like fighting cocks.

"The Cheyennes are up in the mountains placing their women and children in safety before offering fight. They are seventy-five miles from Bent's Fort."

To his Father.

"CAMP ON HEAD WATERS OF WALNUT CREEK,
K. T., *August 3d,* 1857.

"We came up with the Cheyennes on the twenty-ninth of July. There were between three and four hundred of them drawn up in line waiting for us, and confident of victory. Col. Sumner charged with the cavalry, (the infantry were three miles behind,) and broke them instantly. There were eight Indians killed, one taken prisoner, and there is no telling how many were wounded. We lost two men killed and five men wounded. When within a mile of the Indians, Col. Sumner ordered me to halt the artillery, of which he gave me command, and wait for the infantry; so that I was not in the fight at all.

Lieutenant Steuart, commanding my company, was severely wounded. Had Sumner let me bring up my battery and commence the action, I could have raked them with canister, and he would have counted the killed by tens instead of *units*. I only took command of the artillery on the express condition that I was not to be kept behind if there was a fight.

"We lay over the next day to take care of the wounded. Captain Foote was then ordered to throw up a breast-work and remain with the wounded, and the rest of the command pushed on after the Indians. Foote has a hundred men. Steuart being wounded and left with Foote, I resumed command of my company. On the thirty-first of July, we commenced pursuit of the Indians, and in the afternoon came up to their deserted camp, consisting of about three hundred lodges, which we burnt, and everything else belonging to them. We crossed the Smoky Hill yesterday, and after a march of twenty miles camped here.

"We shall continue to follow their trail, even if they cross the Arkansas and go down into the Camanche country. Now that I am in command of my company again, I hope not to be cheated if we have a fight, by being kept out of it."

To his Father

"FORT KEARNEY, *Sept.* 10*th*, 1857.

"Long before this reaches you, you will see from the papers, that we are not to go to Utah, but will return to Leavenworth. Though I should be very glad to go to Salt Lake in the spring, I rejoice that we do not have to go this fall, as we should certainly lose three-fourths of our horses were we to go this season.

"We had a pleasant march across the country, from the Arkansas river. We left there on the sixth, camped on the Smoky Hill river on the eighth, crossed the Grand Sabine on the tenth, Solomon's Fork on the twelfth, on the fourteenth the Little Blue, and struck the Kearney and Leavenworth road. The next day we met Sacket returning to Leavenworth from Kearney, who told us that there were orders at Fort Kearney for us to proceed to Leavenworth. Major Sedgwick halted thirty-two miles from here, and sent quartermaster Wheaton to bring down the train. As I felt some desire to see this fort, I accompanied him.

"It was exactly a year since I left Philadelphia when I arrived here. As a mail leaves to-morrow, I write this to send. I have not received a letter from home since the sixteenth of May.

"I enjoyed my visit to Kearney very much, and had a fine wolf hunt while there."

To his Father.

"CAMP NEAR RICHMOND ON THE NEMEHA, }
    Oct. 3d, 1857. }

"The election comes off to-morrow for the Territorial Legislature. I believe I am stationed here to see fair play. But there was no necessity for that, as the Free-State men won't vote. This place consists of three grog-shops and a blacksmith's shop, and you may therefore infer that the inhabitants in the vicinity are a peculiarly enlightened and intelligent set. Horse-stealing is one of their manly pastimes, and making soldiers drunk the prime article of their religious faith. There will not be more than forty or fifty votes polled here.

"You ask me to give you my opinion of Colonel Sumner, and Major Sedgwick. I like them both, but of course am on more intimate terms with Sedgwick.

"Sumner is a good soldier, and shines as post commander as well as in the field. He is a brave man and generally esteemed in military circles as a gallant gentleman.

"Sedgwick or "*old Sedge*" as he is called, is an universal favorite. He is an old bachelor of forty-five or thereabouts, a gentleman in every respect, generous, social, and excellent company. He is rather too easy in command, and somewhat fidgety, but he knows his duty and performs it well, and is a noble and gallant officer.

"Major Sedgwick left here on the thirtieth ult., with the other three companies of his command. Beall with his company goes to Claytonville, in Brown county, Stockton to Palermo, in Donaphan county, and Sturgis to Atchison, the several companies to be under orders of the U. S. Marshal or sheriffs or such other miserable scamps as may be honored with a U. S. civil commission. Acting *posse comitatus* for sheriffs, etc., is not at all relished, though I suppose our services are necessary."

The following extract from a letter from Kansas which appeared in one of the St. Louis papers, refers to an incident not mentioned by Lieut. Bayard in any of his letters, probably because he deemed it of no importance. But it certainly shows with what energy and promptitude he performed his duty as an officer.

"The election went off quietly—there was no disturbance at any of the polls ; but on the night of that day several soldiers belonging to Lieut. Bayard's company, who were encamped near Richmond, the county seat of

Nemeha county, were induced by some drunken abolitionists to make an attack upon the residence of Mr. Cy.
Dolman, the Democratic Representative of that county,
and member of the Constitutional Convention. Some
nine of them broke in the doors and windows of Mr.
Dolman's house, and treated him and his clerk, Mr. Joseph A. Brown, of South Carolina, rather roughly, and it
is impossible to tell how far the outrage would have extended, had not several Free-State men, who were personal friends of Mr. Dolman, interposed. Mr. Dolman
sent a messenger to Lieut. Bayard, who had retired for
the night, but that young officer leaped from his bed and
ran all the way to Mr. Dolman's house and reached there
just as the now drunken soldiers were about to make another attack. He ordered them to desist, and upon their
failing to do so promptly, he struck two of them to the
earth with his sabre, when the balance at once submitted
and were marched to quarters. Lieut. Bayard deserves
great credit for his decisive action. Mr. Dolman and his
friends had armed themselves with revolvers, pitchforks
and axes, and had not Lieut. Bayard arrived and checked
his men just as he did, there would have been much blood
shed."

To his Mother.

"CAMP NEAR LECOMPTON, }
          Oct. 21st, 1857. }

"I arrived at Fort Leavenworth with my company on
the ninth, and on the twenty-first received orders to
march promptly to this delectable place. Governor Walker has been alarmed by some hostile demonstrations of
the contending parties, and wants the cavalry. My cap-

tain, his nephew, has been acting as the Governor's aide, with which I am well content.

"Fort Leavenworth, when I arrived there, I found very much changed in appearance. I found troops encamped all around it, and everywhere. I passed officers I had never seen before ; orderlies were riding about constantly in every direction, going and returning from the different camps. In fact the fort now has all the appearance of being the headquarters of a large army."

To his Sister.

" FORT LEAVENWORTH, *Nov.* 11*th*, 1857.

" Fort Riley is to be my post during winter, which will be more pleasant than Leavenworth, which is much crowded. Riley is built of stone, and has large and commodious quarters. The detail has been modified by substituting McIntosh's company in place of Sturgis' This sends Lomax to Riley."

To his Father.

"FORT RILEY, *Dec.* 1*st*, 1857

" Lieutenant Long arrived from Leavenworth this evening, bringing us quite a batch of news. He says the information from Washington is that six new regiments will be authorized by Congress, at the ensuing session.

" Of course, you will do all you can to secure my appointment as captain in one of the new regiments. I am known at the War Department, as a good officer. Colonel Sumner and Major Emory will back the application for me—so will Major Sedgwick. With senator Thomson's aid, and that of the N. J. members, there can be no difficulty. But remember a mounted regiment

6*

is my preference, though I should not refuse to go into the infantry as a captain, as I could subsequently, by exchange, get transferred to the cavalry or dragoons.

"There is an order here from "headquarters of troops serving in Kansas," for a detachment consisting of one commissioned officer, one sergeant, and two corporals, and twenty privates, to be furnished from the mounted troops, as an escort for the mail for New Mexico. The escort is to meet the mail at the *Little Arkansas*, and escort it to the crossing of the main Arkansas. It is then to await the arrival of the mail from New Mexico, and escort that as far as the *Little Arkansas*. These escorts are furnished on the requisition of the mail contractor. The mail goes twice a month, and as there are but seven or eight officers here detailable we shall be kept pretty busy. There will be three officers on the road going and returning at one time, and we shall hardly get back before we shall have to get ready for another trip. Long brought the requisition, but also an order for the meeting of a general court-martial on which I am detailed. I am sorry for this, as my turn will now come the first week in January in the depth of winter.

"Both my horses were used up in our expedition last summer, and I have had to purchase another. I gave one hundred and seventy-five dollars for him. He is a first-rate animal and stood the Plains last summer admirably. He is well gaited and very fleet, and is the best horse in the regiment."

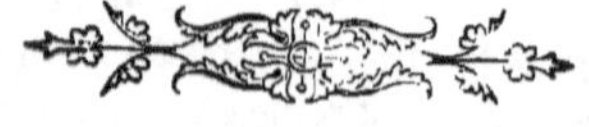

CHAPTER X.

To his Father.

"FORT RILEY, K. T., *Feb. 1st*, 1858.

"I LEAVE for Arkansas with recruits, and will not
be back for three months or more.

"General Orders 1, 2, 3, 4 from headquarters of the
army, show considerable activity as to the *Mormon war*.
I think they indicate an early start, perhaps as early as
the first of April."

To his Father.

"FORT RILEY, *Feb. 21st*, 1858.

"I have nearly recovered from the sickness which
has prostrated me so long, and prevented my going to
Arkansas.

"Col. Johnson is to be breveted Brigadier-general.

"The report is now, we are not to start before the
twentieth of May. I don't care much about going if we
start so late, as all the fighting will be over, (if there is
any,) before we could possibly arrive. I am afraid the
government is disposed to back down. The grass will
be more forward this than last year."

To his Father.

"Fort Riley, *May 23d*, 1858.

"The latest intelligence from Utah is that which announces the flight of Brigham Young, and the advance of Col. Johnson.   The death of Gen. Smith, will probably cause some changes in our movements.   I do not expect to get off from here before the tenth of June.   I am to go with Major Sedgwick's column.   Sedgwick, Walker, Steuart and myself mess together.   Major S. thinks we will go to Utah.   I do not think so."

To his Father.

"Camp thirty-five miles from Fort Kearney, *June 6th*, 1858.

"As I shall probably meet the mail to-morrow, I will write to let you know that we are getting along on our march pretty well, now that we have struck the Kearney and Leavenworth road.   We will reach Fort Kearney day after to-morrow, and I will write from there.

"P. S.   Fort Kearney, *June 8th*.—We made a march of thirty-five miles yesterday, and came into this fort to-day.   We lay over to rest our horses and complete the assignment of our trains.   One of the trains has gone on, and one has not come up.   But the Major will proceed, as no escort is needed here.

"General Johnston's command commenced eating their mules on the 20th of May.   The troops at Laramie have also been out of their meat ration.   You can form no idea of the utter confusion on this road.   Trains are a month behind their time, and by strange and gross mismanagement provisions, which are by far the most required, have been sent last, instead of going in the foremost trains. The prospects of General Johnston are at present rather gloomy. The Governor and Marshal of Utah were sent back to Camp Scott, rather Fort Bridger, where Johnston now is. We expect to take fifteen or sixteen days to Laramie, and then we will have to await, I presume, the arrival of the trains for Utah. The first one arrived here this morning, and will not, I fear, reach Laramie for a month or six weeks.

"The Cheyennes are perfectly quiet this year, and will give no trouble.

"Colonel Hoffman has been delayed on his way above Laramie by rains and high streams. We hope he has reached General Johnston before this. We take twenty days' rations from this place."

To his Father.

"Camp on the North Platte,
two miles beyond Laramie,
June 28th, 1858.

"We reached Laramie on the twenty-fifth, having marched thirty miles that day; there being no grass below the fort. We passed three or four trading-posts during the day, one of which is at Gratiot Point, six miles below the fort, the scene of the Gratton massacre.

"The country about here is as bleak and desolate as you can imagine, and it is only in the valleys and on the borders of the streams that anything will grow, except the sage plant, which for the most part covers the sand hills. The houses at Fort Laramie are built, some of *adobe*, and others of frame, without any particular order of arrangement. It used to be a trading-post belonging to a Frenchman of that name, but was made a military post in 1849, I believe. The latitude of the Fort is 42° 10'. Gill, of the 4th Artillery, arrived here yesterday from Bridger. He went out as quartermaster and commissary. General Johnston was at Bear river getting along very well ; everything was peaceable, with no prospect of a fight. We expect to reach Fort Bridger by the first of August and by the 10th will probably be in Salt Lake city. Most of the Mormons, it is said, have gone south into some of the numerous valleys among the mountains, but Gill says some of them have already begun to come back. There were seventy or eighty seceding Mormons here when we arrived ; they were on their way to the States, and a more miserable set of wretches I never beheld. Major Graham reports the train we are to escort as two days behind. We shall not start before the second of July."

To his Sister.

" Camp on La Presle Creek, seventy-
five miles beyond Laramie,
July 8th, 1858.

" Here in this beautiful valley of the Black Hills, I will while away the evening by renewing converse with the loved ones far away in their quiet home, until twelve o'clock, when I must visit my guard, and then to the realms of Queen Mab when in dreams I will revisit it.

" We left our camp near Laramie on the fifth and camped that night again on the Platte. Our road during the day passed through a rough and hilly country. We have been going over the Black-hill spur of the Rocky Mountains. We will probably be three days more in reaching the Platte bridge, being detained by these ox-teams, which get along slowly, making scarcely fifteen miles a day. It is an absurdity, making cavalry escort ox-teams. However, it is only on a par with the management of the whole expedition.

"I am afraid that these trains will detain us so long upon the road that we shall hardly get into Salt Lake city as early as I expected."

" CAMP AT WILLOW SPRINGS, THIRTY-
THREE MILES ABOVE PLATTE BRIDGE,
July 14*th*, 1858.

"Owing to the mail taking the hill road between *La Presle* and *Box-elder* while we took the lower one, I failed to get my letters in it ; so that several weeks will elapse before you receive this.

"We camped that night on the *Box-elder*, a fine stream of the same character as *La Presle*—water clear, cool and sparkling. We were visited that night with a tremendous hail storm, which came near stampeding our horses. About thirty broke loose, more would have done so, but the ground was very hard ; so that the picket pin could not be drawn out very easily ; we soon caught the loose horses."

To his Mother.

" CAMP ON NORTH PLATTE,
FIVE MILES ABOVE ASH HOLLOW,
August 2*d*, 1858.

"We have got thus far on the *back track*. I always had a presentiment that we should never go to Utah.

"We left Fort Laramie on our return, on the thirtieth ult., and will probably reach Kearney on the fifteenth of this month, and Riley, (unless stopped by orders) by

the twenty-eighth or twenty-ninth. I hope as you saw
the orders in the papers for our return, that I shall find
plenty of letters awaiting my arrival. I am anxious to
hear from you all, as I have not heard since the nineteenth of June. We are all glad of the countermarch,
for all accounts we receive describe Utah as the most
miserable place on the face of the earth, and the people
there the most wretched. I received a letter from Dr.
Corey dated "Camp Floyd, Cedar Valley, July twenty-
second." He is very much disgusted.

"The government have made more than a *failure*.
They have acceded virtually, to every demand made by
the Mormons. The troops are removed far from the
towns, while the civil officers are in fact powerless, Brigham remaining as omnipotent as ever.

"The administration has disgraced itself and acted
most culpably. After making immense contracts for all
sorts of supplies, and after a great display and flourish
of trumpets, they have backed down from every position
they assumed. Of what use are our judges there? The
juries are Mormon and will convict no one without the
permission of Brigham. Our Governor is a mere figure-
head, while Brigham's word is respected as gospel. This
is the ridiculous conclusion of the great expedition to
conquer the Mormons !

"By the time we reach Fort Riley, the summer will
be over, and nothing will have been accomplished. We
have had a tedious march to Laramie, and will have
as tedious a march back again, and *that* is the whole
story.

"If our illustrious masters at Washington, knew in
what estimation their wisdom is held in the army, they

would, doubtless, feel a little indignant, but not more so than we are, on account of their blundering."

Lieutenant Bayard returned as he expected to Fort Riley about the first of September, and soon after obtained leave of absence, and returned home. The most of his time during the fall of 1858, and the two first months of 1859, was passed at his father's residence near Woodbury, New Jersey.

CHAPTER XI.

Life on the Plains in 1859.—*Buffalo Hunting.*—*The Frog-man.*—
His Oration 4th July.—*Conference with Chiefs of Kiowas
and Camanches.*—*Encounter with a Buffalo.*—*Kills Pawnee.*—
Captain Walker's Official Report.—*Hunt with Grantley Berkeley.*—*Mr. Berkeley's Letters.*

LIEUTENANT BAYARD returned to Fort Riley
early in the spring of 1859, after the expiration of
his leave of absence, and remained there until his company was ordered on an expedition to the Arkansas, to
punish the Kiowas for numerous atrocities.

To his Sister.

"FORT RILEY, *April* 17*th*, 1859.

" My translation from the pleasures of home and the
attractions of civilization has been completed ; and again
I experience the rough privations of a western post, and
the wild winds of the prairie : and speaking of the winds
of the prairie, I have never known them excelled in ferocity but once, and that was on the occasion when we
ascended the steeple of Trinity. On that day we had a
prairie blow fresh from Riley. I am confident it came
in a direct current from the Smoky Hill above here,
and where I am inclined to believe King Eolus holds
his court and reigns supreme.

" Our band is now in front of our quarters, discoursing

sweet strains as I write. This is an addition to the post, and a most delightful one too ; and quite proud are we of our new band. They have scarcely been together as yet more than a couple of months, and are already in excellent accord. They are most of them fine musicians, and in time we will have one of the finest bands in service.

"But I began this letter with the view of giving you a superficial sketch of my travels away from home and its precious inmates, to the distant and transient abode to which duty has assigned me.

"I left New York in the eight o'clock train Monday morning. That *Fidus Achates*, vulgarly known as *Lomax*, came out *missing*, nor has he thus far deemed it of sufficient importance to apologize for keeping me kicking my heels round, waiting for him to put in an appearance.

"But like the most amiable and forgiving of men, I stand ready to grant him mercy as soon as he can find time to ask my pardon. As things stand at present, I tend strongly towards the skepticism of Mr. Stevens, (whom I promised I would bring the vagrant to Castle Point,) as to the actual existence of any such person. That in some past age, far back among the darkening shadows of antiquity, there may have existed some such being endowed with human faculties and mortal attributes, I will not pretend to gainsay. But this is a *myth*, or a mythological fiction ; but that there is any such creature at the present day, I am beginning to think, admits of prodigious doubt.

"Alone, therefore—"rapt in the solitude of my own originality "—I turned my back to the Babylon of America, in which and its vicinity I had, during the winter just past, enjoyed many agreeable hours and made many agreeable acquaintances—and I hope kind friends. As I rolled away from the Lelands' Metropolitan, I cast one 'long and lingering glance' upon the Palaces of the Merchant Princes ; and as we went ' pouring forward with impetuous speed' down Broadway—that marble avenue of fashion, luxury, and wealth,—many a familiar edifice brought to mind our sojourn at Hoboken, and our excursions thence to Christy's—Dusseldorf,—Goupil's, etc., and then the tapering spire of Trinity, all and each brought back vividly to mind the pleasant hours, and pleasant friends, with whom we often passed so joyously the fleeting day. And as I receded from the Island City, one of the last objects on the Jersey shore upon which my eyes reposed was Castle Point, with its bold front pro-jecting far out and looking down in proud security on the dark waters which recoil from its solid base. And then from its summit, Mr. Stevens' hospitable home, con-fronting majestically, in rural quiet, the clamorous roar-ings of the *Commercial Emporium.* Before leaving New York, I bought Bulwer's new novel, ' What will he do with it?' —which I soon finished. I could not have made a more agreeable selection of a travelling companion. With that in my hand I could not think myself alone, for did I not admire and revere the noble character, the splen-did talents, and generous impulses of Guy Darrell? Did I not love the sweet face of Sophy, and admire and adore that noble woman, Caroline Monfort, pity and admire the sweet simplicity, the noble generous devoted love and manful struggles against adversity, of poor Waife—noble ' gentleman Waife?' We reached Albany in time for dinner at the Delavan, a hotel worthy of the Knicker-bockers. We were waited on by bright rosy-cheeked damsels, all dressed in a uniform pattern of striped dresses.

" At three o'clock, I renewed my rushing progress westward. We crossed the suspension bridge long after dark, and it was so dark, I could not get a glimpse of the Falls—the thunder of which was, however, somewhat audible. We reached Detroit about three o'clock the next afternoon, and I gladly greeted the green waters of the river of the lakes, for I was wearied and tired of the cramped monotony of the cars, and sighed for a day of rest. I brought up at the Russell House, where Poe and other officers stationed in that city, board. I spent that evening with Mrs. B— and her charming daughters, whose society so embellished Leavenworth. They were all delighted to see me, and to talk of old times in Kansas. They all live with Judge W., Mrs. B.'s father. I dined with them the next day, drove out with the girls in the afternoon, and again passed the evening with them, beating Miss B. at chess. The following morning called again and bid them an affectionate adieu.

" While in Detroit, I saw a great deal of Poe, and introduced him to my friends the B.'s.

" I left that afternoon for St. Louis, where I arrived about four A. M. on Saturday, and immediately retired, pretty well inclined for a good sleep. I did not have long to rest, for Colburn, seeing my name on the hotel register, roused me up soon after eight o'clock, after which, you may well imagine, there was no more sleep for me ; for each had a great many questions to propound to the other on army matters, and next summer's campaign on the Plains, etc., etc. And now since you are informed of my safe arrival in St. Louis, I may bring this long epistle to a close, and defer the further narrative of my travels to some future time."

"FORT RILEY, *May 29th*, 1859.

"This day a year ago we left this fort, *en route* for Utah, little expecting ever to see it again. But three months had hardly elapsed before we were back again. Such is the uncertainty of one's movements while in the army. This year we are going out, expecting not to return before October, and we may not do so at all. But go where we may, we will scarcely find an equal to this as regards *quarters*. I think them superior to those at West Point. Riley has no other attractions, and I should leave it therefore with but little regret.

"*Prairie Dog Creek*, where my company goes before proceeding to the Arkansas, is about two hundred and fifty miles west or northwest from this post. I fear we will have to wait there a month or six weeks before any of the companies from Laramie will reach their destination. My duties as quartermaster and commissary will interfere somewhat with my hunting, but not very materially.

"Major Sedgwick about three weeks ago left on a six months' leave, and I regret that he will not be with us. Taylor, Willie and I have these big *quarters* all to ourselves, and are living in a quiet and domestic way.

"I cannot say when we will get off, but certainly not before the 20th of June.

"We have just heard of Van Dorn's fight in Texas. Fitz. Lee was wounded! of course he would be, if being foremost in the fight were any warrant. Only think, while the Second Cavalry are having these fights, we literally do nothing, unless it is aid and feed the infernal Indians, whenever they come north of the Arkansas.

"It is easy to say 'patience! and your time will come next,' but very disgusting and mortifying, to be in the situation we now occupy. We have but two chances, one is, we may be ordered south of the Arkansas, and the other is, the *Cheyennes* may molest some of the emigrants, and we be compelled to chastise them. Should such be the case, you may be assured we will do it, if there is virtue in spurs and horseflesh."

To his Sister.

"CAMP ON ARKANSAS RIVER,
June 1st, 1859.

"I wrote from Council Grove when we lay over there. We reached the river this evening, being our fifteenth day out from the fort. We are now about two hundred and fifty miles from the fort, and will in a few days enter the Cheyenne country, but there is little chance of our meeting any of that tribe. We will, however, in a day or two, reach the camp of some three or four hundred Arrapahoes and Camanches who are friendly, and on a buffalo hunt, it is said, near Pawnee Fork.

"Of this sport for the last three or four days, we have had as much as our hearts could desire. The first day I killed three, yesterday one, and to-day two. You would hardly believe me were I to tell you what immense herds of them are almost continually in sight. The hills some five or ten miles from the road are black with them. Our *Delawares* generally ride round them down towards the road, when we pitch into the herd, single out a young, fat animal, run it as near the road as possible and shoot it, take the tongue and a rib or two, and sometimes the skin. My horse *Sam* is an excellent horse for chasing them, and seems to enjoy the sport as well as I do, and does not take fright however near I push him to the shaggy beast.

"This sort of hunting is very exciting, especially to those who have not practiced it. Nor is the pleasure diminished by the danger there is from the buffalo, when wounded or closely pressed, turning on the horse, and rending him in pieces before he can get out of the way. One turned on me the other day and did not miss my horse's flank three inches ; nothing but the spring he made when I touched him with the spur saved him.

"But before we reached the buffalo country, we lived on *antelope* for several days. The Delawares killed eight or ten ; but they are so very wild and fleet that none of us pretend to hunt them. We saw a great many of them on the hills at a distance, and they looked very pretty indeed as they strolled off on getting sight of the column.

"We still travel on the Santa Fe road and will continue to do so for some time. A portion of our train starts back to the fort to-morrow, by which I send this."

To his Father.

"CAMP VAN DORN, *July 5th*, 1859.

"Here we are more than two hundred miles from Riley. We shall probably not get off for the Arkansas before the twentieth of next month. We are in a good country for game, and shall enjoy ourselves much.

"Walker will send in an expressman for various official reasons, which I need not detail. He will return in about two weeks, and bring us our missives of love and friendship from the States.

"Yesterday the glorious fourth was celebrated in the most approved style. Scarcely had the " powerful king of day " peeped over the distant hills, when the stars and the stripes were gracefully floating over Camp Van Dorn and its busy garrison. At ten o'clock the oration was pronounced by the orator of the day, the Hon. *Mr. Wisson*, of Ohio, of whom a short account may not be uninteresting.

"A short time previous to our leaving Riley there made his appearance there a very dilapidated individual of a very uncertain age, the collapsed state of whose finances was sufficiently apparent from his seedy appearance and the novel occupation to which he devoted himself for a living. He, like many others of a similar migratory disposition, had started for the new El Dorado, not so much, as he afterward informed me, for the purpose of digging in the mines, as to see the country and enjoy a change of scene. The news, however, which he heard at Riley of disappointment and starvation in the mines, completely staggered him, in short (as Micawber would say) he determined to 'mark time' awhile at Riley. His sole worldly goods, however, consisted (over and above the clothes on his back) of a very long, prodigiously ancient single-barrelled shot gun, which, like its indefatigable bearer, gave unmistakable signs of having weathered many a storm. By this gun he set great store, and with it he supported himself. He one day brought in a fine mess of frogs, which found such a ready sale that thenceforward he daily made his appearance with a long string of frogs dangling in his hand.

7

"The old fellow's quite respectable deportment, his good language, singular occupation, and blithe good nature, soon made him a general favorite, while the choice epicurean delicacies which he vended, caused all the *caterers* for messes to watch his diurnal motions with intense anxiety. To supply their wants, he used to rise with the sun, and sometimes devote the whole day in pursuit of his amphibious game, often up to his waist in water for hours. Such was Wesson's life, previous to our departure from Riley. A few days before we left, he applied to Captain Walker for employment. He wanted to be employed as hunter and guide, which modest request the captain declined, Wesson never having been on the Plains. Finally he begged to be permitted to go along with the command in any capacity whatever, and all he would ask was his daily rations. The old fellow (he was and is to this day known at the fort, and among the men as the 'Frog man') appealed most earnestly to Walker, who finally at the instance of Beall and myself let him go.

"He has proved to us a fruitful source of interest and amusement, and Beall declares that he would not be at all surprised if he should turn out some great man in disguise.

"To see the old fellow trudging along the road, with that long gun of his swung over his shoulder, wearing a shocking bad hat, and a long pointed beard of tawny hue, was an amusing sight. You could plainly read that Dame Fortune had favored him with more kicks than coppers. Yet, I have never seen him in any but a good humor, with a cheerful smile and a kindly word for all who addressed him. Having announced among his other accomplishments that he was a fine cook, a mess of teamsters secured the aid of his invaluable services. Thus cooking in camp and hunting along the road, Wesson arrived at *Prairie Dog Creek*. And there he divulged a portion of his antecedent career. We had already learned from him that he had spent some years of varied life in California, that his father was a farmer of property and respectability in Ohio, and his conversation left no need of his assurance that he had received a liberal education. It was only after our arrival in this camp, that while he was in our tent talking with Beall and myself, he incidentally mentioned his having been at Yale College. Upon questioning more fully, we ascertained that he was a graduate of Yale College. He was, he says, suspended one year, so that it took him five years to get through ; after which he spent one year at the Law School there.

"The oration which he delivered was prepared in a single evening, for it was only on the third that it occurred to some of us to ask him to deliver it. It is a creditable effort, appropriate, neat and marked throughout by sound good sense. There was no attempt by the orator at fine writing or flourish, and on such a hackneyed subject was really original, varied with apt allusions, and quite interesting. We are going to send it to Riley for publication in the *Junction Sentinel,* and I shall direct the editor to send you a copy."

To his Sister.

"Camp Van Dorn, Prairie Dog Creek, }
     July 24th, 1859. }

" Wesson the incomparable who rode our late express

to Riley, brought me many remembrances from " sweet home," and friends elsewhere.

" Walker says he will send in another express in a few days, so I hasten to cancel some of my epistolary debts.

" Walker is going on leave as soon as we return, and I shall again be in command of my company. Lieut. Beall and I get along most harmoniously, and as he is a good hunter we have had much sport chasing and killing buffaloes, and now and then an antelope and elk. We made a short excursion to Solomon's Fork, but did not have much luck, three buffaloes, two elks, and an antelope, being the sum total of game slaughtered. A few days before Beall, and I went over to Solomon's Fork (on which trip we were absent four days, and marched a hundred miles). Captain Walker and myself were down the creek some ten miles below camp ; I had been in pursuit of some antelope among the hills, and had just rejoined Walker, when we were suddenly surrounded by twenty-five Indians. It was a complete surprise. I had been watching for them all day. Though apparently friendly, Walker and I felt no disposition to trust them ; but derived all our confidence from the fact of our each being armed with a couple of revolvers, while I had in addition a double barrelled gun loaded with wire cartridges of buck-shot. After rather hasty salutations, we informed them that we could not wait for any prolonged talk, but would be glad to see them at camp, where we were compelled to go without delay. Whereupon we made our retreat in the most masterly manner, and extricated ourselves from very disagreeable company considering our relative numbers. They afterwards came to our camp and proved to be a party of Arrapahoes. They were all powerful, athletic men. They informed us that the Cheyennes to the number of some hundred are on the Republican near the mouth of this creek. These Indians are all we have yet seen. Both of these tribes are somewhere in our vicinity, and are very suspicious of our intentions, and therefore steer entirely clear of us.

"Wesson, our expressman and orator, was two days behind his time on returning and we became quite uneasy about him. On the morning of the third day of his stay beyond his time I started with twelve men, to go in search of him, fully prepared to '*wipe out*' any squad of Indians, in case I should find his "ghastly remains" by the roadside. Thus breathing war and vengeance, I left Camp Van Dorn intending to march fifty miles a day until I found some trace of our stray *genius*, which would have taken us to Riley in four days. I left here on the morning of the twenty-first, and marched twenty-five miles by about one o'clock, when I halted at an elm grove and spring to rest my horses and pass the heat of the day, intending to make the other half of my day's march in the cool of the evening. Saddling up about five o'clock I resumed my march, but had scarcely risen the crest of the hill when I saw a man mounted on a white mule descending the opposite ridge. I bore down on him at an open gallop, and soon discovered to my delight the never-to-be-mistaken lineaments of Wesson, the 'frog man.' I immediately turned down to the grove and went into camp. It was therefore at elm grove and stretched beneath its refreshing shade that I perused the numerous letters from home and kind friends, brought from Riley.

"You will thus perceive that although we are in a

stationary camp, I still keep moving about the country quite actively. Nor do we always have to seek excitement so far off.

"Every day or two buffaloes come in sight of camp, when sending for my favorite horse Jerry, I am soon enjoying all the excitement of a buffalo chase. There is just danger enough in this sport to make it in the highest degree pleasant. A man belonging to a train that passed here some time ago *en route* for Pike's Peak, was horribly mangled by a buffalo he had wounded. Some people think fool-hardiness, courage, but do not discover their mistake until it is too late."

To his Father.

"CAMP SUMNER, ARKANSAS RIVER, SEVEN MILES
  BELOW OLD FORT ATKINSON,
    August 21st, 1859.

"I have at last, with my company, reached the Arkansas, and joined the other three companies of my regiment.

"On the eighth of August we turned our faces southward, bidding good-by to Camp Van Dorn, round which will cluster many happy reminiscences.

"We had a very pleasant march across the country, reaching this river on the nineteenth, and camped three and a half miles below Fort Atkinson. Beall and myself came to the fort in the afternoon, and Walker and the command next morning. They were all glad to see us. I received a number of letters, two from you. As to the detail for cavalry instructor, Sedgwick will obtain it for me if possible. But I think now I had better wait a year or two before going to West Point. I read the letter of

B., and it is about what might have been expected. The letters from Senators W., T., D., and J., are all that I could wish. Sedgwick, under date of August third, writes that Hardee * will certainly recommend my detail if there is a vacancy in any of the three instructorships which I would accept.

"We shall get back to Riley towards the last of September."

To his Sister.

"CAMP ON LOW CREEK, ONE HUNDRED AND
TWENTY MILES FROM FORT RILEY,
September 20th, 1859.

"We arrived at Walnut creek on the eighteenth and there met *Satanke*, the war chief of the Kiowas, and *Buffalo-Hump*, the chief of the band of Camanches with which Van Dorn has had two fights in Texas. We had a long talk, in which Satanke promised that his tribe would preserve peace with all white men, and Buffalo Hump promised to return to Texas, and make peace. Both these chiefs are remarkably fine-looking men. *Buffalo Hump* has a pleasant face, with a kind and generous expression. *Satanke*, on the contrary, has a cruel, severe expression of countenance, though his features are fine. I should not like to have my life dependent on his mercy.

"We passed to-day through vast herds of buffalo, of which we killed about thirty. I contented myself with slaughtering three, though I could have killed a dozen, but I did not wish to exhaust my horses, as I want to use them to-morrow, when I will write further."

* Commandant at West Point in 1859, afterward Lieut-general in Confederate service.

"Camp on Walnut Creek,
Sept. 22d, 1859.

" How often are we reminded of the uncertainty of everything in this life, and that to-day we know not what the morrow will bring forth. The last two days have been eventful and momentous days for me—one distinguished by the peril of my own life, and the other, by my being compelled to take the life of an Indian, in the performance of military duty.

" Yesterday the 21st, several parties were organized to go after buffaloes. Most of them were very successful, and more than forty buffaloes were killed during the day. Among the other parties which went out was my own, consisting of first sergeant Byrnes, two corporals and one private, all from my own company. After going about five miles, sergeant Byrnes and I dashed after some buffaloes and had quite a spirited chase. I had wounded mine very badly, and spurred my horse close up along side, in order to give him the death shot, but he turned suddenly on my horse before I could fire, and charged down at us. My horse shied, made a false step and fell. I was obliged to let him go, or the buffalo would have killed him. He sprang up quickly and ran off, leaving me standing face to face, with the buffalo, within five or six yards of me. I stood pistol in hand, ready to fire on him should he advance : but I had no hope of killing him ; and I began to think my last hour had come. Never did the sky look so blue, or the grass so green as they did then. Thoughts of home, and an inglorious fate, rushed through my brain with untold velocity. I dare not run, for I knew he would then be upon me instantly. The only safe course, I felt instinctively, was to confront him with a steady gaze. He glared on me intensely for a few seconds, more or less, then shook his head and slowly turning, went off at a sullen walk. Never was a man more relieved than I felt. It was like returning from death to life. You who have never seen a wild buffalo in all his terrible and ferocious aspect cannot fully appreciate the perilous danger of such an encounter. Had the buffalo charged me, most probably he would have killed me instantly. I think if I had moved a step he would have charged. I attribute my escape to my motionless attitude and steady look at him. As soon as I breathed more freely, I began to think of my horse which was following off one of the buffaloes. Sergeant Byrnes' attention I could not attract, as he was several hundred yards off shooting at his buffaloes. Fortunately some of my other men saw what had happened, and galloped up to where I was; one of them dismounted and I sprang on his horse.

" By this time, however, my horse was more than a mile off and out of sight. We searched the country in every direction for fifteen or sixteen miles, but could find no trace of him. We rode all through large herds of buffalo looking for him, but in vain. Finally after travelling about twenty-five miles, we returned to camp with but one hope left, viz., that perhaps he might have returned there. I need not tell you how rejoiced I was on getting into camp to learn that he had found his way back. In the meantime, however, coming as he did with the saddle torn and his side bloody from a cut with the spur when he fell, great fears were entertained for my safety. Parties of officers and men at once went out in scout for me. But my men were soon met by them, from

7*

whom they learned that I was safe, and they all got in again soon after my return.

Sept. 23d.—" I was so tired last night I could not conclude my letter, and McIntyre leaves with the mail in a few minutes, so I can say but a few words now. We left Cow Creek at one o'clock in the morning the night before last in consequence of intelligence from the ranche of Rickman and Flournoy, that the Kiowas had committed some outrage there, and threatened further hostile depredations. We arrived at half past six, A. M., and took one of the offenders prisoner. His name was Pawnee, and was the brother of Tehorsen, head chief of the Kiowas. He was placed in my charge, and endeavored to escape. I pursued him and repeatedly offered him his life if he would stop, but he would not and I was obliged to kill him. We went up the creek to-day where the camp of the Kiowas was, but they had gone. We were much disappointed, as we expected a fight. We got back in the afternoon at four, having marched thirty miles. I will give you as soon as I reach Riley a further account of these events.

" P. S.—I have Pawnee's pony. 'Tis a fine beautiful animal, an iron grey. We have to make very long marches now to get into Riley, as our rations expire on the second of October."

To his Father.

" CAMP ON LITTLE ARKANSAS, ⎱
     September 26th, 1859. ⎰

" I wrote hastily the other day and must do so now ; but as I shall be at Riley in a few days, will defer a more elaborate detail of recent events.

" My conduct in shooting that prisoner when he attempted to escape, has been fully endorsed by both Captain Walker and Captain De Saussure in their official reports, besides meeting the unqualified approval of all the officers who saw the affair and indeed of all belonging to the command.

"I repeatedly offered him his life, and the first shot I fired over his head. I then dashed past him and reined up my horse in front of him, but he dodged to the left and kept on. I then shot him, as a last resort, the ball entering his back, passing through the heart and coming out of the breast, and yet he rode on two hundred yards before he fell. I fired another shot at his head but missed. He was dead within half a minute after he fell. He was the brother of *Tehorsen*, the head chief of the Kiowas.

"Otis after this was detailed to escort the Santa Fe mail as far as Pawnee Fork. Last night an expressman rode in from him, stating that after the mail left him and when five miles beyond, it was attacked by a party of fifteen or sixteen Indians, and two of the party were killed and the third badly wounded, who escaped by jumping out behind the wagon and hiding in the long grass, where they could not find him. A party of Pike's Peakers coming along the next morning found him and carried him into Otis's camp. Otis joins us again to-morrow and Long goes back with forty men on the road for its protection.

"We will undoubtedly have to escort the mail next winter and most probably will be stationed at Walnut Creek."

The following official report from Captain Walker respecting the shooting of Pawnee by Lieut. Bayard has been kindly furnished by Gen. E. D. Townsend, Adjutant-general of U. S., from his office, for use in this memoir.

" CAMP IN FIELD ON WALNUT CREEK,
Sept. 23d, 1859.

" *Capt. W D. De Saussure Comd'g fourth and fifth squadrons First Cavalry.*

" Sir :—I have the honor to report that in compliance with your orders, I started on the march with a squadron of the First Cavalry (Co's. G and K) on the morning of the twenty-first inst., to Alison's ranche, the scene of the difficulty related in Major Donaldson's letter, where I arrived at half past six, A. M. My instructions were to furnish an escort to Major Donaldson to Pawnee Fork, and take such measures in regard to the outrage as I might find the result of an investigation required. I found a letter from Major Donaldson stating that he had started early in the morning on his way to New Mexico, and would not require an escort. On inquiry I ascertained that two sub-chiefs of the Kiowas, Pawnee, the reported brother of Tehorsen, head chief of the tribe, and Satanke, both under the influence of liquor, the latter slightly, went to the ranche occupied by Messrs. Rickman and Flournoy, and demanded a quantity of goods from them. Upon refusal they became angry, and Satanke went out, filled his mouth with blood and spit in Rickman's face. He then twice endeavored to stab him with his knife. Rickman with difficulty and with the assistance of Flournoy avoided his blows. Rickman then got a revolver to defend himself, upon which both the Indians drew their arrows to the head and aimed at him but were afraid to shoot. Satanke then climbed to the top of the house and commenced tearing off the roof; they finally went outside and endeavored to shoot into the house, and after awhile left, threatening to return and demolish it.

"This occurred about two P. M., on the twenty-first inst. Upon my arrival I found Pawnee near the house, and that Capt. Steuart, who with lieutenants Beall and Otis had arrived in advance of the column, had ordered him to remain. He had mounted his horse on some pretence when I ordered him to dismount and go into the store. It was my intention to visit the Kiowa camp to make a full investigation of the affair, and require such satisfaction as I thought the circumstances justified. No violence was offered or intended to Pawnee, who was then perfectly sober, nor did I put a guard over him till he ran to a room in the rear of the house where there were several loaded shot guns. I immediately followed him, called him back and put a sentinel over him. He afterwards attempted to leap the counter of the store to get his bow and arrows. I thought it necessary to detain Pawnee as one of the perpetrators of the outrage, and also to prevent him from reporting our arrival to the Kiowas, and thus enable them to prepare themselves to receive us, should the fears of their hostile intentions expressed in Major Donaldson's letter be confirmed. I therefore ordered Lieut. Bayard, acting Adjutant of the detachment, to take charge of him with a proper guard. The command had been dismounted about a hundred yards from the store, and before the sentinel could return with his horse Pawnee mounted and made his escape. Lieut. Bayard ordered him to stop, and went in pursuit calling out Pawnee! stop! friend! friend! which he understood, as he had been a good deal with the whites as a spy. After a chase of half a mile he overtook him and ran in front of him. The Indian doubled upon him and rode on. Lieut. Bayard then fired his pistol over his head. Having thus exhausted all peaceful means to stop him, he was obliged to shoot him to prevent his escape. He died within ten minutes after he was shot. The whole tribe was reported to be assembled within fifteen miles, and a large band of Camanches were encamped in their neighborhood. They were known to be already exasperated at the refusal of the government to supply them with the usual presents. I believed that in this juncture the presence of the commanding officer of the expedition who was fully informed of the instructions of the government, was advisable either for negotiation or war, in the entire force at his command. I sent therefore by express a brief report of the facts to you, and encamped near the ranche for its defence, awaiting further orders. I make this detailed statement as necessary to a full understanding of events that may materially affect our relations with the Kiowas.

"Very respectfully your obedient servant,
"W. S. WALKER,
" *Capt. First Cavalry Comd'g Squadron.*"

From Lieutenant Bayard's letter of the 29th of September, it appears that the Kiowas immediately commenced hostile operations, attacking the Sante Fe mail-carriers and killing two of them. In 1860, as will be seen hereafter, they took the war path and in such force, that an expedition had to be sent against them for the purpose of giving them an effective chastisement.

Soon after Lieutenant Bayard's return to Riley with his company, the Hon. Grantley F. Berkeley, a member of the British Parliament and a celebrated sportsman, arrived. His visit to the United States was for the purpose of enjoying a buffalo-hunt. He brought letters to officers in command of Leavenworth, and was received with that hospitality and urbanity for which the American officer is distinguished. Letters were given him to officers at Riley, and they were ordered to extend every proper attention to the noble stranger. Accordingly, after resting and refreshing himself in the ample and commodious quarters at Riley, two officers, Major Martin and Lieutenant Bayard, having eight days' leave of absence and a suitable guard, were detailed to accompany Mr. Berkeley on the Plains. Major Martin having lost an arm in the Mexican war, was not capable of taking much part in the proposed hunt, and it therefore fell to Lieutenant Bayard to accompany personally the English sportsman, and give him every opportunity which could be afforded to enjoy the exciting and often dangerous amusement of chasing and shooting buffaloes.

To the monthly English paper devoted to sporting subjects, " THE FIELD," Mr. Berkeley, while in the United States, forwarded several letters giving an account of his delightful pastime with Lieutenant Bayard. But in a more elaborate work * entitled the " English Sportsman in

* Mr. Berkeley forwarded a copy of his book to General Bayard's father, and on one of the blank leaves wrote as follows :

" This book is presented by the author to the father of the late General Bayard as a mark of the sincere friendship and regard he felt for his son—as gallant a soldier and as true a gentleman as ever lived, his loss by the author now so deeply deplored.

GRANTLEY F. BERKELEY."

America," he gave in detail a more full account of their hunting expedition. It is handsomely got up and embellished with many engravings, several of which display the personal encounters of the sportsmen with their gigantic game.

Mr. Berkeley seemed much pleased with his escort, Major Martin and Lieutenant Bayard, and especially refers to their abstinence from tobacco and whiskey as very agreeable to him.

In preparing this memoir, Mr. Berkeley was applied to for copies of letters to him from Lieut. Bayard. The following was his reply to the application.

"ALDERNEY MANOR, POOLE, DORSET,
April 25th, 1873.

"DEAR SIR:—I do remember sub-Lieutenant Bayard. He was at that rank when I met him at Fort Riley, and I have never ceased to regret his gallant, but unfortunate death. In hunting together on the Plains we became sincere friends. A better rider, a better shot, or a more high-minded and graceful soldier and gentleman I never knew.

"We were to have corresponded, and he promised to tell me of the war against the Indians; but, as you know, he was severely wounded in the cheek by an arrow, which could not be cured till they got him to St. Louis, and from the time I left the United States until his gallant death I never heard from him, * so it is not in my power to comply with your request. On my return to England I wrote

* This is evidently a mistake, as Mr. Berkeley in his letter (which we give) May 9th, 1861, acknowledges the receipt of a letter from Lieut. Bayard.

and published from letters which had appeared in the *Field*, a more elaborate work, called "The English Sportsman in America." It is, I believe, very nearly out of print; but if I can get a copy, it would give me great pleasure to send it to you, if only to prove to you the high estimation in which I held your son.

"If you will tell me the best way to send the book to you, and if you would like to have it, I will then pay immediate attention to the matter.

"Yours very faithfully,

"GRANTLEY F. BERKELEY."

"*To Samuel J. Bayard, Esq.*"

To his Sister.

"FORT RILEY, *Oct.* 16*th*, 1859.

"I had a pleasant hunting excursion with Mr Berkeley, an English gentleman, and Member of Parliament. He brought letters to the officer in command here, who detailed Major Martin and me to accompany him with a guard. We killed sixteen buffaloes, and should have killed more if we had not had bad luck with my horses, they having fallen lame. I have not time now to give you the particulars of the hunt. I killed four alone and Berkeley two, together we killed six, and the man Mr. Berkeley brought as guide, killed four. Mr. Berkeley intends publishing an account of the hunt. He insists on my making him a visit to England, to enjoy fox-hunting there, and I have promised I would go, in a year or two, if I could get leave. I like him much, for he is certainly a fine old gentleman of the old school. Think of a gentleman about sixty years of age, coming over here, and chasing buffaloes on our Plains! Precious few Americans at that age could do it.   He says if I will visit him at his estate in Hampshire, I shall have the best horse in his stables at my command."

The following letter of Mr. Berkeley to his friend Bayard, will be read with interest; thoroughly like John Bull, but breathing kind and generous thoughts of his American friends.

   " WINKTON HOUSE, [near Kingswood] }
      HANTS, *May 9th*, 1861. }

"MY DEAR BAYARD :—Your letter of the 15th of April gave me much pleasure, but your *first letter* to which you allude never reached me, and I wondered why you had never written, attributing your silence to the wound from the redskins.   You have a hard and a cruel duty before you, but I am sure you will do your duty wherever the scene of it may be ; and I wish you individually all success, but there my wishes end, save that I always hope to see your country once more at peace.   The cause of war originated in the North, and the source whence sprung that war lies in the overwhelming masses of all grades under the sun, whom the Federal government thought fit to trust with universal suffrage.   An universal suffrage so lavishly bestowed on *rowdies*, having no vested property in the state, of course sends demagogues to Congress, and the event of that bad selection is to keep the army on so weak a footing as to be powerless in certain exigencies.   The privates composing that army are foreigners, and though splendidly officered, by American gentlemen, the enlistment for a short period mars the drill ; while at the same time pay and promotion for the gallant gentlemen of the profession are so low and slow, that really insulted as they are by the assumed rank above them of the generals, colonels and captains *I saw*, Heaven save the mark! I only wonder at the officers whose acquaintance I made at Fort Riley, including Col. Sumner, having taken to the profession of arms.

"To all my friends, whose acquaintance I made, give my sincere and kind remembrance.

"In your letter you have not told me anything about the way in which you got your wound, or how those rascally redskins were cut up, as I have no doubt they were; or if the infernal *Sitting Bear*, Setauke, still keeps that head-dress we talked about, and of what tribes the enemy consisted.

"I take an immense interest in the first battle, day after I left you. We none of us can understand how that first fort came to fall without anybody being killed. What on earth was Major Anderson about? To us here it looked like a grand review or party of pleasure. People are at me about it, knowing my high opinion of the officers of your army, but I can give no explanation.

"My friends in America up to this last week have been sending me over prairie grouse and quail for naturalization for our Society for that purpose here, and I am charmed by being put in mind of the *Plains*, by having a male prairie grouse walking about my garden, tamer than an English pheasant, and coming to my whistle for food and making the *devil's own howls*, with the skin blown out on either side of his neck, strutting round and round, and calling for his mate. But I have no mate to give him. The four prairie grouse that came over are all males. A friend of mine, Lord Malmsbury, has imported some of your wood grouse, and they are doing well.

" I have sent out to different places a great number of quails, some from Canada and some from New York. You will be sorry to hear that week before last your friend my bloodhound poor old David, died. Chance, Bar and Brutus are all well. The latter lies by my writing table now.

" About a fortnight ago, while hunting a deer in the royal forest, I came to grief. I had never seen the horse before, having been mounted by a friend ; but having carried me well for an hour and ten minutes, he fell at a bank, with a double ditch, and while we were on the ground together he struck me with his forefoot on the chest, and then getting up without me trod on me twice. My doctor says the two upper ribs ought to have been broken, but that their strength just resisted it enough to save a fracture. I cannot yet quite use my right arm. The fall put me in mind of yours when Martin gave you a mount, and we came into that low place with long grass after the bison.

" The bisons' tails, two of them, hang from my bell ropes as I write this. We had a deal of fun together— at least I thought so.

" When you see any of the ladies to whom I had the pleasure of being introduced at Fort Riley, be sure to give them my compliments, and ask them not to forget the hunter from the old world. To Willie Martin sing of " Hoot-a-wa, Hoot-a-wa, wandering Willie," and tell him not to forget to grow out of my recollection.

" Hoping some day or other to see you, ever yours sincerely,　　　　　" GRANTLEY F. BERKELEY."

"P S. Is West Point near New York? If so and you see my English friends Cunard and the Major, whom I left at the Clarendon Hotel inspecting arms and improvements, remember me kindly to them."

To his Sister.

"FORT RILEY, *Oct. 24th*, 1859.

"We have a delightful society at Fort Riley at present. We are in full enjoyment of a glorious Indian summer. And, when not on duty, riding, driving and walking with pretty girls and flirting in the day, parties and dancing in the evening, serve to make the time agreeable.

"I am waiting for Sedgwick's return impatiently. There is no one I miss so much when absent as dear "old Sedge." Living alone in this large house (my quarters) my only relief, when getting too solitary, is visiting the ladies.

"Steuart's company will return to Riley, and an infantry company take its place on the Santa Fe road. Col. Sumner approves of everything that has been done, and says, "The Lord willing, I will take the field next spring against the treacherous devils." He says he will take these four companies of cavalry and the three companies of dragoons, making seven in all, and I hope we will be able to strike terror into the hearts of all these savages. We consequently already begin to look forward to the ensuing campaign and the stirring events it promises. If we have good luck and can catch the Indians, the colonel, I think, will be in such good humor when he returns, that there will be no difficulty whatever about getting a *leave*, if I desire one. Already, however, I have changed my mind, and should there be nothing *special* to call me home, I shall wait till next spring a year, and then getting permission to cross the seas, spend a few months in Europe. I could pass a week or two, hunting with Mr. Berkeley, very pleasantly. His acquaintance would, I doubt not, make my stay in England very agreeable. He is a most genial and companionable gentleman, with great vitality for a man of his age."

To his Sister.

"FORT RILEY, *Nov. 20th,* 1859.

"Major Sedgwick has not yet arrived, but I expect him certainly this evening. How glad I shall be to see him! I am very sorry I cannot stay here at Riley with him this winter coming. I am ordered to Jefferson barracks on recruiting service for the regiment. You think I am delighted, do you? well you are mistaken; I do not want to go at all. I am very thankful to Colonel Sumner, for I am confident he thought I would be pleased to spend the winter at St. Louis. Also Major Sedgwick and Colburn, and they all imagined that I would be charmed with the order. Such, however, is not the case. I had determined to devote myself this winter to reading and study and economy. This order puts an end to all such fine resolutions and renders them simply *impossible.*

"St. Louis, you know, is one of the gayest cities in the Union, and army officers there have to visit in a wide circle. So you may set me down as a permanent attachment to hoops and crinoline for this winter, unless I am relieved, otherwise my next letter will give you some account of the "beautiful and attractive" in St. Louis."

CHAPTER XII.

Life on the Plains 1860.—Trip to Arkansas.—Returns to his Command.—Expedition against the Kiowas.—Encounter with an Indian.—Wounded.—Goes to St. Louis.—Arrow-head extracted from Cheek.—Hemorrhage from Wound.—Dr. Pope ties his carotid Artery.—Return Home.

To his Sister.

" CHEROKEE NATION, FORT WASHITA, }
Feb. 19th, 1860. }

" I ARRIVED here yesterday after a twelve days' march from Fort Smith. Weather delightful. To-morrow my train and men start early for Fort Arbuckle, which I hope to reach by the twentythird. I shall not start until afternoon, in time however to reach camp before dark. Iverson and I start at daylight in the morning on a fox-hunt. They have a fine pack of hounds here, and I anticipate a deal of sport. Ingraham is to overtake me at Arbuckle and go up to Fort Cobb with me. Washita is a beautiful place, and the best built fort I have yet seen, with the exception of Riley. But they have such a splendid climate here! In February they sit here with their doors open and without fire, in the middle of the day. The officers of my regiment here are Carr, Iverson, Ingraham and Church. I am staying with Iverson, whose father is Senator Iverson, and was a class-mate of father's at Princeton. I have received letters from Beall at Arbuckle, and Lomax at Cobb, insisting on my staying with them at their respective posts. I leave on the twentyfifth for Cobb, which I will reach if not delayed by high water, on the second of March. There I will stay probably some days. But I expect to be back in St. Louis on the second or third of April, and get to Riley towards the last of that month."

To his Mother.

" PLANTERS' HOUSE, ST. LOUIS, }
April 28th, 1860. }

" I wrote to father this morning that I would leave here on Tuesday for Fort Riley. But since I wrote an entire change has taken place in my *programme.*

" Recruits have to be sent to the posts in the Indian Territory which I visited last winter, and there is no one here to take them but Colburn and myself. Colburn has given me the choice of going there again, or taking his place here as Adjutant until his return. I told him if he desired to remain, I would go, but otherwise I was satisfied with one trip there. Accordingly I will remain here for the present. I cannot express how much I am disappointed by this arrangement ; for I fear that it will prevent my going out on the Kiowa expedition and keep me here all summer. I shall still hope that I will get off by some means or other. I know Major Sedgwick will be terribly disgusted, if both Taylor and I fail to go out with him. I cannot conceive of anything more horrible than to be condemned to stay here all summer. It appears my luck to miss all fights. Some day it will be quoted against me by some '*kind friend*' as '*remarkably peculiar*' that Bayard was not in that fight.

" But I shall reconcile myself as well as I can to fate,

and enjoy the fascinations of St Louis in compensation. St. Louis is a most pleasant city. Life here for the army officer is a constant round of festivity in the most charming society of ladies, excelled by those of no other city in the United States. It is really a pleasure to leave awhile such a place, to enjoy the flattering cordiality with which your return is greeted."

To his Sister.

" PLANTERS' HOUSE, ST LOUIS,
    May 2d, 1860.

" In my last letter home, I expressed the fear that I would have to remain here all summer. I am now happy in being able to say that Col. Sumner has promised to relieve me from duty here in time to go out with the Santa Fe mail and overtake my command before it crosses the *Arkansas*. My horses and general camp effects will go out from Riley when the command starts, so that everything will be there when I join it. I shall probably leave here by the twentieth of this month."

To his Father.

" CAMP ABOUT PAWNEE FORK,
    June 1st, 1860.

" I arrived here last night about eleven o'clock, after a rapid trip from St. Louis, making the whole distance in six days. The command leaves this morning, in fact, has already gone, but camp is within twelve miles of this, and I will overtake it.

" We start on a pack mule scout of thirty days and have strong hopes of catching the Indians. I have a mule and one of my horses in fine condition. I write in great haste ; you may not hear from me again before I return from the scout."

To his Father.

"CAMP SIX MILES BELOW AUBREY CROSSING, ARK. RIVER, *July 6th,* 1860.

"Our wagons arrived with our provisions on the morning of the third, and reported Captain Sturgis with the six companies of our regiment from Cobb, seventy miles below here. So Taylor and I went down and spent the fourth with them, and returned to this camp yesterday. Pretty good riding, is it not?

"We hear that the Kiowas and Camanches are near Denver City with Sioux and Cheyennes, in all, some three or four thousand. We start to-morrow in pursuit and hope soon to give them a Waterloo defeat.

"When we will get back to Riley I cannot say, but I presume about the first of November.

"Colonel Hardee wrote Major Sedgwick that he would apply for me * in the department of cavalry at West Point.† I wish you to get a friend to go to Floyd and Buchanan and make them promise that I shall have the place, if Hardee applies for me. The appointment will be made about the middle of August."

The object of the expedition in which they were engaged, was to chastise a band of Kiowas, who, led by their chief, Setaukie, had been guilty of many outrages and murders.

* To be Instructor in Cavalry Tactics.

† Colonel Hardee was commandant at West Point ; and according to *routine,* it was his duty when a vacancy occurred among the Instructors at West Point to designate the officer he desired to be appointed.

Pawnee Fork, where Lieutenant Bayard joined the expedition, is about one hundred and forty miles from Fort Riley. Starting from thence they scoured the Plains and country watered by the tributaries of the Arkansas, as far as Bent's Fort, about three hundred and fifty miles from Fort Riley. On the eleventh of July, having discovered traces of the Indians they were pursuing, Captain Steuart, to whose command Lieutenant Bayard was temporarily attached, immediately followed with all despatch their trail. After a pursuit of more than twenty miles, some Indians were seen at a distance. Lieut. Bayard, being mounted on a superior horse, whose speed surpassed that of any in the command, led the way in the chase. He soon came up with an Indian warrior, and, presenting his revolver, demanded his surrender. The Indian, as Lieut. Bayard rode up to him, had dismounted from his pony for the purpose of dodging the shot from the pistol he anticipated, or to enable him the better to use his bow and arrow. At this moment, while in this attitude, Lieut. Bayard saw some Indians running at a distance, and turned to see if any of his men were near enough to receive a signal from him that other Indians were in sight, and as he turned again towards the chief he had brought to bay, the latter shot him with his arrow. The arrow was steel-headed, in shape like a spear head, and the head two and a half inches long. It struck Lieut. Bayard under the cheek bone, and penetrated the *antrim*. If the Indian had not been so near he would have drawn his bow more taut, and probably killed his enemy. With arrows of the same sort they kill buffalo, and it is and, often shoot their arrows entirely through the animal. Of course the wound disabled Lieut. Bayard, and the Indian

instantly renewed his flight.   But Sergeant Ocleston, of
his command, fortunately came up in time to pursue the
Indian, and after a severe chase on foot, (both parties
having abandoned their horses), overtook and killed him.

Lieutenant Bayard was wounded on the eleventh of
July, and solicitous that his parents and family should be
relieved of anxiety respecting him, wrote home by the
first mail opportunity as follows:

To his Father.

" CAMP ON ARKANSAS, TEN MILES ABOVE }
    BENT'S FORT, *July 13th*, 1860. }

" I write you a few hasty lines to set your mind at
rest regarding my wound, which, perhaps before you receive this, you may see announced in the papers.

" We killed two Indians and captured above a dozen
women and children, and about forty ponies.   The former are the wives and children of Setaukie.

" I was shot with an arrow in the left cheek just below the eye.   The *arrow-head remained in the wound*,
when the arrow was pulled out.   Dr. Madison is just
about to attempt its extraction, and Lieut. Steuart * will

---

* This officer kindly forwarded the following extract from his
official report :

" Finding further pursuit fruitless, and that Lieut. Bayard had
received a severe arrow-wound in the face, I rallied the men in
advance and conducted him safely back a distance of six miles to
Capt. Steele's camp, as he belonged to that detachment.   Though
not of my command, I deemed it proper to add my testimony to
the gallant bearing and personal daring he displayed."

" Most respectfully your obedient,

       " J. E. B. STEUART,

    " *First Lt. First Cavalry Comd'g Detachment.*

add a P. S. as to the result, as I will feel rather exhausted after the operation. Even should he not succeed in extracting it, the doctor says it can remain without any injury. Give yourself no uneasiness in regard to this, it will soon be well.

"P S. *July* 14*th*. The doctor was unsuccessful in his attempt yesterday, and so it must remain. He says it will soon be well."

To his Mother.

"CAMP ON ARKANSAS, TEN MILES
ABOVE BENT'S FORT,
July 17*th*, 1860.

" Knowing that you will feel some solicitude on my account, I will send you a few words by Mr. Robert Bent, who starts for the States to-morrow. My wound is healing very well, and the doctor says I am getting along famously. Of course I suffer some pain, but I hope it will diminish soon. I shall probably go into Pawnee Fork early in August, and should my wound continue to trouble me, I shall go on to Philadelphia or New York as quickly as possible, and advise with the best surgeons."

To his Father.

"CAMP ON ARKANSAS ONE HUNDRED AND TEN
MILES BELOW BENT'S FORT, *July* 25*th*, 1860.

" I believe Major Sedgwick goes no further down the road but to-morrow strikes north for the Smoky Hill country in search of the Kiowas and Camanches. I go on to Pawnee Fork with an escort of ten men under command of Lieutenant McIntyre. My wound continues to heal, but as the cheek bone is somewhat shattered, I suffer a good deal of pain from neuralgia. I have Dr.

Madison's certificate and recommendation for a leave of absence for sixty days on that account, and am authorized by Major Sedgwick to proceed to St. Louis to apply for such leave.

"I shall go into Pawnee and there wait a few days, to see what *rest* will do for me. Should there be a very marked improvement such as to induce me to believe that I would soon be enabled to return to duty, I will not take advantage of this certificate of the doctors. But otherwise I shall go on via. Riley and Leavenworth to St. Louis. I shall take steamboat to St. Louis from Leavenworth, as the overland route, by Santa Fe road, would be too trying."

To his Father.

"St. Louis, *August 9th*, 1860.

"I arrived here yesterday considerably enfeebled and suffering much pain. The importance of getting the arrowhead out as quickly as possible, with the fact of my weakness and suffering, have caused me to resort to Dr. Pope of this city, who stands here at the head of his profession as a surgeon of celebrity.

"Should the operation prove successful, Colburn will telegraph you at once. I will then remain here only long enough to permit me to recover strength sufficient to travel homeward. I am surrounded by the kindest and most attentive of friends. I am staying at Colburn's rooms. Mrs. W. insists on sending me my meals, so you see I receive all possible attention, and I trust I will be with you by the twenty-fifth a well man again."

As will be seen from the foregoing letters Dr. Madison,

the army surgeon, after a critical examination, thought
it best not to extract the arrow-head at that time, fearful
that excessive hemorrhages might ensue. As a prudent
and skilful surgeon, he wisely preferred that Lieutenant
Bayard should have the benefit of the best surgical advice to be obtained. Lieutenant Bayard and his family
always have believed that Dr. Madison did his full duty
in the case, and exercised the soundest judgment in the
course he pursued.

Immediately after his arrival at St. Louis, Dr. Charles
A. Pope, the celebrated surgeon, and President of the
Missouri Medical College, was called in. He determined,
after due examination of the case, to extract the arrow-
head, which he did, to the great relief of Lieutenant
Bayard. His face continued quite swollen, and he still
suffered much pain. At last he experienced a severe
hemorrhage, and lost so much blood as to bring him to
death's door. His father was telegraphed for, and immediately came on. He found his son very low, and
feeble in health, and confined to his room in the hospital
of the Sisters of Charity. In a few days, however, he began to recover strength, and improved so rapidly that his
father, after being with him a week, proposed returning to
New Jersey. But the night before the day he intended to
start, about one o'clock, A. M., Lieutenant Bayard suffered
a severe hemorrhage, which again reduced him very low.
He was put under the influence of morphine all the next
day, the doctor remaining with him for the greater part
of the day. Dr. Pope was now fearful that another hemorrhage would prove fatal. He, accordingly, determined
to tie the carotid artery. This he did on the morning

of the sixteenth of September. The following is Doctor Pope's statement of the operation performed :

"CASE I. The late General Bayard, who was killed at the battle of Fredericksburg, received an arrow-shot wound in the left upper jaw, on the eleventh July, 1860, while a lieutenant in New Mexico, in a skirmish with the Indians. The iron point, spear-shaped, and two and a half inches long, with a small neck for the attachment of the wooden shaft, was driven with force, entering a little below the middle of the orbit, and with a slight obliquity backward. The surgeon of the post immediately endeavored to extract the foreign body. At first it was hoped that this might be accomplished by traction upon the arrow itself, but this was thereby only separated from the iron point, which remained firmly impacted in the bone. Different forceps were then resorted to, and after a trial of two hours the effort was abandoned.

" The absence of suitable instruments, the slight hold which could be obtained on the offending body, as the small neck was all that could be seized, and above all the firm impaction, sufficiently account for the failure of extraction. Slight hemorrhages from the corresponding nostril followed within the subsequent four weeks, and on arriving at St. Joseph, a more serious one occurred.

" The patient reached St. Louis five weeks after the reception of his wound. There was some tumefaction of the left side of his face. The wound at the time had skinned over, so that no foreign substance could be seen, but on gentle pressure with the finger, a hard point was perceptible beneath the integument. There was a muco-purulent discharge still issuing from the nostril, proceeding doubtless from the antrum. On incising the imperfect cicatrix, I felt the projecting neck, and supposing that the arrow point, after so long a time, might be somewhat loosened by the efforts of the organism, I attempted its extraction with the dressing forceps of the pocket case, but found them wholly inadequate. I at once supplied myself with instruments of various kinds, and with a powerful forceps succeeded in one or two efforts in extracting the offending body. This was followed by a troublesome bleeding, both from the nostril and the external wound. By rest, opium, cold, plugging and pressure, this was duly arrested. Several slighter hemorrhages subsequently occurred, but they gave rise to no uneasiness.

"The case now progressed favorably, and the patient was able to get about the streets. He walked to my office, and complaining of some inability to separate the jaws, a difficulty, by the way, which had existed all along, I directed him to use gentle and gradual efforts at opening the mouth. In less than an hour his troubles recommenced. The whole cheek and jaw became hot, swollen, and painful. Fever, with renewed hemorrhage, set in, and caused me much anxiety. The same means of arrest first tried did not avail. Extensive extravasation of blood took place, and in order to relieve the pain, tension, and possible sloughing, I deemed it proper to make free counter-openings, both in the mouth and on the cheek and neck. From these, large grumous clots were turned out, and through the inner opening the finger's point could be carried round the almost denuded bone, and lodged high up in the pterygoid fossa. The hemorrhage continuing with various and delusive intermissions, the case became critical. Finally, for three successive nights, these came on regularly at midnight, and were copious and exhaustive. From such repeated losses of blood the patient had now become reduced to the lowest degree, when the further issue of a few ounces more might have turned the scale against him. I then determined to tie the carotid. This was done on the night of the sixteenth of September, more than two months after the reception of the wound. Such was the extreme condition of the patient, that he fainted during the operation, although in a recumbent position.

"The operation was a delicate and difficult one, as the parts were very much swollen and altered by sanguineous extravasation and inflammatory effusion, and the incision being correspondingly deep, the effect of artificial light in such cases, at all times bad, was only the worse, for while the surface of the wound was well lighted, the sharp deep shadow rendered its depth almost invisible. The touch therefore superceded sight. There was no more hemorrhage. Opium and nutritious ingesta were freely given, and the patient continued to do well.

"From the thoroughly anæmic state and the effect of interruption of the cerebral circulation, caused by the ligature, the patient's mind was somewhat impaired, and I feared some altered nutrition or softening of the brain. These symptoms, however, gradually yielded and after several weeks he was again up and about. Being rather impatient and self-willed, he went out before I deemed it prudent for him to do so. The ligature was slow in coming away, and for some weeks after its fall a small fistulous opening remained."

The Lieutenant now left St. Louis for West Point, to which place he was assigned for duty. When on a

visit to his family in New Jersey and travelling by railroad at night between New York and Philadelphia, after
much bodily fatigue, a further hemorrhage occurred from
the still unclosed fistula of the cervical wound. By rest
and moderate pressure this was relieved. This bleeding
was the last ; the wound healed and the patient recovered
his usual health. There always remained, however, an
unpleasant fullness of the affected cheek and masseteric
portion of the face.

The following letter was written before the operation
on the carotid artery was performed:

To his Mother.

"St. Louis, *August* 10*th*, 1860.

" I telegraphed yesterday that the arrow-head was extracted from the wound. It was a great relief, physic-
ally and mentally, and I hope the wound will now soon
heal. It is still very painful.

" I trust I will be able to go out in a week, in which
event I will probably be home by the 29th.

" I have received the utmost kindness and attention
here. The gentlemen have all called repeatedly and offered every attention in their power. Mrs. W. sends my
meals and every delicacy which can tempt the appetite.
Other ladies supply me with fruit of all sorts, flowers, etc.

" If I wish I can be stationed here, but would prefer
going to West Point, could I be ordered there as Instructor in Cavalry. If ordered there I would at once commence the study of law and at the end of my four years
service, be qualified for practice."

To his Mother.

"St. Louis, *August* 31*st*, 1860.

" Although I scarcely feel able as yet to give you a daily journal of the convalescence of an invalid, I will however, during the few minutes I sit up this evening, jot you down a few lines by way of showing that I am still in the land of the living and with a very fair prospect of remaining there for the present.

" I think I am getting stronger every day. I never was so tired of anything in my life as I am of lying in bed. My face on the left side continues highly inflamed, and my jaws I cannot use. I have lost the West Point detail ; Hood, of the Second Cavalry, being ordered to West Point as cavalry instructor."

CHAPTER XIII.

IN the letter of Lieut. Bayard, July 6th, 1860, he says
that Major Sedgwick had been informed by Col. Hardee, Military Commandant at West Point, that he would
apply for him to be appointed Instructor in Cavalry Tactics. This we have no doubt he did. It is usual for the
Secretary of War to leave to the professors and officers at
West Point the designation of appointees in their respective departments to supply vacancies. The Secretary of
War almost invariably acts in accordance with such de-
signations. He did not, however, do so on this occasion,
but appointed Lieut. Hood.*

Early in 1860, at the instance of Lieut. Bayard's father and other friends, the Hon. Vincent L. Bradford, of
Philadelphia (whose personal relations to President Buchanan were those of intimate friendship), asked the
President to appoint Lieut. Bayard Instructor in Cavalry
Tactics at West Point, should there be a vacancy in that
position. This the President promised he would do,

* General Hood, of Confederate army.

and was quite indignant when he found that Governor Floyd had appointed Lieut. Hood. Subsequent events made it probable that Lieut. Hood was appointed because of his known sympathy with the South. He was then in Texas, and doubtless well posted with respect to the designs of the southern leaders, and was better able to co-operate with them in his position in Texas, than he would have been at West Point; and he, therefore, promptly declined the appointment conferred on him. Governor Floyd now, therefore, in obebience to President Buchanan's wishes, appointed Lieut. Bayard.

On the expiration of his leave of absence, Lieut. Bayard reported for duty at West Point. But the condition of his health was such that it was necessary that he should abstain from active duty, and a further leave of absence was obtained.

In returning from West Point home, as he was coming over in the ferry boat at Camden, he experienced another hemorrhage from the still open fissure in his neck. Wrapping his handkerchief tightly around his neck to check the flow of blood, he reached the La Pierre House in Philadelphia. There for several weeks, under charge of Doctors Mitchell, Pancoast, and Brinton, he lay in bed, until, by their skilful treatment, the external aperture, where the artery was tied, became closed, and all apprehensions of future danger from his wound ceased. His face, however, continued, for a year, more or less swollen, and through his mouth, for several months, there was a flow of viscous matter, and sometimes small fragments of bone. During changes of weather, or after exposure in the camp or field, the swelling of the face would increase, accompanied with much neuralgic pain.

In March, 1861, about the middle of the month, he once more reported for duty at West Point, and was assigned to duty, as will be seen from the following letter:

To his Father.

"WEST POINT, *March* 14*th*, 1861.

"I found every thing here *in statu quo.* I will be ordered to duty to-morrow. I thank you for the letter enclosed which was from Grantley Berkely. He had heard of my being wounded, and wrote a very kind sympathizing letter, and repeated his invitation for me to go over and make him a visit. I see that Sumner is at last a Brigadier-general. That makes me a first lieutenant. All such favors thankfully received."

To his Father.

"WEST POINT, *March* 20*th*, 1861.

"A piece of bone is coming out in my mouth, and I went down to New York and let Dr. McDougall have a pull at it. He said, however, I had better let it come out a little further. I think I will let Dr. Perin, who will relieve Dr. Hammond here on the first of April, pull it out: and I then hope my face will very soon get entirely well."

To his Father.

"*April* 13*th*, 1861.

"War has now begun, and I suppose it will very soon extend over the whole length and breadth of the land. Where I am to go or stay, and what to do, I have of course as little idea as yourself. But I think it is my duty to write to the Adjutant-general and tell him that I hold myself in readiness for any duty.

"If McIntosh resigns, my company will be without an officer, and I think that I ought to be with it. Don't you think so? The capital will very soon be the object of attack and I think it the duty of all good Americans to march to its defence. My heart is too full to write you anything about *Sumter.* The southerners have made a great mistake in attacking it. All my sympathy with the south is now gone. It is now war to the knife.

"If New Jersey should be called on for any troops, I will take a Majorship in a Jersey regiment. Write to your friend Governor Olden on this subject. I will also write."

To his Mother.

"WEST POINT, *May 29th,* 1861.

"That portion of my regiment which was west of Arkansas, I see, will in a day or two be in Leavenworth, so my regiment is all *right.* I see Riddick and Ingraham have resigned. So I am third for promotion to a *captaincy.*

"I am pretty well, though my face continues much swollen and the discharge through the mouth does not abate. The cold weather no doubt retards my improvement."

To his Father.

"NEW YORK, *July 26th,* 1861.

"I am now in this city, buying horses which I will get I think in the next two weeks. I will then be busy training them, and after that drilling the cadets.

"That Bull Run affair was a disgraceful and cowardly rout. The volunteers will not stand without experience and drill. But I suppose the southerners are no better. But perhaps the lesson will be useful for the North. It will teach us not to despise our enemy. I must go to this war. I cannot stay here and rust while gallant men are in the field. This rebellion is a much more serious thing than many suppose. I pity the southern officers in our army. They cannot but condemn the madness of their politicians who have brought on this war, and yet they feel in honor bound to go with their section."

The *animus* of the southern officers is well depicted by the following letter of Lieut. Lomax—(Gen. Lomax, of Confederate Army,) addressed to his friend Bayard :

"WASHINGTON, *April 21st*, 1861.

"I cannot stand it any longer and feel it my duty to resign. My State is out of the Union, and when she calls for my services I must go. I regret it very much, and feel that it is almost suicidal.

"As long as I could conscientiously believe it a war on the Union and the Flag, I was willing to do my part. But it is a war between sections, the north against the south, and I must go with my relatives and sympathies. I only hope all my friends in the army will act conscientiously, and I beg of you not to let my action alter the relationship between us. Tell Mac * and all my friends that I love them more than ever. I will hand in my resignation about the first of May, and I want to hear from you before then. I feel too badly to give you all the rumors.

"I believe Baltimore is to be the field of battle. The authorities say that they will bring troops through Baltimore if it takes all the north to do it. I hope to God

* Macallister, of his class.

there are some Conservatives yet left in the North. All the southern officers are going. God bless you.

"S. L. LOMAX."

Almost half the officers of the first cavalry, (Lieut. Bayard's regiment) resigned in 1861, and entered the southern army, with few exceptions, if any.

They were Lieut. Col. Hardee, Captains De Saussure, William S. Walker, George H. Stewart, James McIntosh, W N. R. Beall. First Lieutenants Alfred Iverson Jr., Philip Stockton, J. E. B. Steuart. Second Lieutenants Richard H. Riddick, Edward Ingraham, S. L. Lomax, O. H. Fish, Andrew Jackson Jr., J R. B. Burtwell.

July first, Lieutenant Bayard applied for leave to take the commission of Major in a regiment being raised at Albany by Col. Frederick Townsend. He was curtly informed officially by the Adjutant-general of the United States, that " the Secretary of War had decided that officers of the regular army cannot be spared for service with volunteer regiments." This dispatch was dated third of July, 1861. It shows that the government had then no adequate appreciation of the crisis. The Hon. Simon Cameron was then Secretary of War.

On the sixteenth of April, 1861, Lieut. Bayard wrote to Governor Olden* of New Jersey, offering, in case leave could be obtained at Washington, to take a commission in one of the New Jersey regiments. It is believed that Governor Olden could not obtain for him the desired leave. But as the magnitude of the rebellion became better known, the administration found out that " officers

* Foster's History of New Jersey troops in the war, p. 28.

of the regular army," *could* " be spared for service with volunteer regiments."

About the first of September leave of absence was obtained for Lieutenant Bayard to take the commission of Major in a regiment being raised by General Van Allen, of New York. On his arrival in Washington, on the evening of a day in the first week in September, he went in half an hour after his arrival to the headquarters of General McClellan, to see his friend Colburn, acting as aide to the commanding General.

As soon as they met, Colburn said that General McClellan wanted several army officers for colonels of regiments, and that he would not permit him to take such a subaltern position. Colburn insisted that it would be unjust to himself for Lieutenant Bayard to accept a Major's commission, and have all the labor of putting the regiment in condition, while the credit would be given to his superior officer.

General McClellan knowing well the reputation and merits of Lieutenant Bayard as an officer, was desirous of putting him on his staff as aide :—but tendered him the option, of becoming an aide on the staff of the commander-in-chief, or the Colonelcy of a Pennsylvania regiment. He preferred the latter, and was accordingly commissioned as Colonel of the First Pennsylvania Cavalry.

The mutations of time bring about singular coincidences. In the Revolutionary war, John Bayard was Colonel of the first troop of Philadelphia cavalry, and now nearly a century subsequent his great grandson George D. Bayard was placed in command of the first regiment of cavalry of the State of Pennsylvania.

Pennsylvania, in the law authorizing the organization of State regiments of volunteers, provided for the
election of officers by each regiment. The following
official letter informed Colonel Bayard of his election as
Colonel of the First Pennsylvania Cavalry :

> " HEADQUARTERS PENN. RESERVE,
> CAMP TENNALLY, *Sept.* 14*th*, 1860.
>
> " *Col. George D. Bayard, 1st Penn. Reserve Cavalry* :
>
> " DEAR SIR,—I have the pleasure to inform you that
> at an election held the twelfth instant, you were elected
> Colonel of the First Cavalry of the Pennsylvania Reserve.
> Should you accept, I would request you to join the regi-
> ment with as little delay as possible, as the presence of
> an officer of experience is much needed.
> " I am very respectfully, your obt. servt,
> " GEO A. McCALL,
> "*Brig-Gen. Comd'g.*"

A few days after the above election Colonel Bayard
received from the War Department the following letter :

> " WAR DEPARTMENT, *Sept.* 16*th*, 1861.
> " SIR—you are hereby informed that the President
> of the United States has promoted you to the rank of
> captain in the fourth regiment of cavalry in the service
> of the United States, to take effect from the twentieth of
> August, 1861, vice Beall, resigned, should the senate at
> their next session advise and consent thereto. You will
> be commissioned accordingly.
> " SIMON CAMERON,
> " *Secretary of War.*"

He was commissioned the following February. Col. Bayard was much pleased with the *matériel* of which his regiment was composed, with the exception of some of the officers, whom he found it expedient to supersede with others. The men were principally gentlemen, farmers, farmers' sons, mechanics, from the counties along the Schuylkill, and from the interior, and became devoted friends of their colonel. In the following letter to his father he refers to the character of his men and officers :

To his Father.

"CAMP REYNOLDS, NEAR TENNALLY TOWN,
             Sept. 25th, 1861.

"General Reynolds (Col. Reynolds of West Point) has command of my Brigade. General McCall commands the Division, about twelve or thirteen thousand men.

"I have got seven companies of my regiment mounted here, and shall have ten to-morrow. I am just now having a pretty rough time with some of my officers, and I intend to bring four or five of them before a board of officers, as deficient in military instruction, and incompetent to learn. The men are first-rate, and do the best they know how, and as well as could be expected. I think after awhile I shall have a very good regiment.

"I hope Beauregard will hold on a couple of weeks, and by that time I shall have my regiment in some kind of order and drill. I belong to McCall's division, and will advance with it. I expect McCall and Smith will command the advance guard of the advancing army. So I will have an early chance of winning laurels. I am coming out of this war with a *yellow* **sash** on, if I don't get higher."

The following letter from Governor Curtin shows that the officers who were relieved from duty in the regiment had preferred complaints to the Governor, and how well Col. Bayard was supported by the patriotic governor of Pennsylvania :

"HARRISBURGH, *27th October*, 1861.

"*Col. G. D. Bayard, Commanding First Reg't Penn Cavalry :*

"DEAR SIR :—I am much gratified with the report Colonel Ball brings me of the condition of the First Pennsylvania Cavalry, under your command.

"You must not imagine that the complaints of the incompetent or the rejected, had any effect on my mind, but inasmuch as the friends of these men were uneasy, I wished to be informed, so as to assure inquirers truly.

"I feel much pride in your command, and satisfaction with your performance of all your duties, and rest assured that you can command me for anything, that will make the men comfortable and efficient, and the regiment the pride of the State. I am with sentiments of the highest respect, your obedient servant,

"A. G. CURTIN.

To his Father.

"CAMP PEIRPONT, *October* 23*d*, 1861.

"We move to-morrow with four days' rations and forty rounds of ammunition ; where I do not know, but presume somewhere towards Leesburgh.

"Was not that Ball's Bluff affair awful? Almost every colonel killed or taken prisoner. *Raw troops will not stand fire* unless *intrenched*. I hope my fate will permit me to see a little more of this war. I send a list of my few creditors. If I live I shall pay them all before six months. If I fall, you must not permit my memory to be tainted by unpaid debts."

The few months previous to November, 1861, were distinguished by many disasters to the Union troops. Big Bethel, Bull Run, Vienna and Ball's Bluff, were affairs discreditable and depressing in their influence. The rebels were elated with their uniform success, and the popular feeling in the loyal States was indignant with, and impatient of, that series of defeats which the Union forces had experienced.

The first gleam of victory which shone through the darkness of those sad days, was that afforded by Col. Bayard's affair at Drainsville, Va., on the twenty-seventh of November. It was comparatively a small affair; but it had a most inspiriting influence on the public mind throughout all the northern States. It proved that our men would fight gallantly when properly led, and showed that we had officers who knew how to lead and how to fight.

To his Mother.

" CAMP PIERPONT, VA., *Nov. 29th*, 1861.

" I suppose you have read in the papers the result of my expedition into *Secessia*, and the narrow escape I had. Poor Alexander died this morning, and one man died night before last. So that my loss is one officer and one man, and then I have one man wounded. I killed four and captured three of the party which fired on me. I was hit myself twice, and my horse was killed. Surgeon Stanton had three balls through his clothes. I have a slight touch of the quinsy this morning, but the doctor is here, and I hope to avert the attack."

The following are the official reports of General McCall and Colonel Bayard of the Drainsville action:

"HEADQUARTERS McCALL'S DIVISION, *Nov. 27th*, 1861.

" *General S. Williams, A. A. G.*

"General,—I have the honor to transmit herewith the report of Colonel G. D. Bayard, First Regt. Cavalry Penn. Reserve, of a very successful expedition made during the last twenty-four hours, in the direction of Drainsville, where I had ascertained that a picket force of the enemy was stationed. The men who were sent by the colonel for ambulances, reported to me a strong force opposed to the colonel, whereupon, I put the first brigade of my division under arms, and with Kinney battery was marching to his support, when we met the colonel's command returning. The troops all evinced praiseworthy alacrity on the occasion.

I am very respectfully your obedient servant,

"GEORGE A. McCALL,

"*B. G. Comd'g Div.*"

"CAMP PIERPONT, VA., *Nov. 27th*, 1861.

"SIR.—In obedience to orders, I started from this camp yesterday with my regiment at nine o'clock in the evening, for the purpose of marching on Drainsville. We reached positions above and behind Drainsville shortly after five in the morning, after a very tedious and toilsome march.

"Major Barrows advanced on the town by the northern pike which leads to it, with two companies of the regiment, while I with the other eight gained the rear of the town, and advanced by the Leesburgh pike. There were but two picket-men in the town ; these were cavalry men belonging to Col. J. E. B. Steuart's regiment of Virginia Horse, and were captured with their horses and arms by Capt. Stadelman's company B. I arrested six of the citizens of Drainsville who are known to be Secessionists of the bitterest stamp.

"The names of the citizens taken are as follows :

1. John T. Day, M. D., Drainsville.
2. R. H. Gannel, Great Falls, Va.
3. John T. D. Bell.
4. C. W. Coleman, Drainsville.
5. W. B. Day, M. D.
6. J. B. Farr.

" Upon my return, some miles from Drainsville, a fire was opened upon the head of the column from a thick pine wood. Ass't Surgeon Alexander was seriously wounded, and private Joel Houghtaling, Co. — was badly wounded, and I had my horse killed. Surgeon Stanton received a ball in his overcoat, and his horse shot twice. The woods were instantly surrounded and the carbineers dismounted and sent into the woods. We killed two, and captured four, one of whom is shot twice, and is not expected to live. Private Houghtaling, Co. — is, I fear, mortally wounded. I captured two good horses, five shot-guns, one Hall's rifle, and two pistols. The names of the prisoners are as follows :

1. W. D. Farley, 1st Lieut S. C. Vol. Capt. on Gen. Bonham's staff,

9

2. F. De Caradene, Lt. Seventh S. C. Vol.,

3. P. W. Carper, Seventh S. C. V.,

4. Thos. Coleman, citizen of Drainsville and dangerously wounded,

5. F. Hildebrand, private Thirtieth Virginia Cavalry,

6. A. M. ,Whiten, private Thirtieth Virginia Cavalry, taken at Drainsville on picket.

"We killed and captured all we saw. I cannot close this report without speaking of the splendid manner in which both men and officers behaved, the fine manner in which Major Jones, Byrnes, (Second Lieut. Fifth Cav.) and Barrows acted, cannot be too highly commended or appreciated. All acted well and I cannot but thus publicly express my admiration for their truly admirable behavior.

"I am, sir, very respectfully your obt. servt,

"GEO. D. BAYARD,

"*Col. First Penn. R. Cavalry.*"

To Col. H. J. Biddle, Ass't Adj't-Gen., McCall's Div.

The camp of the First Pennsylvania Cavalry was stationed about twenty-two miles north of Washington, a few miles from the chain bridge, on the Virginia side of the Potomac. There Col. Bayard remained the greater part of the winter of 1861-2. He was occasionally compelled to go to the hospital in Washington on account of the condition of his old wound in his cheek. That at times was quite painful, and his face became much swollen, doubtless owing to his exposure in all kinds of weather. But the ardor of his military spirit was such and his desire to discipline his regiment and make it competent to perform the severe duty which he foresaw that coming events would exact from it, was so great that he was in the field much of the time that prudence dictated his remaining in the hospital.

To his Father.

"CAMP PIERPONT, *Dec.* 15*th*, 1861.

"I send you an extract from some country paper in relation to Drainsville, from which you can gather all I could tell you. I cannot come home at Christmas, however I should delight to do. We are liable to be at any moment ordered to advance. I have been in bed for a few days past, but am about well again.

"I thank mother for what she says about my not exposing myself. *That* is precisely what it is the duty of the soldier to do."

The extract from the country paper, to which he refers, is as follows. On the margin of the paper slip he sent appears the following line in his hand-writing. "I send you this as I have been too lazy to write anything about this affair."

"CAMP PIERPONT, *Nov.* 28*th*, 1861.

"*Dear Register* As it is your request to hear from all parts of the country, I will drop you a few lines from this neck of timber. I do not pretend to be a letter-writer, but still I may be able to give some news or information that will be interesting to some of your many readers. I am a member of the First Penn. Reserve Cavalry, company G, and we are encamped in Fairfax County, Virginia, about eleven miles from Washington city. We have been in this vicinity near three months. The sacred soil in this county is very rough and broken, but the farms have the appearance of being well taken care of, and have fine buildings on them ;

but the most of them have been vacated, the occupants have gone to places of safety, some north and others south. This regiment is under the special orders of Gen. McCall, but is not attached to any Brigade. It is commanded by Col. George D. Bayard, of the regular army, and he has the name of being one of the most resolute and best cavalry officers in the service. He keeps a very strict discipline in the regiment, and the officers and men under him have all got to come to time, or they are attended to. I have no doubt but that the boys will all give a good account of themselves under him.

"Jacob Higgins is Lieut. Colonel, and he is a man well worthy of the position he holds ; he is always ready and willing to assist or accommodate any of his men. Our company is commanded by Capt. David Gardner, of Plane No. Ten, Blair Co.; Hampton Thomas, of Chester county, is our first lieutenant; H. C. Wier, of New York, second lieutenant. They are a whole-souled set of fellows, and are liked and respected by all their men. We are styled the Black Horse Company, our horses being all jet blacks, and the company is composed of men from twenty-four different counties of the old Keystone State.

"We are armed with revolvers, sabres and Sharpe's improved carbines, but we have had but one opportunity of using them as yet. On the twenty-sixth of November, we received orders to be ready to march by eight o'clock that evening, with one day's rations, and we started at half-past eight, with six hundred men, headed by Cols. Bayard and Higgins and a guide. We rode all night at a break-neck gait, crossed the Leesburgh pike on a by-road, and followed it until near daylight, when we struck the pike again within four miles of Leesburgh, and between the Rebel camp and their outside pickets, which were posted at Drainsville. We made a charge on and surrounded the place in double-quick time, and succeeded in capturing two mounted sentinels, and arrested five notorious characters who were guilty of deeds almost too horrible to relate, such as cutting the heads off of wounded Union soldiers that fell in the battle of Ball's Bluff, putting them on poles and placing them before their houses, throwing their bodies to the hogs, etc. Our men were all eager to tear them to pieces, and would have done so, if the colonel had not interfered. He said they should be treated as prisoners of war. Of all the crying and screaming that ever was heard came from the women and children, who were running around in their night clothes, pleading for us to spare their fathers, brothers, sons, husbands etc. It was, indeed, a deplorable sight. It was now daylight, and we started for home by the pike, riding carelessly in the walk. After we had proceeded* about three miles from Drainsville, the head of the column was fired upon by a party of rebels concealed in ambush, shooting Colonel Bayard's horse from under him. We were ordered to surround the thicket, which was done as quick as possible, as there was a high fence that had to be thrown down before we could get the horses across. There was a sharp fire kept up for some time between both parties, the cedars being so thick that we could not

* I sent a company ahead to scour the road, but the captain did not do his duty, and turned off on a *by-road* not fifty yards short of where those men were hid.—*(Note on margin.)*

ride through them. Our company dismounted and patrolled the woods with carbines, killing three, and wounding and taking six prisoners, among them being a captain and lieutenant. Col. Bayard was slightly wounded in the shoulder and thigh with buckshot; Assistant Surgeon Alexander was shot in the abdomen and died the next day; a private of company D. was wounded, and has since died, and one man of our company was wounded in the thigh, but is recovering. The wounded secessionists are dead. Everything was done in order, and the men did not get excited. The regiment received great praise from Colonel Bayard for their coolness. He said that he had a set of men that he could rely upon hereafter. We left the dead ones lay, as we had not time to bury them, for we could hear the long roll beat and the bugle sound in different directions from the enemy's camps. So we had to get on double-quick, for fear our retreat would be cut off. We met Gen. McCall coming with two batteries of artillery and six regiments of infantry. The firing had alarmed the pickets, and the old General thought we had got in a tight place, and he would come and help us out. Bully for him! We arrived in camp pretty well worn out, both horse and man, having been in our saddles sixteen hours, and travelled forty miles without taking time to water our horses."

The following is from the New York *Evening Post,* of *Dec. seventh,* 1851 :

"They tell a good story of Bayard, in connection with his wounds, which were by no means trifling. On the morning after the skirmish General McClellan sent a messenger to ask how he was.   His reply was that he was hit on the shoulder, had a bullet in his thigh, had had his horse shot under him, and had been somewhat stunned by the fall ; but he was 'quite well, I thank you, and able to attend to his duties, and should report in person at headquarters very shortly.'   He has the true gallantry and endurance of his namesake, Bayard of old."

CHAPTER XIV.

Camp Pierpont.—First Pa. Cavalry.—In the Field.—Moves South.— Affair at Falmouth.—Col. Bayard appointed a Brigadier-general.—Stationed below Fredericksburg.—Goes to Shenandoah Valley.—Fremont.—Jackson.—Shields.

To his Father.

"CAMP PIERPONT, *January 3d*, 1862.

"WE will move, I hope, next week. I have been so often fooled with such a hope, that I say nothing more about it. But all the generals think and expect to do so. Buell, I hope, will thrash them in Kentucky, Burnside will take the Potomac batteries, or at least attempt it. And then we will move, to victory I trust."

To his Father.

"CAMP PIERPONT, VA, *Jan. 9th*, 1862.

"I have no news of any importance to communicate. We are waiting on McClellan. It is a work of immense labor to put an army of raw inexperienced men in condition to fight successfully ; none but military men can understand the difficulty of performing properly such a labor. We ought to have a certainty of victory before we move. Another such a victory for the rebels, as that of Bull Run, would prolong the war indefinitely.

"Burnside will strike in a day or two, and then comes our time. Buell I hope will make a good move in

Kentucky and do something to encourage our men; but like all new troops they are too much affected by the current rumors of the day, and allow them to affect their spirits and conduct. They all have the utmost confidence in McClellan, however, and believe he will lead to victory. Halleck, I hope, will not take much longer to prepare for his move down the Mississippi. A few great victories to be achieved soon, would crush out the rebellion. I feel more confidence in the success of Buell and Halleck, than in our own. All the best Confederate generals and troops are in our front. And Jefferson Davis knows that victory for him in Virginia is more important than anywhere else. God grant that the Union army may win ; for we are fighting in a holy cause! We are fighting for the existence of free government. The people are all rebels in this part of Virginia. The sword's fierce blows alone will conquer them. When the clash of arms does come, it will be a terrible conflict, and many a fine fellow will grace a ' sacred grave.' "

To his Mother.

" CAMP PIERPONT, *March 1st,* 1862.

" The movement of the Grand Army has begun. When you hear from me again I shall be on the road to Richmond. God grant that we may go through with honor. I have caught cold in my face and it is very painful, but it will not detain me."

" EXAMINING ROOMS, WASHINGTON, }
March 3d, 1862. }

" I am here on an examining board to test the competency of subaltern officers. Banks and Sedgwick are

9*

across the river, and in a very few days you will hear of something *important.* After that we will not much longer remain here, in inglorious inactivity. Of course we are gnawing with impatience the bonds of discipline which hold us here. But the hour of our release is soon to come."

To his Father.

"WASHINGTON, *April 8th,* 1862.

"The order for my embarkation with McClellan has been countermanded. I am to be assigned to General McDowell's command. I suppose I shall have two regiments at least, and perform a Brigadier's duty. We will remain till after the fall of Yorktown. I am much disgusted. But it is the part of a good soldier to obey orders and hope for the best."

To his Father.

"MANASSAS, *April 10th,* 1862.

"I have just camped about three miles from this place, and will march beyond to Bristow to-morrow. I camped at Fairfax last night; had a fire; much trouble in putting it out; I thought at first my men did it, but I know now the contrary. I will not permit my men to burn and ravage; it demoralizes them."

To his Mother.

"HUNTER'S MILLS. *April 11th,* 1862.

"We got here last night at eight, P. M. The rebels have burned a bridge in front, which stops our progress a little. But we shall go ahead to-morrow. The weather is splendid, and challenges us to brilliant deeds. I am very well, never better in my life."

To his Father (written with pencil).

"CAMP AT FREDERICKSBURG, ⎱
April 18*th,* 1862. ⎰

"Last night I left camp with eleven companies of cavalry at two, A. M., to go by a secret route to Falmouth, and occupy the bridge and hold it. I was ambuscaded. I had five men killed and something under twenty wounded. My pretty black mare, my pet, was shot two or three times, and, I fear, is ruined for some time to come. Thanks to Almighty God! I am safe and un-harmed, though I heard the balls whistle close to my head. They say I committed but one fault ; I charged once too often. We have driven our enemy across the river, and they have burned the bridge."

The following is the report of the Falmouth affair made to Governor Curtin by Colonel Bayard.

"CAMP AT FALMOUTH, VA. ⎱
April 20*th,* 1862. ⎰

" SIR,—I have the honor to report, that on the morning of the 18th, I was ordered with one battalion of the First Pennsylvania Cavalry, and seven companies of the Har-ris light cavalry, to take possession of the bridge lead-ing from this place across the Rappahannock, and hold it till Gen. Augur, commanding, came up.

" I started at two A. M., and about four in the morning I reached the vicinity of the enemy. They were posted on a high hill, with a brush on either side of the road, and had erected heavy barricades of rails across the road. Ignorant of these obstructions, as soon as their pickets were driven in, I ordered Colonel Owen Jones, commanding the battalion of the First Pennsylvania Cavalry to move forward and to seize the bridge at all hazard. He moved forward at a rapid gait, and as soon as he reached the vicinity of the barricades, a very heavy infantry fire was opened upon him.

"Capt. Richards' company M, and Capt. Davidson's company F, acted with the utmost gallantry. Capt. L. M. French, of company E, and Sergeant Jesse Fry, of same company, with Lieut. William Bayard, adjutant of the second battalion, all acted with courage. Capt. Davidson was taken prisoner, but finally captured the man who had charge of him, and brought him and his horse into camp. Lieut. Sample, of Capt. Richards' company, had his horse killed. Lieut. Leaf, of same company, acted through the affair with bravery, while the good conduct of Capt. Richards is spoken of in the highest terms by Col. Jones. Of Col. Jones it is sufficient to say that he rallied his men with the same coolness with which he led the advance under the withering fire opened upon him. A second charge of the Harris light cavalry, led by myself, first made me aware of the obstructions in the road. I have since learned that behind the barricades were posted four hundred infantry, and in their rear, on their flanks, were three or four companies of cavalry. Immediately after the affair, the enemy deserted the barricades, and I advanced with Gen. Augur's command in pursuit.

"That I lost so few men, I attribute to the darkness of the night, which caused them to shoot too high. I had three men killed, nine wounded, and eleven horses killed and five badly shot.

"It was quite a brisk little affair, and but added to the confidence I have in the bravery of the men, and the good conduct of the officers of my regiment. I think, sir, you can trust this regiment.

"I am, sir, very respectfully,

"Your obedient servant,

"GEO. D. BAYARD.

"*Colonel Pennsylvania Cavalry.*"

To his Excellency, Gov. A. G. Curtin, Harrisburg, Pa.

To his Father.

"WILLARD'S HOTEL, WASHINGTON, }
April 20th, 1862. }

"I left camp at four o'clock this morning, went to Acquia Creek and came up in a revenue cutter. Gen. Mc-Dowell took me to the President, Secretary of War and Treasury and demanded that I should be made a Brigadier-general.

"The Secretary of War says my nomination shall go in in a couple of days. I presume it will go through without difficulty. If I find there is any need of it, I will see Senators Harris, Thomson and Ten Eycke.

"McDowell will give me a brigade of three or four regiments of cavalry and a battery. He expects much of me, daring deeds and gallant conduct, and I must not disappoint him. I drove up to-day with the President and Mr. Chase ; carriage broke down ; horses attempted to run, excitement. No one hurt.

"William Bayard * did well in the fight. Weir was not in it. I think I will make Weir Asst. Adjutant-general, and William Bayard an aide, as soon as I receive my commission as brigadier.

"Give my love to all dear ones at home, and say

* See Appendix F.

although I shall have to lead the way in every fight, I yet trust a merciful Providence will protect my life, and keep me for some greater service in defence of the Union.

" I am the youngest brigadier in the army, hurrah ! My eyes are fixed on the future, and new lustre for my name will be achieved, if I survive."

To his Sister.

" CAMP NEAR FREDERICKSBURG,
 May 3d, 1862.

" I am in the saddle so much that I have little time to write. I had intended telling you of my excursion down to King George Court-house, but defer doing so to another time.

" I have been confirmed as brigadier, as you have seen in the papers, and I have received my commission.

" I think we will be across the river next week, and advance. Tell father I sent, (I believe) to McClellan, his plan of advance by way of Urbana. I regret that he does not approve McClellan's movement entirely. I think it all right. The sequel will show. I am sorry I have not been able to come home while your St. Louis friends are at Woodbury. I shall always be grateful to them for their kindness while I was sick at St. Louis."

To his Mother.

" CAMP BELOW FREDERICKSBURG,
 May 11th, 1862.

" I fear I shall not be able to see you this summer. I do long to see you once more, dearest mother. To you and father I owe all my success in life. I have always looked for smiles of approval from you ; I have longed to hear of your approbation of my appointment as general, and have thus far been disappointed.

"You must write to me, mother ; I do not wish to be spoiled ; but I am in a fair way for it. My will is law over eighteen hundred men, and almost every one approaches me with flattery on their lips. They call me the 'bravest of the brave,' etc., etc."

To his Father.

"CAMP McDOWELL, *May* 14*th*, 1862.

"I am here resting on my arms, and weary of resting. My quarters are a fine, large brick house, deserted by its owners. I enjoy my position with all the *nonchalance* of a soldier of fortune. Flowers of all kinds are blooming around us, and in the evening the whippoorwills serenade us with their melancholy notes, as we sit on the porch. But I am tired of this easy life, and am anxious to get under way once more.

"My regiment is to present me with a fine horse and equipments. I am to be in the advance when we do take that step, and will, therefore, have further opportunity for distinguishing myself. McDowell has promised me *that*. If he will give me three regiments of cavalry and one battery, I think I may be able to do something. This is a hard country for cavalry, being so heavily timbered. But I shall do the best I can."

The following in relation to the organization of the First Penn. Cavalry, after the appointment of General Bayard as brigadier, and his formal leave-taking of the regiment as colonel, appeared, we believe, in the Philadelphia *Inquirer*

"The brigade to be commanded by Gen. George D. Bayard is being rapidly organized. Under such a gallant and able officer as Gen. Bayard, this brigade will bring renown upon itself and glory to the Union. Col. Owen Jones, late lieutenant-colonel of the First Pennsylvania Cavalry, having been elected to the colonelcy of the regiment, has assumed the command. Major S. D. Barrows, late major, has been promoted to the lieutenant-colonelcy. The following is a list of promotions in the same regiment :—

"R. S. Falls, Major of first battalion,

"J. H. Rae, Major of second battalion,

"T. S. Richards, Major of third battalion,

"H. S. Thomas, formerly adjutant, captain of company M.,

"Lieutenant George D. Leaf, company M, to be regimental adjutant.

"Captain R. R. Corson, formerly quartermaster of the regiment, has received the appointment of Assistant-Adjutant-general on the staff of General Bayard,

"Lieutenant H. C. Weir has also been appointed as aid-de-camp to General Bayard.

"General Bayard took leave of the First Penn. Cavalry, as its colonel, a day or two since. Every member of the regiment, while gratified at the appointment, deeply regrets the loss of General Bayard as their colonel. While on dress-parade, the General took leave of his men in the following address, at the conclusion of which he was enthusiastically cheered :—

"'Soldiers :—I have been summoned to a larger and more extended field of duty, and to-day we meet for the last time as colonel and men commanded. Last

September, when this regiment was offered to me, it was
with many doubts, and against the advice of many of
my military friends, that I assumed the command.
Need I recall to you your disorganized state then, or
picture to you the contrast now.   If at any time I have
been too strict, or turned a deaf ear to justice, I beg of
you to remember that man is not always infallible, and,
as a military man, I may have expected too much of you.
From being but a disorganized mass, you are now a
regiment, the pride of the State—a source of satisfaction
to your friends, and a pleasure to yourselves.   Officers
and men, I thank you from my heart for the obedience
I have uniformly had from you ; and my associations
and friendships here formed shall always be remembered
with the warmest feelings, and to the last day of my
life.   It is a source of satisfaction to me to leave you in
such good and brave hands.   Colonel Jones I have
confidence in, and, also, in all of you.   I feel proud to
have you in my brigade ; I feel a confidence in your
courage, and 1 know that whenever I call upon you
every man will strive to do honor to the noble old Keystone State.   Good-bye.' "

Pyne, in his History of First N. J. Cavalry, pages 38,
39, says : " After a delay incomprehensible to the army
then, and uncomprehended still by the majority, at last on
Sunday, twenty-fifth of May, Bayard's Brigade moved
across the river and passing through Fredericksburg, advanced on the plank road as far as Salem church.   On
the afternoon of Monday, it went to the front of the army;
and on Tuesday, penetrating through a barren country,
and fording with difficulty streams whose bridges were

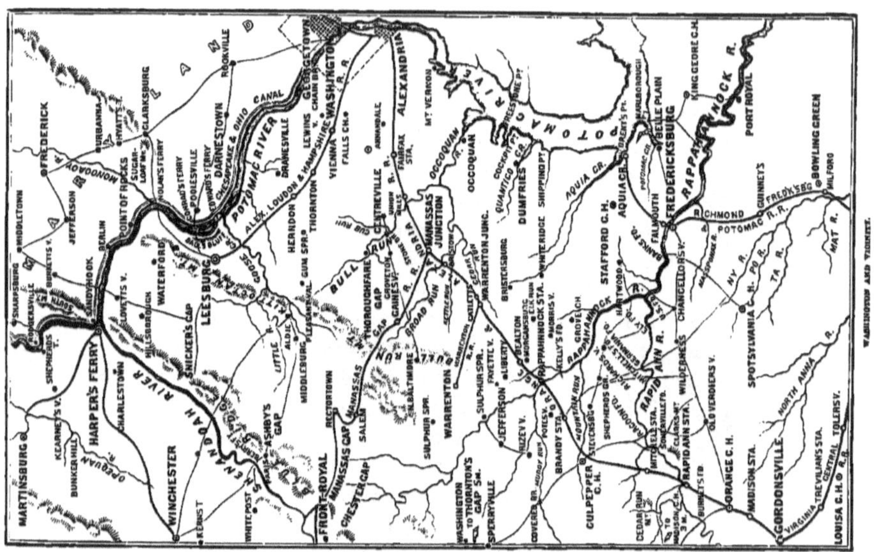

MARYLAND
POTOMAC RIVER
CHESAPEAKE & OHIO CANAL
SHENANDOAH RIVER
RAPPAHANNOCK R.
MARTINSBURG
FREDERICK
MIDDLETOWN
JEFFERSON
MONOCACY
HARPER'S FERRY
SHEPHERDSTOWN
SHARPSBURG
KEARNEY'S V.
BUNKER HILL
WINCHESTER
KERNST
CHARLESTOWN
HILLSBOROUGH
WATERFORD
LEESBURG
POINT OF ROCKS
BERLIN
CLARKSBURG
DARNESTOWN
ROCKVILLE
POOLESVILLE
DRANESVILLE
GEORGETOWN
WASHINGTON
ALEXANDRIA
VIENNA
HERNDON
CENTREVILLE
FAIRFAX C.H.
FAIRFAX STA.
ANNANDALE
MT. VERNON
FALLS CH.
FRONT-ROYAL
CHESTER GAP
ASHBY'S GAP
SNICKER'S GAP
MANASSAS GAP
SALEM
RECTORTOWN
MIDDLEBURG
ALDIE
BULL RUN
MANASSAS JUNCTION
BRISTOE STA.
WARRENTON
WARRENTON JUNC.
SULPHUR SPR.
JEFFERSON
CULPEPPER C.H.
BRANDY STA.
RAPPAHANNOCK STA.
CEDAR MT.
MADISON STA.
GORDONSVILLE
ORANGE C.H.
RAPID ANN R.
SPOTSYLVANIA C.H.
NORTH ANNA
LOUISA C.H.
VIRGINIA CENTRAL R.R.
OCCOQUAN
DUMFRIES
QUANTICO CR.
AQUIA CR.
STAFFORD C.H.
FALMOUTH
FREDERICKSBURG
CHANCELLORSV.
WILDERNESS
BELLE PLAIN
KING GEORGE C.H.
PORT ROYAL
BOWLING GREEN
MILFORD
RICHMOND
MAT R.
TA R.
NY R.
WASHINGTON AND VICINITY.

still smoking, it pressed forward meeting with no enemy, and hoping soon to unite with the army of the Potomac. Halting upon a rising ground, we heard, far in our front, a dull, thunderous sound, notifying us that a mighty conflict was going on between two distant armies. In a far off quarter of Virginia, after a series of events, we learned that we in the advance of McDowell's corps, had listened to the cannonade of Porter at Hanover Courthouse."

They were in fact, but fifteen miles from Hanover, and in another day would have united with McClellan's army. That junction, if it had taken place, would have changed the current of events, and probably precipitated the collapse of the Rebellion by two years.

But a panic had struck with terror the Washington Government. Jackson had forced Banks to retreat, and thundering after his flying troops the rebel general was approaching the Potomac at Harper's Ferry. It was feared that the daring chief would march on the capital. Under the influence of this alarm, McDowell's advance on Richmond was arrested, and Shields' corps of twenty thousand men ordered to the Shenandoah Valley with the design of cutting off Jackson's retreat.

General Bayard was now attached to Shields' command and ordered to the Shenandoah Valley. Fremont with fifteen thousand men who was north of the Valley, a day or two's march, was also ordered to march on Strasburg to coöperate with Shields. The President ordered him to take a route, by which, if he had obeyed the order, Jackson would have been intercepted. This he failed to do, and by this error suffered Jackson to escape.

The best account of the advance of Bayard's brigade to the Shenandoah Valley will be found in Pyne's History of the First New Jersey Cavalry. It is accurate in detail, eloquent, and interesting. No narrative of military events during the war, which we have seen, is more worthy of perusal. Inspired by McDowell with the necessity of a rapid movement, General Bayard pushed forward with all the speed which horse-flesh was capable of attaining.

Pyne, page 43, says : " Passing the house of Turner Ashby, in a beautiful valley among the mountains, we came upon a road swarming with moving infantry and artillery, until there was no room left for further travel upon it. With no pause, however, to attend to their dilatory motions, Bayard forced forward his brigade. Down went walls and fences on the hill-side, and along declivities, which scarcely afforded foothold for the horses, where they slipped and staggered ; over ditches, which they leaped, scrambled through, or fell, the dashing leaders, Wyndam and Bayard, side by side, led the way. Through the fragrant clover, and the waving sea of thick-growing grain, the troops swept along like a gallant fleet, while the hills grew steeper, narrowing the gorge, until we wheeled around an intervening bluff, and saw before us the glittering ranks of Ricketts' infantry passing into Front Royal."

Late in the afternoon of the fourth day after their movement commenced, Bayard's brigade approached Strasburg. The First Pennsylvania regiment was sent to reconnoitre in advance ; and its colonel reported that the enemy were in force there, and strongly intrenched. Other portions of the brigade not having come up, an attack on the enemy was deferred till morning. Nothing was heard of Fremont. But General Bayard determined not to wait for him, and ordered a movement forward as early as possible.

The following evening and night was very dark, and a heavy fall of rain made the bivouac of the brigade cruelly cheerless.

Pyne says, page 46: "Munching in the dark such fragments of wet crackers as remained in their haversacks, the men, wet, cold and miserable, lay down in the continuous rain to sleep upon the soaking grass, and in deep discomfort waited for the dawn."

At sunrise the brigade pressed forward, fording the swelling Shenandoah, which the flood was feeding to turbulence, and rode into Strasburg to find it deserted by Jackson, and filled with his sick and wounded. Without a pause, the brigade hurried on, making prisoners at every step. There were no signs of Fremont's army when the brigade entered Strasburg. Though having more than twice the distance to move that Fremont had, after the orders for the advance on Strasburg had been issued, Bayard was there before him.*

Pyne says, page 47: "Just as the rear departed from the town," (Strasburg,) "the sound of cavalry in motion was heard upon the northern road ; the head of a long column appeared and an officer rode up, wearing on his shoulders the stars of a major-general. He (Fremont), could not realize the truth that the town had been

* A dispatch in the *Tribune* of June 11th, 1862, asserts that Fremont was there first. My authority is Pyne, and Col. Karge and Col. Cumming, both present.

taken before him, and that McDowell's troopers were leading the 'path-finder' in the chase of the enemy; and he seemed scarcely pleased to find it so. When Capt. Gray, the provost-marshal, told him that we had come from Fredericksburg, his astonishment was by no means lessened."

The brigade in advance of all, continued the pursuit with unabated vigor. Karge and Wyndam overtook the retreating Ashby, and had some desperate encounters with him. Some of Fremont's men came up near night after the fighting was over.

Pyne, page 50, says: "With trumpets sounding and waving banners, Bayard's brigade marched the next morning through the town of Woodstock, pressing upon the rear of Jackson."

Still ahead of all others, the brigade reached that branch of the Shenandoah river on which Mount Jackson is situated. The river was too swollen to be forded, and the rebels had fired the long bridge over it, and so commanded it with their artillery, that nothing could be done to save it, Fremont's guns and infantry being in the rear. Two days afterwards, the bridge being rebuilt, a crossing was effected and the pursuit renewed. At Cross Keys a battle ensued, in which Fremont was worsted. General Bayard had been ordered to the rear, and was not engaged in this affair, as will be seen by one of his letters. The escape of Jackson was entirely owing to the inefficiency of Generals Fremont and Shields.*

" The following telegram was sent by General Bayard.

* See McDowell's testimony, report on conduct of the war. Vol. first. Pages from 260 to 269.

To his Father.

"Telegraph office, Cattlet's Station,
May 29*th*, 1862.

"I arrived here from Fredericksburg this morning—am going to move up towards Front Royal to-morrow morning. We hope to meet the enemy soon. I have two regiments of cavalry, four howitzers and four companies of bucktails."

To his Father.

"Camp at Mount Jackson,
June 4*th*, 1862.

"We have been in rapid pursuit of Jackson for two days, and have only been stopped by the flood, which has swollen all the streams so that pontoons will not stand. I captured two hundred prisoners and got back thirty of Banks' men. I joined Fremont three days ago at Strasburg, with two regiments of cavalry, two batteries and two hundred infantry (sharpshooters.) I have had the advance ever since. Yesterday I commanded about five thousand cavalry ; shells burst thick and fast around us for two days ; but I have only had one man killed by them. I am in good health, although I have not had on dry clothes for three days, and we were two days with nothing to eat but what we picked up on the road. I have not heard from you or any one at home for three weeks, so long and so fast have I travelled ; no mails can reach us. We have not seen our wagons, even, for a week. I am now in the Dutch army. Fremont has about fifteen thousand men ; but he expects Banks to join him with ten thousand, and a little below here Shields with ten thousand men. If he knew how to handle them he ought to be able to threaten Richmond in a few days.

To his Father.

"CAMP NEAR HARRISONBURG, VA., }
June 7th, 1862. }

"Col. Wyndam was ambuscaded yesterday, and taken prisoner. Lieut. Col. Kane, of the bucktails, was also surprised, and lost about thirty men, and was wounded and taken prisoner. Captains Sherman and Haines are also prisoners ; all good officers ; among my best. Shells and shot flew around me in all directions ; but I am still unhurt. We lie over to rest to-day, and will go forward to-morrow."

To his Mother.

"CAMP AT MOUNT JACKSON, }
June 13th, 1862. }

"I received yours of the twenty-fifth ult., the first I have received for a month. I have halted here to recruit my exhausted horses and men. Day after to-morrow I will march from here to join Shields. Whether I shall go by Front Royal, or by the New Market pass, I do not know yet. Shields' force is very much demoralized. We have had none but citizen-generals in command in this valley. Hence results are inconclusive and nugatory.

"Carroll's brigade was badly cut to pieces the other day. He is with Shields.

"My command, owing to the men being without rations, and the horses without shoes, was about broken down, and I halted here to let them shoe their horses, and let the men recuperate. My wagons just came up to-day,

not having seen them since the day before I was at Front
Royal.

" We are now expecting to go to Richmond by way
of Fredericksburg. There's where we should have gone
long ago, instead of doing nothing effectual here under
Fremont. He has been very kind to me, and I esteem
him as a gentleman. But he is utterly deficient in all
military ability, and all his officers know it. Jackson has
completely outgeneralled him, and I am glad to get away
from here before he is defeated.

"P. S. I am ordered to go by Strasburg, and will
start on the fifteenth."

The testimony of Gen. McDowell, as given by the
Committee on the Conduct of the War, vol. i., pages 260
to 269, fully sustains Gen. Bayard's opinions as to the
mismanagement in the Valley of Shenandoah. There
were at the same time there three generals, each with ten
thousand or more troops (Fremont had more); yet
Jackson, with a force not quite equal to that which
either two of the Union generals had, after chasing
Banks to Harper's Ferry, and worsting both Shields and
Fremont, escaped, and was soon fighting McClellan's
army.

The inefficiency of Fremont and Banks was about
equalled by that of Gen. Shields. Gen. McDowell says,
Conduct of the War, vol. i., p. 285 : " After some time
in getting Ord's or rather Ricketts' division together, I
started out to the front. I met one of Gen. Shield's
aide's-de-camp coming in from Front Royal, and asked
him how far out he had met Gen. Shields. He said he
had not met him at all. I told him he had started to

go out ; and he said he must have lost his way.   Without stopping to see what had become of him, I took
Bayard's cavalry brigade—*the only one ready to move*—
and sent it forward by the direct road to Strasburg.   I
then went to see where Gen. Shields was, and found
him over on the road towards Winchester"—he was
ordered to Strasburg.   "He had sent his troops on
that road instead of the one I had ordered him to send
them on.   He said that he had received information
from his aide-de-camp that Jackson had fallen back.
When I got up there, they were coming in.   Well, it was
too late to get ahead of Jackson then."

The following is an extract from the Orders, June
eighth, 1862, of the War Department, Adjutant-general's
Office, addressed to Gen. McDowell :

"Instructions have been sent to Major-general Fre
mont to order the cavalry force known as Bayard's cavalry brigade, with the artillery and battalion of Bucktails, to join your command at Fredericksburg.

"S. Thomas,
"*Adjutant-General.*"

To his Father.

"Camp ten miles from Strasburg, }
June 15th, 1862.   }

"I started from Mt. Jackson this morning.   I shall
make short marches, so as to get the remainder of my
horses shod, and get them along in as good order as
possible.

"We are now bound for Richmond, and I hope we
may reach there before long.

10

"I am thoroughly disgusted with this department. Fremont's army is a rabble. He is a perfect gentleman but not adequate to such a command. He has been outgeneralled by Jackson who made a splendid retreat. Ashby was killed in the fight with my bucktails, and it is shameful that newspaper correspondents should attempt to rob them of the credit of that. We did all the hard work, but the fighting at *Cross Keys* on Sunday. That day I was rear guard, and the bucktails alone of my command, got in the fight. I stopped the men withdrawing from the field, about five hundred declaring themselves all *very sick*. It was a drawn battle. The next morning we advanced and the enemy had gone, carrying off many of our wounded. The papers may say what they please, but God preserve me from all such victories! While I am very grateful to General Fremont for his kindness, I shall to-morrow shake from my boots the dust of his department, and thank God that my service here is over. I regret much the loss of Captain Haines, son of Governor Haines. He was a gallant and most worthy soldier. Carroll's brigade was badly cut up. We lost five hundred or six hundred men. The next day we pushed on to Port Republic. Jackson got off and we returned.

To his Mother.

> "CAMP NEAR MANASSAS,
> *June 22d,* 1862.

"My brigade has been so completely broken down by my long and rapid journey to, and with the "*Pathfinder,*" that I need two weeks' rest at least for my horses. I have sent to Washington for six hundred horses to replace those lost and broken down. We are going to Richmond this time, unless they become stampeded at Washington again.* I have not heard from home since the twenty-fifth of May. My letters may be at Fredericks-burg.

"You will see in the *Inquirer* of the eighteenth, a description of the sword to be presented me by the First Pennsylvania Cavalry. The following is the account of the presentation given by the Inquirer."

From the Philadelphia *Inquirer*, July the 12th, 1862.

"WARRENTON JUNCTION, *July 9th*, 1862

"General Bayard's brigade has changed its recent position from Manassas to this place. After the late trip down the Valley of Virginia, the men and horses were so completely broken down, that it was imperatively

---

* The panic produced at Washington by the defeat of Banks, and the advance of Jackson to the Potomac, is here very gently referred to by General Bayard. Tenney in his " *Military and Naval History of the Rebellion*," (the best History yet written of that event) pages 235, 236, says: " The effect of this causeless panic on the part of the authorities at Washington was extremely disastrous to the Federal cause." Mr. Stanton telegraphed to the Governor of Massachusetts, May the twenty-fifth, that " the enemy in great force were marching on Washington." The President took possession of all the railroads in the United States. The Governors of Pennsylvania, New York, Ohio, Massachusetts and other states, ordered an immediate movement of all available forces. Almost half a million of men offered themselves in twenty-four hours for the defence of Washington. And this, while Jackson was in a dilemma, from which he escaped with great difficulty, and only because the superior force by which he might have been intercepted was not properly handled.

necessary that they should have a good resting-spell.
There was scarcely a horse in the brigade with a full set
of shoes left upon his feet ; some of them, as well as the
men, had gone two and three days at a time without a
mouthful of subsistence, and the brigade was reduced to
a truly woful condition.   But matters have now changed.
Both men and horses have regained their strength and
former excellent condition, and we are ready again for
service.   As a consequence, we are now removed to the
outposts.   Our camps are situated in a beautiful and
healthy locality, and every one is as comfortable as this
intensely hot weather will allow.

"We are now beginning to have summer in earnest,
and the heat, at times, is almost unbearable.   Those of
our friends in the north who are enjoying all the comforts
of home, have but very faint ideas of the privations and
sufferings of the gallant fellows here, who are battling
amid the tempests, the blistering heat, the floods of fire
and blood, for the dear "Old Union."   But all these will
be of small account, if our divided land can be restored
to its once prosperous and happy unity.

"The glorious Fourth was enthusiastically celebrated
by the men in camp.   General Bayard's brigade made
especial use of the day.   They not only made it an
occasion to give vent to their patriotism, but also to give
tangible evidence of their love for, and confidence in,
their commander, General George D. Bayard.   Some
time since, the officers of the First Pennsylvania Cavalry
raised a large amount of money for the purpose of pur-
chasing a magnificent sword to be presented to the general.   The enlisted men, musicians etc., of the same
giment, also subscribed a large amount to be expended

in the purchase of a handsome horse, saddle and accou-trements, to be also presented to General Bayard. On the fourth, the First Pennsylvania Cavalry determined to present the gifts. The First New Jersey Cavalry and the Bucktail Rifles were invited to be present. The occasion was a spirited and magnificent affair.

" The regiments were drawn up in close column of bat-talions, forming three sides of a hollow square. A com-mittee, consisting of Major R. J. Falls, Adjutant Buffing-ton, Quartermaster Baker and Chaplain Beale waited upon General Bayard, inviting his presence in the field. Amid vociferous cheering the general made his appear-ance, when, after formal introductions to Colonel Owen Jones and other officers, the party dismounted, and the ceremony of presentation was commenced. Colonel Jones, on the part of the officers of the First Pennsylvania Cavalry, then presented the magnificent sabre (made by Bailey & Co., Philadelphia), in an eloquent and able speech, to which the general replied as follows :—

"' *Officers of the First Pennsylvania Cavalry :*—If good words could properly express or indicate my thanks to you for this truly handsome gift, be assured they should not be wanting, but would come freely and be thankfully spoken to you all. I am no orator, as Brutus was, or my honorable friend Col. Jones is ; and therefore speak to you but the homely words of thanks. To you, officers of the First Pennsylvania Cavalry, let me say that this sabre, saddle and bridle shall always bring back to my heart those happy days of yore, when I rode the chief of the First Pennsylvania Horse, and when you and I alike pictured to ourselves gallant deeds bravely undertaken

and fearlessly performed. The dream of my youth has
been to command a regiment of cavalry, where officers
and men alike ask not where they go, or what they do,
but bravely follow where'er my hand should point the
way. I consider it a proud honor to command a Pennsylvania regiment. During our Revolutionary struggle
my great-grandsire led, on other fields, a regiment of
the Pennsylvania line, and it is now a happy duty for
me to emulate his deeds. Gentlemen, let me again
thank you for your handsome gift.'"

" At the conclusion of the general's speech, it was
received with immense cheering, and every demonstration of enthusiasm.

" After order had been restored, the magnificent horse
'Falmouth,' caparisoned with the gorgeous saddle,
bridle and accoutrements, was led forward towards the
position occupied by the general and staff, when Private Higginbottom, company F, First Pennsylvania,
came from the ranks, and dismounting, made the presentation speech to General Bayard, on behalf of his comrades, the privates, musicians, etc. The effort of Mr.
Higginbottom was an able one. He repeated for his
comrades their undying confidence in, and love for, their
commander. At the termination of his remarks, amidst
vociferous applause, Gen. Bayard, deeply affected, again
responded as follows :

"' Pennsylvanians ! I thank you for the feelings which
dictated this gift, but I feel my utter incapacity to properly reply to the remarks of Private Higginbottom. You
all know how my affections and pride were wrapped up

in this regiment, and in your performances, believe me, I felt the deepest interest ; but nobly did you sustain and vindicate that trust in our late arduous march through the Valley of Virginia. Moving from a point ten miles south of Fredericksburg, we rapidly passed the Bull Run Mountains, and appeared in the Valley of the Shenandoah. So fast did we travel through the stony mountain roads, that wagon-trains and supplies were left behind. Yet, still onward we pressed towards Strasburg. Just at dusk, there we see the heavily-massed columns of infantry, the artillery and the cavalry of Jackson's rear-guard. With that in our front we are obliged to pause ; yet forward we go in the morning, and Strasburg is ours !

"'We turn it over to General Fremont, and forward we go in pursuit of the retreating enemy, leading General Fremont's advance. How nobly you struggled to keep that advance, in the absence of rations, and with foot-sore horses, here let me say to all Pennsylvanians. A soldier's life is often hard, and full of privations ; but the trials and privations of the past are often our dearest remembrances. To them we can look back, and recall, that *there* we did our duty to ourselves, our country, and our God ! Again, Pennsylvanians, let me thank you all for your generosity, and, I trust, your approbation ; and when the time comes to lead you forward to an attack where the balls fall thick and fast, I only trust this horse may bear me where undying glory shall forever hover around our heads.'"

" At the conclusion of his speech, the general mounted his beautiful steed and passed along the whole line.

The scene was one of intense interest; the general never exhibited his splendid horsemanship to greater advantage than on this occasion. As he charged before the Pennsylvanians, Jerseymen and the gallant 'Bucktails,' he was greeted with cheers, from the men who idolized their young and gallant chieftain, that might have been heard for miles. The enthusiastic shouts were repeated innumerable times. The scene was worthy of an artist's skill, and will never be forgotten by those who participated in the joyous festivities of the occasion. May the brigade, and 'Falmouth' and his fearless rider, live many days to win new laurels to add to those unfading chaplets which they have already won!"

The following excerpt is from the Philadelphia *Inquirer*—about the last of April:

"We cannot fail to call to the minds of Pennsylvanians that they have the best equipped, best drilled, and best officered regiment of cavalry in the service.

"At some future time, when we have more leisure, we shall endeavor to say more of this truly splendid regiment. Suffice it to say, it has performed more active service than any other cavalry regiment in the employ of Uncle Sam. Col. G. D. Bayard is a regular graduate of West Point, and has been connected with the regular army for several years. Although youthful, he bears his honors and position with an amount of grace that we have considered a scarce commodity in several of our hot-cake brigadier-generals. He is universally beloved by his command."

CHAPTER XV.

ON the twenty-sixth of June 1862, General Pope was placed in command of all the Union forces in Virginia. They comprised about fifty thousand troops scattered from Winchester to Fredericksburg. It was originally expected that McClellan, instead of his movement to Harrison's landing, would have come north, so that Pope could have united with them. McDowell's advance (General Bayard's Briagde), when Shields' division was taken from him, was within fifteen miles of Hanover then, held by a corps of McClellan's army. As soon however as it was known where General McClellan had gone, it was apprehended that Lee would make a demonstration on Washington, and crush General Pope's army before it could be reinforced by McClellan's troops. General Pope immediately disposed the different corps of his command, so as to confront the enemy, whenever he advanced. The cavalry were ordered to the front and picketed the line from the Blue Ridge to the Rapidan.

August sixth, General Bayard wrote from camp, ten miles below Culpepper, giving only his position. General Pope in his Report says, that on the seventh of

August, "General Bayard with four regiments of cavalry
was posted near Rapidan station, the point where the
Orange and Alexandria railroad crosses Rapidan river,
with his pickets extended as far east as Racoon Ford,
and connecting with General Buford on his right at Bur-
nett's Ford."

Pyne says (Hist. page. 71) : "On the night of Thursday, seventh August, the portion of the Pennsylvania cavalry then picketing at Barnett's Ford was driven back by
the rebels, who threw a force across the river. Bayard
after consultation with Karge, directed him to take a portion of the regiment, and sweep round the enemy's flank and
fall upon their rear ; while the general led the remainder,
under Major Beaumont to join the Pennsylvanians, prepared, if circumstances favored them, to make an attack
in front.

"Before dawn therefore the bugles blew to arms. As
the detachment filed off upon its appointed route, Bayard rode up and anxiously whispered to Karge. 'No
matter,' responded the latter, half aloud ; 'I will go on.
It may do good.'

"Not till hours had elapsed were we made aware
that in that short colloquy Bayard had imparted the intelligence, that there were fifteen thousand men in that
position, where we had calculated to encounter less than
as many hundred ; and that our resolute commander had
engaged to lead his hundred and fifty troopers around
the rear of this formidable body, while Bayard as stoutly
engaged to face their front with about one-twentieth
their number.

"Karge, with consummate skill and daring, performed
the duty assigned him. He soon found himself almost

enveloped by different bodies of the advancing foe. But with prudence he checked and alarmed the enemy without loss to himself. One of his companies, under Captain Janeway, surprised a party, and captured twenty-two prisoners, one lieutenant, and a colonel of militia. His skirmishers constantly threatened the line of the enemy, forcing him to keep within support of his reserves. So the day was consumed, the enemy retarded, so as to be able to advance only five miles, and time given to Pope and Banks to concentrate their commands."

Pyne, page 70, says : " To Karge's manœuvre was no doubt due much of that over-caution on the part of Jackson, which enabled Bayard to check the rebel advance so far from Culpepper." Pyne says further, on the same page : " To Bayard's brigade, and to General Crawford, belong the credit of having saved the army of Virginia, and of having enabled General Banks and General Pope to close the door, which would otherwise have been opened into Washington."

Sigel, with his troops (formerly Fremont's command), was posted at Sperryville. General Pope says : " During the whole morning of the eighth, I continued to receive reports from General Bayard, who was slowly falling back in the direction of Culpepper Court-house, from the advance of the enemy, and from General Buford, who also reported the enemy advancing in heavy force upon Madison Court-house."

He then ordered General Sigel to march to Culpepper Court-house, which he failed to do by the time appointed.* General Banks, with a force of eight thousand, which General Pope supposed from the return made

* Pope's Report, page 8.

by General Banks was fourteen thousand strong, was ordered to move towards Cedar Mountain. General Pope directed General Banks, "if the enemy advanced to attack him, he should push his skirmishers well to the front, and notify him." Instead of obeying his orders, General Banks left the strong position he was directed to take, and advanced a mile to assault the enemy, not knowing his strength, but considering it not very formidable. The consequence was he was severely handled, late in the afternoon of the ninth. General Pope having brought up Rickett's division, and Sigel at last having come up, the enemy were finally, after a renewed attack on the morning of the tenth, compelled to retreat.

In the battle of Cedar Mountain, Bayard's brigade was posted in advance, and long held the enemy in check. *Pyne* page 85 says, "The rebels unable to comprehend why cavalry held the front of our line of battle, and apprehensive that we might design a desperate charge right through their centre, did not venture to make their grand assault while we maintained our ground. Little did they think that we held them so long with the mere shadow of a line—and that cavalry had been holding a place which we had no infantry to fill.

But now as the balls continued to hail around us, a grave calm voice in our rear was heard to say, "It has been bravely done, they stand like veterans "—and there was the iron face of General Banks, his proud eye softening with a smile of approbation. But our position was fast becoming untenable. A fresh battery of the enemy had been so placed as to command the whole field in which we stood and its missiles threatened us all with annihilation. Bayard spoke for a moment to the command-

ing general. "You retire the Pennsylvania," was the
answer—"I myself will show these where to go."

The obstinancy of the cavalry and Crawford's small
brigade of infantry—kept back the enemy so long—that
night was approaching when he made his last desperate
but fruitless assault. The New Jersey cavalry were
placed in a position upon the left flank, to charge if
necessary, but had no further call upon them. The
Pennsylvania cavalry, as preparing to withdraw, were
suddenly attacked by two brigades of the enemy, who
were upon them before their guns could be limbered up.
The ground was such that the whole regiment could not
make an effective charge. But just at the critical moment Bayard saw that his guns would be lost unless a
decisive movement was made.* He then ordered Major Falls to charge with his battalion, and rescue the
guns. With loud hurrahs the Pennsylvanians dashed
upon the enemy. One company of the squadron was
almost annihilated. But the battery was saved, and the
gallant Falls returned unhurt.

During the night of the eleventh, Jackson retreated
across the Rapidan in the direction of Gordonville. The
cavalry force under Bayard and Buford pursued the
enemy to the Rapidan capturing many stragglers. The
whole cavalry force then resumed their original positions,
and again occupied the Rapidan from Raccoon Ford to
the Blue Ridge.† On the eleventh, there was a truce to
enable both the combatants to bury their dead and
remove their wounded. The following incident as stated
in a Washington paper, then took place.

"General Bayard went forward under a flag of truce,

* Pyne's History, page 89.   † Pope's Report.

to meet and confer with his old comrade in arms, the now famous J. E. B. Steuart, of the rebel cavalry.   Less than two years ago Jeb. was first lieutenant in the same company ; but Jeb. is now a Major general and Bayard a brigadier.   During the interview, a wounded union soldier lying near was groaning, and asked for water. 'Here, Jeb.' said Bayard—old time recollections making him familiar, as he tosses his bridle to the rebel officer—'hold my horse a minute, will you, till I fetch that poor fellow some water.' Jeb. held the bridle.   Bayard went to a stream and brought the wounded man some water.   As Bayard mounted his horse, Jeb. remarked, that it was the first time he had 'played Orderly to a Union general.'   The business upon which they met was soon arranged, and the old friends parted—a fight, which had ceased while they were engaged in talking, recommenced with great fury on both sides the moment each got back to his own ranks."

General McDowell in his report to General Pope,[*] says : " The First Pennsylvania Cavalry under Colonel Owen Jones, the First New Jersey Cavalry under Colonel Karge, (Colonel Wyndam being a prisoner of war under parole), the First Maine under Colonel Allen, the First Rhode Island under Colonel Duffie, all under General Bayard, had been engaged (the evening of the ninth July) in the battle before we came up, and I am assured by your chief of cavalry, Brigadier-general Roberts who was present, they performed good service, not only before but during the action.   General Bayard who had himself rendered most valuable service, speaks warmly of a charge made about five o'clock P. M. by that gallant old

* Pope's report, page 33.

soldier, Major Falls, First Pennsylvania Cavalry, who led his battalion against the enemy's lines and charged completely through them. All the regiments above named, especially the Pennsylvania and New Jersey, had severe duty to perform in holding the enemy in check."

On the morning of the eighteenth, intelligence was brought to General Pope by one of his spies, that the enemy, massing his forces, was about crossing the Rapidan at Racoon Ford, with the design of interposing between General Pope and the troops of McClellan arriving at Acquia Creek. General Pope immediately ordered his whole army to retire beyond the Rappahannock. The several corps of McDowell, Sigel, Banks and Reno, were directed to cross at different fords of the Rappahannock. Bayard's cavalry was charged with covering the rear of the retiring army. He accordingly fell back no further than Culpepper Court-house on the evening of the nineteenth. The next morning he took position at Brandy station, half way between Culpepper Court-house and the Rappahannock, and sent out strong detachments on all the roads by which the enemy could approach. The cavalry sent out on the Racoon Ford road soon came upon the advancing column of the enemy, who followed them up to the Brandy station and thence to the Rappahannock, while the army was pressing rapidly across the Rappahannock. General Bayard so disposed his brigade as to check any interruption of the retreat. As was expected, the enemy would not suffer the escape of his foe unmolested. As the last of Pope's trains were rolling over the bridge, a formidable cavalry force was seen approaching Bayard's position. The First New Jersey Regiment was placed on the right, the Tenth New York on the

left, the Second New York in the centre and held together to charge the advancing enemy. The First Pennsylvania, was to act as the Reserve. As the two oppos-
ing forces, came in sight of each other, and as Kilpatrick
was riding to the front, to order a charge, the lieutenant
at the head of his line, proved to be a coward and
backed his horse through the ranks behind him. The
leading column become panic-stricken and halted in confusion. At this moment the rebels charged, scattering
and riding down the New Yorkers. They were met gallantly however by Karge and Sawyer and severely handled and the First Pennsylvania finished the day's work,
repulsing and dispersing the rebel troopers and effectual-
ly securing the safe retreat of the whole army without
the loss of a gun or a wagon.*

The next day after crossing the river, Bayard's brigade
was hurried to Thoroughfare Gap, where without guns or
infantry, he was sent to check Lee from supporting Jackson, until our army and its trains could be prepared to
meet them. Towards evening, Ricketts with two brigades
of infantry came up, and the rebels were compelled to
seek another route by which to continue their advance.
Pyne says, page 104, and Foster page 432 : "That Bayard and Ricketts had to decide absolutely for themselves,
and without orders from the Commander-in-Chief, on
their own independent movements, with Jackson con-
fronting them, and Lee thundering on their rear. No intelligence reached them to direct their movements in
combination with other corps. Accordingly, after effect-
ually arresting the progress of Lee, they retired from the

* Pyne, page. 97.

Gap, and fell back on their only way of retreat to Manassas."

Gen. Bayard's Report to Gen. McDowell.

"HEADQUARTERS CAVALRY BRIGADE,
THIRD ARMY CORPS,
CAMP NEAR CULPEPPER, VA.,
August 14th, 1862.

" *Major S. F. Barstow. A. A. G., Gen. McDowell's corps.*

" SIR.—I have the honor to make the following report of the operation of the Cavalry Brigade under my command on the eighth and ninth of August, just past.

" On the seventh, my line of pickets extended from a point three miles east of the railroad, to beyond Barnett's Ford, some three or four miles ; and on that day I rode along the entire length of that picket line, examining the headquarters of the pickets, and seeing that the videttes in front were properly executing their duty: about twelve o'clock that night, Captain David Gardiner, First Pennsylvania Cavalry, in charge of the line of pickets west of Robertson's river, reported that his videttes and pickets had all been driven in, that the enemy had crossed the Rapidan in force, and that he (Capt. Gardiner) was falling back towards Robertson's river : I immediately dispatched Colonel Owen Jones with the remainder of his regiment to reinforce the pickets, and he shortly reported that he had advanced again to within a couple of miles of the river.   Before the break of day, Lieut. Col. Karge, with one hundred and sixty of the men of his Jersey regiment, started in order to turn the enemy's left by the Madison road, leading into Barnett's Ford road, while I, with the remainder of the regiment under Major Beaumont, advanced to reinforce Colonel Jones and attack the enemy in front.

"I advanced all the way to the Rapidan, and Major Beaumont's videttes here came in sight of a large train of the enemy, and their camps, with a heavy force of cavalry in front : just at this moment a contraband came in and reported that the whole of Ewell's division had crossed the Rapidan and were advancing. I ordered Major Beaumont to fall back slowly when pressed by the enemy, and sent word to Col. Karge to return at once, as the enemy were in too great force to be attacked by our light force. The Jersey batallion fell back slowly and in good order, and about three miles from the ford. I relieved it by bringing up the Pennsylvania regiment into action. I fell back to the road (on which Col. Karge was obliged to return), halting my command and held that position until Colonel Karge returned with his force and twenty rebel prisoners, captured by Captain Janeway, Co. L. New Jersey Cavalry. During that time we had to stand a heavy fire from the enemy's cavalry, in which we lost two corporals of the Pennsylvania regiment, severely wounded. As soon as Colonel Karge came in, I continued my retreat.

"The enemy now opened upon us with their artillery, and we crossed Robertson's river, under heavy fire of both artillery and musketry. Col. Owen Jones, First Pennsylvania Cavalry, here by my order, destroyed the bridge which for a long time prevented the crossing of the river by the enemy's artillery. As soon as I had discovered the enemy's force, I had sent to camp, and had everything started for Culpepper. Owing to the neglect of duty of Quartermaster Hazen, the New Jersey teams left their portable forge and a great deal of baggage. I continued the retreat to Cedar Run, where I posted the Pennsylvania Cavalry on picket, and fell back a mile further with the Jersey regiment.   I had sent word to the pickets, on the east side of Robertson's river, to fall back, but, the order reaching them so late, it was impossible to do so. They remained in the woods till next day, when they succeeded in getting back to Culpepper, Captain Boyd, the commanding officer of that picket, rejoining my command, after a hard race, by abandoning his horse.   The picket lost two videttes, who were captured, which was the only loss sustained by my command during the retreat.

"That same evening, the First Maine Cavalry, Col. Allen, and the First Rhode Island Cavalry, Col. Duffie, reported to me, and I relieved the Pennsylvania regiment by the latter.   General Crawford also arrived during the evening with his brigade, the next day I advanced with the three regiments of cavalry, to Col. Duffie's support. I drew up the cavalry to the right and left of the road, taking down the fences, so that they would have an unimpeded field of action.   By direction of General Roberts, chief of cavalry, I detached the Maine regiment to the rear and left, in order to watch and patrol all roads to our left.   Two battalions of the Pennsylvania regiment performed the same duty on the right.   About half past one o'clock the enemy opened on us from three batteries, to which our batteries replied.   General Banks soon arrived, and shortly after the infantry fight begun.   When our infantry fell back, the enemy advanced, endangering Best's battery, and General Banks ordered me to order a charge of cavalry on the enemy's advancing lines to try and check the pursuit.   I ordered Major R. J. Falls, commanding First Battalion, First Pennsylvania Cavalry, to lead up his battalion, and charge.

"He led the charge bravely, and executed it well. The enemy, though advancing in force, were astonished, and could not think that so small a body of men would execute such a charge, unless supported by large bodies of troops behind them. And accordingly they halted, and soon fell back. Second Lieut. Butcher was killed, and Captain McDonald was severely wounded, with four balls in him. Major Falls, in advance of his men, ran through the neck, with his sabre, a rebel soldier. Officers and men behaved admirably, and I cannot speak too highly of the good conduct of all the brigade.

"The cavalry was held in the edge of the timber, and covered the retreat of the artillery and ambulances. Of my staff, I cannot but speak of the uniform gallantry and bravery of Captain H. C. Weir, my assistant adjutant-general, and First Lieut. W. C. Patterson has my thanks for the manner, in which he promptly transmitted my orders. I have the honor to be sir,

"Very respectfully, your obedient servant,

"GEORGE D. BAYARD,

"*Brigadier-general commanding cavalry.*"

General Pope in his Dispatch, August twenty-fifth, to General McDowell expressed the opinion that the enemy had marched off by way of Fort Royal to the Shenandoah Valley. But he was soon apprised of his error. The enemy had advanced to crush him, and to that end all their efforts were directed. They went round him and attacked on the twenty-seventh. On the twenty-eighth they were reported to be near Centreville and on the other side of Bull Run.   During the twenty-sixth, seventh and eighth, the cavalry were constantly employed, in the advance, making reconnoissances and guarding the outposts of different corps.   On the twenty-seventh, General Pope ordered the several corps to concentrate at Manassas junction.   But at four P. M. of that day, learning that the enemy had gone as far as Centreville and Bull Run, he ordered a concentration at Centreville.

On the twenty-ninth there was severe fighting.   "Bayard's cavalry attacking, to the left of General Hatch, on the south of the road on which Seymour's squadron suffered severely.   These were the finishing strokes of the day, which we could now claim as ours." *   On the thirtieth, the fighting continued, General Bayard, by order of General Pope, was temporarily attached to General Porter's division, who was ordered to pursue the enemy which he did vigorously.

The battle of the thirtieth and thirty-first, resulted unfavorably, the enemy inflicting on us serious injury. There was continuous fighting on the twenty-seventh, twenty-eighth, twenty-ninth and thirtieth.

On the evening of the twenty-ninth, and early on the morning of the thirtieth, General Pope was under the delusion that the enemy were retreating, (see Report pages 24, 25) but by twelve o'clock found out that he was confronted by the whole army of Lee, reinforced by fresh arrivals every hour.   (Page 47 of Pope's Report.) There is an order from headquarters, dated August thirtieth, to General Porter concluding thus : " Organize a strong advance, to precede your command and push on rapidly until you come in contact with him.   Report

* McDowell's Report to Pope. Pope's Report page. 46.

frequently, Bayard's Brigade will be ordered to report
to you : push it well to the left as you advance.

" ED. SCHRIVER.

" *Colonel and chief of staff.*"

Major general Porter commanding etc,

" In all these actions the cavalry participated as far
as they were able. But incessant service for a month
had much reduced their strength. General Pope says
(Report, page 26) : " Generals Buford and Bayard, commanding the whole of the cavalry force of the army,
reported to me that there were not five horses to the
company that could be forced into a trot. Our cavalry
at Centreville was completely broken down, no horses
whatever having reached us to remount."

A severe action took place on the first of September,
in the afternoon, near Chantilly, in which Generals Kearney and Stevens were killed. On the second of September, General Pope was ordered by General Halleck from
Washington, to retreat, which he did.

In his General Order of Sept. second, prescribing the
order of retreat, General Pope says : " The cavalry, under
General Buford, will follow, and cover the march of the
three corps of Porter, Sumner, Sigel and Bayard the
troops marching on the road south of it."

In his final report, Jan. twenty-seventh, 1863, of his
whole conduct in this campaign, General Pope pays a de-
served tribute to the services of the cavalry generals in
these words (see Report, page 29) : " Generals Bayard
and Buford commanded the cavalry belonging to the Army
of Virginia. Their duties were peculiarly arduous and
hazardous, and it is not too much to say that through-

out the operations, from the first to the last day of the campaign, *scarcely a day passed that these officers did not render service which entitles them to the gratitude of the Government.*"

On the second of September General Pope resigned his command of the army of Virginia.

General Bayard, during the campaign, wrote very few letters home, and those chiefly to inform his family of his position and his health. Indeed his correspondence during the fifteen months of his service in the war is in striking contrast to that of previous years. When at West Point, and on the Plains, his letters were replete with interesting details. But, during the war, his duties were so severe, and his mind so engrossed upon the proper performance of them, that his letters were extremely laconic, and comparatively few in number.

To his Mother.
" Camp on Rapidan, *August 3d,* 1862.

" I am guarding a long line on the Rapidan, pickets extending fourteen miles. Be assured I shall take good care of myself.* I had a great deal rather live than die. You need not think that I am such a desperate fellow. I hope to live to enjoy the laurels I shall win in this war. I have three cavalry regiments with me now. I have been in the saddle for two days continually till late at night. My health is excellent."

* In reference to a letter from his mother, urging him not to expose himself unnecessarily.

To his Father.

"CAMP TEN MILES BELOW CULPEPPER, }
           August 6th, 1862. }

"We are here in the advance, and our army is advancing, with I think inadequate forces.

"McClellan applied to the War Department for me to command a brigade of Pennsylvanians in his army. They cannot spare me from here. The government has never properly appreciated the value of cavalry for such a country as this. We ought to have a cavalry force ten times greater than it is at present."

To his Mother.

" FIVE MILES FROM CULPEPPER, }
           August 11th, 1862. }

"We had a fight. I was in the front, and on the flanks protecting the right and left wings. Shells and bullets showered around me, a merciful Providence protected me. Had a parley under flag of truce with J. E. B. Steuart ; our greeting was cordial; nothing said except about old times on the plains. I am well, but almost worn out."

To his Father.

" CENTREVILLE, }
           August 31st, 1862. }

"Pope was beaten yesterday. He is not a match for Lee. There must be a change of commander on our side, or the rebels will be in Washington soon. Oh, if I only had a sufficient cavalry force, things would not have gone thus ! As it is, our meagre cavalry regiments are about used up. They have been overtasked. I thank my God I am conscious of having done my duty.

I had some very narrow escapes. But though weary, worn and sad, my health is good."

To his Mother.

"HEADQUARTERS BAYARD'S CAVALRY
NEAR LONG BRIDGE,
Sept 3d, 1862.

"Here we have been driven at last. I think Pope will resign. I trust Wyndam and love Karge, no one can hurt them in my estimation."*

To his mother.

"WASHINGTON, *Sept 11th,* 1862.

"I have gone into Hospital, but hope to be out in a few days. I shall get leave in December to go home and get married, if possible. It will take some time to reorganize the army for a movement 'On to Richmond,' where we ought to have been long before this."

The following is the report of General Bayard of his movements during the Campaign of General Pope in Virginia.

"HEADQUARTERS CAVALRY BRIGADE,
THIRD ARMY CORPS, ARMY OF VIRGINIA,
CAMP AT UPTON'S HILL, VA., *Oct 13th* 1862.

"*Col. Edmund Schriver, Chief of Staff.*

"SIR.—I have the honor to acknowledge the receipt of your communication, announcing your desire to have a

---

* Considerable efforts had been made by certain parties, principally from New Jersey to prejudice General Bayard against Lieut. Col. Karge and Col. Windam. But knowing them to be good officers, he gave no ear to their disparagement. It is to these efforts that General B. refers in this letter.

11

report of the operations of my brigade during the advance towards Gordonsville, and on the subsequent retreat.

"At this late day I must depend much upon my memory, as many of my papers have been misplaced, and it is impossible at present to find them.

"The last ten days in July were occupied in scouts towards Madison Court-house and the Rapidan river.

"Madison we occupied, and our parties also went to the Rapidan, which was uniformly reported to be strongly picketed upon the opposite bank by the cavalry of the enemy. On the first of August, I was ordered by Gen. Crawford, commanding the U. S. forces about Culpepper Court-house, to proceed to Barnett's Ford and make a demonstration there, so as to attract the attention of the enemy.

"At the ford there is a mill which was occupied by the enemy as the headquarters of their advance picket, and from which they were driven by a battalion of the First New Jersey Cavalry under Major Beaumont.

"The skirmish was quite brisk, and I had two men wounded, but owing to the enemy keeping at long carbine range, I lost no more, although for some hours there was a constant cracking of carbines.

"The enemy suddenly disappearing, the cause was shortly explained by an express from Gen. Crawford, stating that he had taken Orange Court-house.

"The next five days were occupied in establishing my line of pickets along the Rapidan from a point five miles below the railroad, up as far as Cave's Ford, while my headquarters were moved from Elm Farm, between the Robertson and Crooked rivers to a point two miles beyond Cedar Mountain.

" This made a line of at least fourteen miles in length to be picketed by two regiments of cavalry, much reduced by long and hard marching.

" I marched into Madison Court-house one day and returned the same evening with First Pennsylvania Cavalry. Along the entire line skirmishing was continually going on, and the men were obliged to exert themselves continually to maintain this line of pickets so far in advance, and supported only by the weak and worn out reserve that I could give them.

" On the night of the sixth, the enemy captured two men, and the horses and arms of six men at one of my advanced posts. For this negligence. I at once reduced to the ranks the commanding non-commissioned officer.

" My headquarters were now moved to a point two miles south of Cedar Mountain. On the night of the seventh, the enemy crossed the river at a private ford, Walker's, and also at Cave's Ford, from which I had been compelled to withdraw all my forces, and not at Barnett's Ford, as General Pope states in his report.

" At daylight on the eighth, doubtful of the report that the enemy had crossed in force as reported, I advanced to reestablish my pickets.

" Lieut. Col. Karge with one battalion of his regiment, (the New Jersey), took a road to the right with orders to get around the enemy and cut off his retreat to the river, while I with another battalion of the regiment moved to reinforce Col. Owen Jones of the First Pennsylvania Cavalry, and with our combined forces drive the enemy back upon Colonel Karge.

" I advanced beyond Slaughter's house, when my

advanced guard reported large infantry forces and long lines of wagons in plain view.

"I at once sent word to Col. Karge to withdraw his force, and fell slowly back myself to the road by which he would have to return.

"The enemy advancing in force, I nevertheless succeeded in checking his advance with Major R. J., Fall's battalion of the First Pennsylvania Cavalry, who deployed his men as skirmishers and held the position for half an hour under a heavy fire. He had two men wounded.

"Colonel Karge now returned, having captured one captain, one lieutenant and twenty-four men of the infantry force of the enemy. I now sent word to the pickets along the river, below where we were to return to camp, and all reached camp the next day by a roundabout road, except Captain Boyd, First New Jersey Cavalry, the commanding officer, who was compelled to take to the woods, and finally reached us just before the fight at Cedar Mountain, losing horse and equipments.

"We now fell slowly back, and just as my rear guard reached Robertson's river the enemy opened, with their artillery.

"Over that stream I destroyed the bridge, which detained them for some time, and enabled me to break up my camps leisurely.

"All was conducted in the best order and manner by all the men and officers, except Quartermaster Hazen, First New Jersey Cavalry, who deserted his camp, leaving a portable forge and the regimental books to fall into the hands of the enemy, and one more exception I have again to make. All the men who were left in camp became panic-stricken and went rushing into Culpepper in a disgraceful manner.

"Those in the field did admirably. I fell back beyond Cedar Run and reported the facts occurring in my front to you. General Crawford arrived the next day and assumed command.

"On that day was fought the hard fight at Cedar Mountain. Colonel's Allen and Duffie reported to me according to order. I enclose a list of my losses. I must again speak of the admirable behavior of my men, and of the gallant charge led by Major R. J. Falls, First Pennsylvania Cavalry, and herewith enclose his reports.

"The next two days was employed scouting in the direction of the enemy's flanks, and then we had a few days for a rest.

"On the eighteenth, I received orders to cover the retreat from Cedar Mountain with five regiments of cavalry. viz., First Pennsylvania, First New Jersey, First Rhode Island, First Maine, and Second New York Cavalry.

"We waited all that night and the next day for General Sigel's train to pass, reaching Culpepper just at dark on the nineteenth. I received orders to halt at Brandy station that night. In the morning, according to order, I sent out reconnoitering parties on all the roads. A squadron of the Maine Cavalry which I sent out on the Raccoon Ford road, first came up with the enemy and finding them advancing in force, they fell slowly back.

"The Harris Light (Second New York Cavalry), Col. Kilpatrick kept them at bay until all the reconnoitering parties returned. He lost several men badly wounded.

" As soon as the reconnoitering parties returned, I slowly fell back toward the river, following the Maine and Rhode Island regiments which I had already sent on.

" Just before reaching the ford of the Rappahannock the country is open, and for two or three miles offers for cavalry an open and uninterrupted field for their operations.

" I crossed this and drew up the Harris cavalry beyond the strip of timber which separates this plain from the river. The Jersey cavalry I placed to the right of the Harris cavalry and some six hundred yards in the rear.

" Lieut. Col. Karge 1 instructed to support Col. Kilpatrick if he needed it.

" I sent an order to Col. Toms to form his regiment just beyond the timber, so that he could charge the enemy should they get through the timber.

" From the hill on which was drawn up the Harris light cavalry the long columns of the enemy's cavalry could be marked by the clouds of dust arising and the quick sharp report of the carbines proved that our skirmishers were already engaged.

" Our skirmishers drove back those of the enemy but this was but a temporary success.

" I had the general's orders not to bring on a general engagement or I should have brought into action the whole of my force.

" As soon as the leading regiment of the enemy came up, they formed and quickly charged with loud shouts and wild yelling. They caught Col. Kilpatrick executing a manœuvre and his men at the time had their backs to the enemy. The sudden charge and the yells of the enemy seemed to strike panic in the men so that they soon began running.

"They were rallied by Col. Kilpatrick and Capt. H. C. Weir, my Assistant-Adjutant-general both of whom displayed their usual bravery and coolness.

" Col. Karge from his flank position had a fine opportunity to cut the enemy to pieces and gave the order to charge, but he was followed only by his Adjutant, Lieut. Penn Gaskell and Lieut. Wm. Bayard my aide-de-camp.

. " They rode into the scattered enemy, and here Col. Karge was shot through the leg, making a painful and serious wound.

" The enemy now charged the Jersey cavalry, and, I regret to say, contrary to their previous history, they too began running. I, as soon as I saw this, ordered Capt. Broderick, commanding the rear battalion of the Jersey cavalry, to place his men in the timber just in his rear, and let the men use their carbines, from which position he repulsed the enemy.

" Seeing the enemy going round the timber, I quickly rode through it, and hastened the formation of the Pennsylvania cavalry.

"As soon as the enemy appeared, I ordered Major R. J. Falls to charge them with his battalion, and he quickly cleared the enemy from sight. The enemy now withdrew, and the fight closed.

" I enclose a list of killed, wounded and missing.

" The Maine cavalry recrossed the river, and were formed just in rear of the Pennsylvania regiment.

"As soon as I gathered together all the men to be found, I crossed the river.

" The next few days following, all my cavalry force

was employed reconnoitering and picketing along the Rappahannock river. Two days afterwards, I was ordered to proceed to Lawson's ford, and hold it, if possible.

"I placed the main body of my force at the forks of the road, where the Freeman's ford and the Fox mills' roads join the one to Lawson's ford.

"At Lawson's ford there was some skirmishing, but nothing that amounted to anything.

"The next morning I was relieved by General Sigel's forces, and was ordered to move to the right to feel the enemy in that direction.

"I pushed my skirmishers to the small stream to the east of Warrenton springs, but I there found the enemy in force.

"As I had orders not to engage the enemy, I halted and planted my battery on commanding ground.

"It rained very hard this night and in the midst of it, General Buford arrived with his brigade and declared his intention of going through to the springs. The next morning however I found him in my front having been unable to force his way through. The next night I staid in Foxville and the following day, joined General Sigel in his advance on Warrenton Springs. The next day, the twenty-sixth, I was ordered around to the right and I went as far as Waterloo Bridge where I found General Buford.

"I then received orders to proceed to Warrenton when I was ordered once more to accompany General Sigel in his march on Gainsville, which we reached but a short time before dark.

"I threw out my pickets and we established ourselves for the night.

" The next morning I was ordered forward to hold Thoroughfare Gap until General Ricketts came up. Colonel Wyndam had been already sent forward by General McDowell and had occupied what he took to be the gap. General Ricketts came up, but finding he could not hold the position, he fell back to Gainsville, while my brigade with General Buford's continued to hold Haymarket till daylight the next morning,

"Lieut. Col. Kilpatrick, you will percieve, lost several men at the Gap.

"Colonel Wyndam had detached Lieut. Yorke and six men on a scout to the right of the road; finding himself cut off from our troops, he struck out boldly through the country, and after considerable suffering he led his party up by Leesburg, crossed the river and came down through Washington. I followed General Ricketts' column until we had nearly reached Bristow, when I pushed on to the front and reported to General McDowell. By him the Brigade was taken on the Sadly Ford road, and ordered to take a position to the left of the line formed by our own forces.

" Later in the day, Captain Leske came with an order for me to move forward on the Gainsville road and charge the enemy, but when I reached the point the enemy had retired.

" After dark I moved forward a portion of my command under Lieut. Col. Kilpatrick, to the support of King's Division at that time engaged with the enemy.

"Capt. Seymour's squadron was drawn into an ambuscade and cut to pieces.

" The next day I was ordered to report to Gen. Porter and he ordered me to fall to the rear. Shortly

11*

after our left was turned and all my cavalry was deployed to stop the infantry from running away.

"I reported to Gen. Pope and carried one or two orders for him.

"When he left the field, I reported to Gen. Reynolds and having sent my aids to order the cavalry to fall back on Centreville, I left the field when Gen. Reynolds left, leaving nothing behind except the noble regulars.

"At Centreville I collected the cavalry and was ordered out towards the Little River turnpike, but soon met the enemy, with whom, for the remainder of the day we kept up a desultory firing.

"That night I was awake all night, and just before daylight the last of my cavalry left the town, the whole army having fallen back to Fairfax Court-house during the night.

We lay near the town during the day and just before sundown we evacuated the place, following Gen. Hooker on the Alexandria pike, where we arrived safely the next morning.

"It is natural in closing a report of this character, covering the length of time that this does and including the number of actions and skirmishes it does, that I should have many men to point out as distinguished for their gallantry and good behavior.

"Lieut. Col. Karge I would particularly name, as always ready and valiant and I would particularly ask that the general would notice him.

"Lieut. Col. Kilpatrick was always active and brave. Lieut. Col. Barrows by his personal daring was enabled to give me important information when near Barnett's Ford.

"Capt. Boyd, first New Jersey* "   *   *   *

The foregoing report appears as furnished by the Adjutant-general's office. The note appended to it, *A. G O.*, it will be observed says the "balance of the report is missing, has never been received in the *A. G. O.*" But in the letter of General Bayard to his father, dated October 18th, 1862., he says expressly, "Have sent in my report of operations under Pope." He was uniformly precise and accurate in his statements, and had he sent in an incomplete report he would have said so.

There is reason to believe that the report was mutilated surreptiously.

* The balance of this report is missing, has never been received in the A. G. O.

CHAPTER XVI.

General Bayard, on the eleventh of September, received the following orders from General McClellan, through General Buford :

" HEADQUARTERS, ARMY OF POTOMAC,
ROCKVILLE, *Sept.* 10*th*, 1862.

" *General George D. Bayard,*

" SIR :—The major-general commanding directs that you consult, in person, with Major-general F. J. Porter, as to the strength of the cavalry force necessary for picket duty in front of Washington. If you require more than your own brigade, name the regiments you wish, taking those now on your side of the Potomac.

" You will take the sole charge of the outpost duty in front of the city of Washington. Reporting everything concerning the movements of the enemy to these headquarters, and to Major-general Porter, if immediate action is necessary. Your force must be strong enough to resist the cavalry force the enemy may bring against you.

Herewith you will find a circular, which requires immediate attention.

"I am very respectfully,
"Your obedient servant,
"JOHN BUFORD,
"*Brigadier-general, and Chief of Cavalry.*"

On the twenty-seventh of September the following special orders were issued.

[SPECIAL ORDERS, NO. 18.]

"HEADQUARTERS, DEFENCES OF }
WASHINGTON, *Sept.* 27*th,* 1862. }

"9. All the cavalry south of the Potomac is placed under the orders of Brigadier-general *George D. Bayard,* and will at once report accordingly. General Bayard will organize the cavalry into brigades, and will take immediate measures to bring it, as rapidly as possible, in a state of efficiency.

"He will assign to the different corps and independent commands south of the Potomac, such force for orderly service as General Heintzleman may deem necessary.

"By command of Major General Banks.
"RICHARD B. IRWIN, CAPTAIN, A. D. C.
"*Acting Assistant Ajutant General.*"

General Bayard through General Heintzleman.

These orders will explain why General Bayard's brigade did not participate in the Maryland campaign, and the battle of Antietam. The government had become thoroughly convinced by sore experience of the necessity of a large efficient cavalry force. New regiments of cavalry were therefore organized, and as they arrived at Washington, were put under General Bayard to be disciplined and prepared for service, and assigned to different commands.

But while engaged in this arduous duty, his brigade was not idle. Pyne says, page 122 : " Before the two armies had met together at South Mountain, the First New Jersey Cavalry had reconnoitred the whole country about the battle-field, and while the northern newspapers were speculating upon the numbers of the hostile force still at Manassas, that position was in the hands of our regiment. Many were the stragglers who fell into our hands, and fearful the number of wounded from whom we took a parole.

" Lieut. Col. Karge, who in response to General Bayard's special and urgent request, had returned to duty before his wound was fairly healed, took command of a force composed of several regiments, and swept the country near Leesburg, to the base of the Blue Ridge.

" In the early part of October, Karge received an order to go to Warrenton. So well was the movement executed, that our troops were dashing into the town by three roads, before the rebels had an intimation of our approach."

To his Father.

" HEADQUARTERS CAVALRY DIVISION, }
CAMP AT UPTON HILL. *Oct.* 18*th*, 1862. }
" I am so busy that I cannot write letters. Have sent in my report of operations under Pope.* I have a

* See last page of chapter xv.

force of about eight thousand under me. I shall propose a raid into the enemy's lines, but I fear they have not the *nerve* to authorize it. I could perform a most important service if they would let me."

About the middle of October, General Bayard proposed to General Banks a cavalry raid into Virginia. But with commendable prudence, or lamentable timidity, Commander-in-Chief Halleck would not authorize it, at least, not to the extent recommended by General Bayard. They should have had more confidence in his judgment. He knew the country thoroughly, into which he desired to penetrate. He knew better than General Halleck the forces he would encounter. He had proved himself a discreet and wary cavalry leader. He had been guilty of no rash or imprudent movement. He had been uniformly successful, wherever he alone was the responsible leader. He was therefore entitled to the confidence of the government, and his advice should have been respected.

Below we give the plan of the raid proposed, and the reply of General Banks.

(Confidential.)

" HEAD-QUARTERS DEFENCE OF }
WASHINGTON, *Oct.* 15*th* 1862. }

"*For General Banks.*

" Cavalry expedition projected by Brigadier-general Bayard, commanding cavalry south of the Potomac.

" The expedition, consisting of about twenty-five hundred horse, and six pieces three-inch rifled cannon, is to start from Fairfax Court-house. A special corps of engineers is organized, provided with necessary tools, burning and blasting compositions, and other requisite materials for enabling us to destroy speedily, canals, rail-road-tracks, and structures, and bridges. It is intended to leave behind the caissons, and to mount the cannon-eers, thus enabling the battery to follow the rapid move-ments of the cavalry force.

"In making the expedition, the co-operation of the troops stationed near Centreville is so far desired, to draw the attention of the enemy stationed at Culpepper, and on the line towards the Rapidan.

"Major-general Sigel is acquainted with the plan of the expedition, and is willing to co-operate, making a demonstration towards the Rappahannock railroad bridge.

"The expedition starting at an early hour, is to proceed by the Dumfries road, crossing Occoquan by Hogs-ford, thence fording Chopowansie, Beaverdam Creek, Canon and Deep Creek to Morrisville, from Morrisville to Barnetts ford, Rappahannock, remaining for the night; the advance occupying Ely's ford on the Rapidan. A part of the force is to push on the road north of Stevens-burg, crossing the railroad between Culpepper and the Rappahannock, destroying the track and telegraph wire, and then proceeding to Teetham river, destroy the rail-road bridge, after making a demonstration on Culpepper, is to return back towards Centreville, joining the troops of General Sigel which were advanced to the Rappa-hannock line. The main force after resting for the night on the Rappahannock, is to cross by day-break Ely's Ford, and then passing through Chancellorsville, proceed on the road to Louisa Court-house.

"After recrossing the river Go Ta, N. E. Creek Douglas, arriving at North Anna, take the Orange road, then running southward, cross the South Anna and proceed to Newark, passing the railroad four miles from Louisa Court-house. The command, after destroying railroad communication, would proceed on a forced night-march to the Charlottesville railroad bridge over Rivanna, where it is expected they would arrive by daylight ; while a part of the men are occupied in destroying the bridge and railroad track, another force will be sent east of Carter's Mountain to destroy the bridge south of Charlottesville. Another detachment would be sent to Columbia to destroy the canal, which is believed to be one of the main channels of supplying their army.

"Should there be no indication of a large force near Gordonsville, it is intended to return by the road west of South Mountain and then by Cave's Ford, and passing around Culpepper back to the line of the Rappahannock.

"Should however, a large force of the enemy be posted near the Rapidan and Charlottesville, it is intended to take the road running along the Rivanna on its southern shore, thence crossing by the Union Mills, proceed by Shannon Hill to Potterville, destroying, before reaching the latter place, the railroad track.

"This line of retreat seems to be perfectly safe, as there are no troops in that region, but after crossing Potterville the line of retreat to the Rapidan may be contested. It is intended therefore to proceed first to Spottsylvania Court-house, and then if forces should be near the fords, to take the old-mining road to Fredericksburg.

"Should the enemy have succeeded in assembling a large force in front of Fredericksburg, it is intended to go south to Guiney station and thence to Port Royal. Although the last road is very much out of the way, it presents the advantage of a safe retreat, in case the other lines are occupied by the enemy. It may be added that it would be very desirable to have one or two gun-boats on the Rappahannock to protect the passage of the river, should it be found necessary to take the latter road. This road will only be taken in case of necessity.

"At Charlottesville, I think there are but few troops, and that I can take the place and destroy the depots of provisions which may be there.

"A raid on our part is necessary to inspire our troops and restore confidence through the country in the cavalry force.

"I can move within four days from this line.

"GEORGE D. BAYARD,
"*Brigadier-general Commanding Cavalry.*"

"HEADQUARTERS DEFENCES OF WASH-
INGTON, *Oct. 21st*, 1862.

"*General Bayard, Commanding Cavalry* :

"General, your plan for a movement of cavalry by a route suggested in your memorial of the fifteenth instant, to Charlottesville and Columbia on the James river has been presented to the Commander-in-Chief of the army, who directs me to say, that he regards it as too hazardous at the present time, to undertake the entire route. He also directs me to say, that the march should be limited to the Rapidan and Rappahannock rivers. And that the destruction of the bridges, and communications rebuilt by the rebels on this route, will be advisable. He also directs that information be communicated to these headquarters, before the expedition shall leave, of the time, purpose, and extent of the march. For the reason, that the exigencies of the public service may call for the use of the cavalry in other directions. Information received this morning from a deserter represents that a strong force is posted at Culpepper.

"I am, General, very respectfully,

"Your obedient servant,

"N. P. BANKS.

"*Major-general Commanding Defences of Washington.*"

To his Mother

"HEADQUARTERS CAVALRY DIVISION,
CAMP AT UPTON HILLS,
Oct. 26th, 1862.

"To-morrow I move to the front, and assume command in front of Sigel. I presume the whole army will soon follow, and I fear that we shall have active operations the whole winter. This may interfere with my marriage, which we have intended should take place on the eighteenth of December, my twenty-seventh birthday. Unless I could get a leave of absence then for at least a week, the wedding will possibly have to be postponed until spring. If there be fighting imminent, I cannot ask for leave."

The following letter was written by the volunteer aide of General Bayard, his cousin, William Bayard.

To Mrs. Bayard.

"CAMP NEAR UPPERVILLE, VA., *Nov. 4th*, 1862.

"Although the general commenced this letter by dating it, yet he is so pressed with duties, that he has commissioned me to write for him.

"After our movement commenced, our first camp was three miles the other side of Fairfax Court-house. From there we marched to Aldie, where we came upon Steuart's cavalry, under Fitzhugh Lee, with four guns. Major Falls, with a squadron of First New Jersey Cavalry, attacked vigorously, and the enemy retired. Then came on an artillery-fight, in which some six or eight of our men were wounded, none seriously.

"The general, lieut. colonel and Major Falls went to the front yesterday. This way we have advanced to camp two miles from Upperville with only a ridge of elevated ground between us and the enemy. The general has only his first brigade here now—expects the second very soon—while the third is temporarily under Sigel. So he commands a division and ought to be made major-general and will be we think in a few days."

To his Mother.

CAMP AT RAPPAHANNOCK STATION, }
November 10th, 1862. }

"I am well and we are here, but I am sad that McClellan is removed. I hope no misfortune will result. I had a little shelling last evening. I saved the bridge here and hold it now."

To his Father.

CAMP NEAR HARTWOOD CHURCH, }
EIGHT MILES FROM FREDERICKSBURG, }
November 20th, 1862. }

"We are here. It is raining tremendously. I am in Franklin's grand division—all well."

To his Father.

" HEADQUARTERS BROOKE'S STATION, }
November, 22d, 1862. }

" I am now in Franklin's army and command all his calvary. I am pleased with this, as Franklin and Reynolds are the ablest men in this army. I think our country will be sick of the bargain before they get through with it. We are here trying to get something to eat. It is pretty hard work though. I don't believe the army will move for ten days yet or perhaps two weeks. When we do move we will very soon have a battle. I have been troubled a good deal of late with rheumatism owing to having been thoroughly drenched with the rain. I ought to be in the hospital. But I must go with this army through. I am Senior-general of cavalry. Honor and glory are before me—shame lurks in the rear. It looks as if I should not be able to leave at the time appointed for my marriage, but will have to postpone it till this campaign is over."

To his Father.

" CAMP AT BROOKE S STATION, }
November 29*th,* 1862. }

" We are still lying here and the Lord only knows how much longer we shall be here. My horses have been taken sick. I shall have to send them home to you. My horse Falmouth (the one presented), I shall lose. Rush's lancers are ordered to join me and I will then have about three thousand effective troops."

The following spirited account of them ovement of Gen. Bayard after he left Upton Hills is from the pen of the army-correspondent of the NEW YORK TIMES.

The Occupation of Rappahannock Station by
General Bayard—An Artillery Skirmish—
The Bridge and Railroad in Good Order.

"Rappahannock Station, }
Saturday, Nov. 8th, 1862. }

" The return of one to a place from which he had
been, but a short time before, forced to leave inconti-
nently, and with a sharp shower of grape and canister in
his rear to expedite his movements, as may well be supposed, is fraught with no little degree of interest. It was
with a remembrance of such an occasion, that I approached Rappahannock station last evening, in the
wake of Bayard's cavalry. But a little more than two
months ago, with the whole army commanded by Major-
general Pope at my heels, I was compelled to leave the
very spot from which I now write under a force of circumstances which all are bound to recognize. The ske-
daddle of the Union army from the line of the Rappahannock must be fresh in the minds of every newspaper-
reader, and need not be particularly detailed at this time.
It was a disgraceful, because unnecessary retreat. We
again approach the scene of our former disgrace under
more encouraging circumstances. The Union army,
beaten at Cedar Mountain, was then retreating before an
exultant and overbearing foe ; on the contrary, it is now
advancing upon or to circumvent that same foe, and with
an encouraging prospect of success. Then the army
was, to a certain extent, demoralized, as all retreating
armies, must, to a greater or less extent, necessarily be;
but now the scene is reversed, and the enemy, though
doing it sulkily, is fleeing before it.

" Gen. Bayard, with cavalry and artillery, approached

the scene of their former triumph, last evening after nightfall. A small picket, stationed on the Rappahannock bridge, received the first intimation of the approach of a Union force, by a shell passing over their heads, and landing in the enemy's camp beyond, to which the picket-guard speedily retreated in the utmost consternation ; the camp, consisting of about one regiment of infantry, and a small force of cavalry, and four guns, was at once in a terrible commotion ; the camp-fires were extinguished, and the force fell back to the main camp, after responding to the abrupt salutation they had received from a six-pounder. The lights having been extinguished, left no mark for the artillerists, and consequently but few shots were fired. This morning the enemy, having received reinforcements, took a favorable position for artillery practice, and commenced returning in kind the compliments extended to them last evening. Our six-pounders were put to the work in hand with spirit, and the gunners on the opposite side of the river were forced to retire beyond the reach of powder and ball. The enemy's fire was very much at random, and no one was seriously injured in the Union force. Gen. Bayard, acting under orders, declined to avail himself of a tempting opportunity afforded him to cross the river, and whip the whole camp, and the enemy having retired, we rested in position. Thus matters stand to-night.

" Lieutenant-colonel Blount, Acting Assistant-Adjutant-general to General Longstreet, together with two sergeants and ten men of the rebel army, were captured on Friday, near the Rappahannock river by General Bayard. It seems, from the rebel colonel's own account, that the pickets of his army were enjoying the effects of a little whisky, and, to test their vigilance, Colonel Blount approached the picket line incog., accepted the invitation to "smile" with the pickets, and passed uninterrupted outside their lines. Before he was enabled to retrace his steps, and before he was aware of the reality the matter was assuming, he found himself the unwilling guest of the ever-vigilant Bayard.

"The bridge at this point is in good condition, and we shall not be surprised to see the steam-horse, with the Union flag set, crossing the Rappahannock again, within a few days, headed for Culpepper. The stream at this point is low, and can be forded at many points other than the regular fords. Gen. Pleasanton, on the extreme right of the army, has crossed the river on a reconnoissance, and no one need feel surprised to hear that Gen. Bayard has gone off on a similar project for the left flank, at an early day. The owners of property in this vicinity have not manifested any great degree of enterprise in the way of improvements, since my last visit to the place. A few shanties, with here and there a house in the distance, is all that there is to be seen to relieve the barren waste —made so by the exigencies of the war.

"Gen. Bayard's command, for the last ten days, has been constantly on the move. Starting from Chantilly in the early part of last week, it was engaged with Steuart's force at Aldie—an account of which I furnished at the time. Rebel soldiers captured recently say that in the fight at Aldie, their loss was much more heavy than we had any knowledge of; they estimate the rebel loss to have averaged two men in every company engaged. Almost daily from that time to the present, Gen. Bayard has been skirmishing with the enemy, everywhere defeating him, and taking many prisoners. This force has rendered heretofore distinguished service, particularly when covering the rear of Gen. Pope's army last August, on its retreat from the fatal field of Slaughter Mountain, until that army was in front of Washington. It is now in better condition than ever before, notwithstanding the arduous service it has recently rendered, and to-day equals almost any cavalry force, in efficiency, in the world."

The following letter, was the last except one (exclusively on family subjects), and the despatch after he was wounded, which was written home by General Bayard.

To his Father.

" HEADQUARTERS CAVALRY BRIGADE, }
" CAMP BROOKE STATION, *Dec.* 2d, 1862. }

" My ' Falmouth ' horse died the day after I wrote you last.

" If we are here a week from this time I shall hand in my application for leave. I shall apply for twenty days' leave. Franklin has to sign it, and approve or disapprove, and then it has to go to the Secretary of War. If they contemplate an early movement it will not be granted, nor will I apply for it if there is any certainty of an immediate march onward."

Gen. McClellan was relieved from the command of the Army of the Potomac, by the President, November fifth, 1862, and General Ambrose E. Burnside, appointed Commander-in-Chief in his place.

According to the report of Gen. Burnside, November thirteenth, 1862, the position occupied by the different corps Army of the Potomac was as follows :

'First. Second and Fifth Corps, near Warrenton.

'Sixth Corps, at New Baltimore.

'Ninth Corps, with Stoneman's and Whipple's Divisions, on both sides of the river, in the neighborhood of Waterloo.

'Eleventh Corps, at Gainsville, New Baltimore and the Gap.

'Pleasanton at Jefferson and Amissville, with advance on Hazel River.

'Bayard at Rappahannock Station and neighborhood.

'Slocum was still at Harper's Ferry and Fayetteville.

'There were no pontoons with the moving army at this time, and our supplies had run very low.'

The larger part of the army it appears was pretty well concentrated at, and not far from Warrenton. The President and General Halleck preferred that the advance on Richmond should be from Warrenton to Gordonville or in that direction.

Many reasons favored that route. The streams to be crossed were fewer in number, and generally fordable, the distance not materially different from the route adopted as railroad, for much of the way could be made available for transportation of supplies, the country was well known beyond, and the army was already concentrated there to a considerable extent. Gen. Burnside however, preferred the Fredericksburg route, and prevailed on the President and Gen. Halleck to concur with him in such preference.

But a fatality seemed from the first, to doom the route by Fredericksburg to misfortune.

November fourteenth, Gen. Burnside received the following dispatch:

"WASHINGTON, *Nov.* 14*th*, 1862.
" *To Maj.-Gen.* A. E. BURNSIDE, *Commanding Army of
the Potomac* :
" The President has just assented to your plan.   He
thinks it will succeed if you move rapidly, otherwise not."
" H. W HALLECK, *General-in-Chief.*"

In his report General Burnside says :

" This dispatch was received at my headquarters
Warrenton, at eleven o'clock on the morning of the fourteenth inst., and I at once issued orders for the different
commands to move in accordance with the above mentioned plan.

" The remark in this dispatch, indicating the great
necessity for the speedy movement of the troops was
entirely in accordance with my own views, as the season
was so far advanced that I looked for but little time in
which to move the army effectively.

" The distance from Warrenton to Fredericksburg
does not exceed sixty miles, and from Waterloo, Gainsville, New Baltimore and other points where army corps
were camped, not exceeding one hundred miles."

The " speedy movement " which General Burnside
approved, as executed by him, was dilatory in a lamentable degree.

In his report, he complains that the pontoons which
were promised him by General Halleck should be
" promptly forwarded," were not forwarded with the despatch expected.

Undoubtedly there was sad blundering in relation to
these pontoons, the blame for which must be shared by
Generals Halleck and Woodbury and General Burnside,

himself. Nevertheless the pontoons arrived on the twenty-fifth of November, *two weeks before Gen. Burnside was
prepared to use them.*   For his report says, after speaking
of the movements of the troops: "These arrangements
were made with a view to throwing the bridges on the
eleventh of December."

General Burnside says in his report :

"It was my intention, and I so informed General
Halleck, to cross some of the cavalry, and, possibly, a
small force of light infantry and artillery over the fords
of the Rappahannock and Rapidan, with a view to moving rapidly upon Fredericksburg and holding the south
bank of the river while bridges were being laid."

And why should not the whole army have been
crossed at these fords ? If the enemy could have dictated
to General Burnside, *where* he should have crossed the
Rappahannock, without doubt they would have designated
the very point which he selected.

General Burnside says : "Before issuing final orders,
I concluded that the enemy would be more surprised by
a crossing at or near Fredericksburg, where we were
making no preparations, than by a crossing at 'Snicker's
Neck,' and I determined to make the attempt at the
former place.

We should think he did *surprise* them, crossing the
river at the very point where they were best prepared to
meet him.   But we do not propose to make any plenary
criticism on the movements which resulted in the battle
of Fredericksburgh.   Yet those who have studied that
disastrous event cannot when speaking of it, fail to remark some of the mistakes by which it was signalized.

The whole army on the evening of the twelfth of De-

cember was in the position designated for attack. But
when the attack was made, it was not simultaneous. Gen.
Meade's division, part of Gen. Franklin's corps, did not
advance until nine o'clock. This was the first advance
of any part of the army. But Gen. Sumner with his corps
was not ordered to attack until after eleven o'clock, and
Gen. Hooker's support, was not ordered to his aid until
half past one o'clock.

From General Franklin's report it will be seen*
that the pontoons, by which his wing of the army crossed,
were finished, one at nine A. M., and another at eleven
A. M., on the eleventh of December. Franklin's whole
force was across the river by one o'clock P. M., on the
twelfth. "At daylight on that morning of the twelfth,
Smith's corps began to cross. It was followed by
Bayard's brigade, which went immediately to the front to
make a recognizance.

The following order was issued to General Franklin :

" HEADQUARTERS ARMY OF THE POTOMAC. ⎰
          Dec. 13*th*,—5 : 55 A. M. ⎱
" *Major-general* FRANKLIN, *Commanding Left Grand
Division, Army of the Potomac :*

" General Hardie will carry this dispatch to you, and
remain with you during the day. The General Commanding directs that you keep your whole command in
position for a rapid movement down the old Richmond
road, and you will send out at once a division, at least,
to pass below Smithfield, to seize, if possible, the heights
near Captain Hamilton's, on this side of the Massaponax,
taking care to keep it well supported and its line of re-

* See Appendix I.

treat open.   He has ordered another column, of a division or more, to be moved from Gen. Sumner's command up the plank road to its intersection with the telegraph road, where they will divide, with a view to seizing the heights on both of those roads.   Holding those two heights with the heights near Captain Hamilton's, will, he hopes, compel the enemy to evacuate the whole ridge between these points.   I make these moves by columns, distant from each other, with a view of avoiding the possibility of a collision of our own forces, which might occur in a general movement during the fog.   Two of General Hancock's Divisions are in your rear, at the bridges, and will remain there as supports.

"Copies of instructions given to Generals Sumner and Hooker, will be forwarded by an orderly to you very soon.

"You will keep your whole command in readiness to move at once, as soon as the fog lifts.

"The watchword, which, if possible, should be given to every company, will be 'Scott,' I have the honor to be, general, very respectfully, your obedient servant,

"JNO. G. PARKER, *Chief of Staff.*"

It will be perceived that General Franklin was ordered to send "at once" only a single division.   He obeyed this part of the order by pushing forward Gen. Meade at nine A. M.   His *whole command* however, was ordered not to move until the fog rose.

General Burnside says in his report : " At half past ten A. M., I sent Captain P. M. Lydig of my staff to Gen. Franklin, to ascertain the condition of affairs in his front, as I was anxiously expecting to hear that the hill near Hamilton had been carried." Captain Lydig returne l and reported in person to General Burnside at half past twelve o'clock. But it was not until an hour afterwards that General Burnside sent to General Franklin a peremptory order to attack.

A strict construction of his orders justified General Franklin in not attacking with his whole force, until the fog rose. But Gen. Burnside should have been *absolutly certain* of his orders to Gen. Franklin being executed as he himself understood them. Franklin's force constituted nearly half of Burnside's whole army ; and its early, prompt movement, Burnside well knew, was indispensable to success.

Mr. Greeley, in his history of the " American Conflict," says of the order of Gen. Burnside above, dated at 5. 55., A. M :

" It was after seven A. M. of the fatal day, when Franklin received his orders ; which if they were intended to direct a determined attack in *full force*, were certainly very blindly and vaguely worded ; whereas a military order should be as precise and clear as language will allow, and as *positive* as the circumstances will warrant."

Time in military movements is an element of success; —and this, General Burnside does not appear to have properly appreciated. The movement of his troops on the thirteenth and previously, as well as that of his pontoons, were dilatory to a sad degree.

Gen. Franklin in his examination by the Congressional committee, March twenty-eighth, 1863,* testifies : " About five o'clock in the afternoon of the twelfth, Gen. Burnside came down to look at the condition of things.

* Conduct of War, part I, page 707.

He appeared to be pleased with the appearance of affairs on the left, and had a long conversation with Gen. Smith and myself. I urged him to give orders which would enable me to put my command in such a position, that *a very strong attack could be made there at daybreak the next morning.* He left at six o'clock, without consenting to make the attack, or without saying that he would not do it. The last thing I said to him was to give me the orders, as soon as possible, at any rate, whatever they were. He said I should have them in the course of two or three hours. I then said I hope they will be here before twelve o'clock to-night, at any rate.' "

It seems very probable, from the official reports of both Generals Burnside and Franklin, that if the entire army had advanced simultaneously, even when Meade advanced, the victory might have been ours. If the fog did not prevent Meade's moving, it need not have deterred the rest of the army from attacking.

The advance of the right wing of the army met with no such success, as that of Franklin under General Meade. Sumner's grand division encountered insuperable obstacles, and was only a *forlorn* hope.

A belt of hills girdles Fredericksburg on the south and southwest. There the enemy were entrenched, and unseen by our troops, poured upon them as they approached a deadly stream of fire. Again and again did our gallant men march upon the positions of their foe, until their commanders saw that the carnage was fruitless, and would no longer permit the slaughter to be continued.

General Bayard was posted, with the batteries attached to his command, on the left of Gen. Franklin's force. There he was engaged all the morning of the thirteenth, more or less, with the enemy's skirmishers and advance. His last directions, before leaving his troops to go to the headquarters of Gen. Franklin, were given to his artillery officer to change the position of some of his guns. A little before two o'clock he rode to headquarters, to receive such orders as Gen. Franklin might deem proper to give. He found the general in a grove of trees with some of his staff and other general officers. The enemy were then throwing their shells at and around this grove. Gen. Bayard, soon after he arrived, having dismounted, seated himself at the foot of a tree ; but with his face towards the quarter from whence the shells came. He was warned by a brother-officer of his needless exposure, and invited to change his position. This he did not do, but remained for some time participating in the conversation of those around. In a little while, however, he rose from his seat, and hardly stood erect, when he was struck by a shell just below the hip, shattering his thigh near the joint. He was immediately removed to the hospital in the neighborhood.

The surgeon, after examining the wound, inquired if he desired that amputation should be performed. The wounded general asked in reply what chances for life amputation would afford, and when told very few, if any, he declined the operation, and resigned himself to his fate.

He preserved that calm, cool, intrepid self-possession by which he was always distinguished, to the last. He dictated a telegram home, one to his betrothed, and one to his friend Col. A. V. Colburn,* who was with him at

---

* A more gallant and noble officer was never in the service of the people of the United States. See Appendix G.

12*

West Point, and on the Plains ; and to whom he was much attached.　He took an affectionate leave of several of his army friends, particularly of his aide, Major H. C. Weir, and Lieut. Colwell.　Being placed under the influence of morphine, he did not appear to suffer much pain, but gradually sank in his last sleep about twenty-four hours after he was struck down.

The following note was dictated by Gen. Bayard, about twelve hours after he was wounded, and forwarded by his aide, H. C. Weir.

" HEADQUARTERS TWO MILES BELOW
"FREDERICKSBURG, Dec. 14th, 1862.　1.45 A. M.

" *Dear Father and Mother*,

" I have to dictate to you a few words ere it becomes too late.　My strength is rapidly wasting away.　Good bye, dearest father and mother; give my love to my sisters.　I send you, mother, my watch and my pay due for November and part of December.

*　　*　　*　　*　　*　　*

*　　*　　*　　*　　*　　*

My black mare and sorrel horse I give to you, father. There are about sixty dollars in my pocket-book.　There are papers in my trunk to be turned over to the Department (Quartermaster's), to settle.　Once more, good bye, beloved father, mother, sisters, all.
" Ever yours,
" GEORGE D. BAYARD."
" My sabre goes to father."

About three o'clock of the thirteenth of December, his father received the following telegram from General Bayard. " I have been badly hurt, come on."

His father started that night from Philadelphia at eleven P. M., and reached Fredericksburg the next evening. He found that his son had died that day at two, P. M., and that his remains in charge of his aide, Major Weir, had gone to Acquia Creek, and would go up the Potomac by steamboat the next morning. His father reached Acquia Creek the next morning, in time for the steamboat, and accompanied the remains to Washington. They were left there on Monday to be embalmed. They were forwarded thence to Princeton, where the funeral took place.

The following letter from the *Philadelphia Inquirer,* gives a correct statement of the funeral ceremonies :

" THE FUNERAL OF GENERAL BAYARD."

[Special Correspondence of the *Inquirer.*]

" PRINCETON, N. J., *December* 19*th*, 1862.

" The funeral obsequies of the late Brigadier-general GEORGE DASHIELL BAYARD took place here to-day, being among the most imposing and solemn that have ever occured in this ancient borough. The arrangements were made and orders given by the Adjutant-general of the state, General Robert F. Stockton, for a military funeral. The body was received here on Wednesday evening, and lay in state with a military guard from the Governor's Guards of this place, who acted as body-guard throughout the ceremonies.

" The Marshal of the day was Major Cummings,

late of the First New Jersey Cavalry. The pall-bearers were the following Brigadier-generals :—

 "General Cornelius Van Vorst, of Jersey City,

 "General Joel Parker, of Monmouth (Gov. elect),

 "General George M. Robeson, of Camden,

 "General Palmer, of the United States Army,

 "General N. N. Halstead, of Newark,

 "General Theodore Runyon, of Newark.

 "General Bayard's Aides were also present.

"The military escort was one regiment of infantry, Col. Napton, of Trenton; one company of cavalry, the Princeton Troop, Captain Hamilton; with two pieces cf artillery from the State Arsenal, being manned by Webb's artillery-cadets of Trenton—the whole escort being under the command of General Hatfield.

"A large number of distinguished persons were in the procession, among whom we recognized Edwin A. Stevens, Com. Stockton, Major-general Cook, General Stevens, of Gloucester county, and Judge Carpenter.

"Between thirty and forty of the principal citizens of Woodbury, neighbors of the father of the deceased, S. J. Bayard, Esq, were also in the procession.

"The clergymen of Princeton and several of the professors were also in the procession.

"The remains were inclosed in a metallic coffin, with a glass over the face, and were placed in the Canal office for public view. A large number availed themselves of this opportunity to look upon the face of one who made such great promise of usefulness in his profession. The features were natural and easily recognized by those even who had looked upon the photograph, where he appears as a cavalry officer.

" The body was borne by United States soldiers, detailed by Major Jones, and United States officers stationed at Trenton. Many military officers, as well as distinguished citizens, were present, who followed the hearse, together with the escort, in the inverse order of their rank. The arms of the escort were all reversed. The religious services were held in the First Presbyterian Church, and were conducted by Rev. Dr. Hodge, assisted by Rev. Dr. McDonald and Rev. Dr. Baird, of Woodbury, N. J.

" The discourse by Dr. Hodge was very impressive, embracing a brief history of the brilliant career of the young and daring officer; but as I understand it is to be published, I will make no further comments. At the grave—which was prepared in the Princeton Cemetery, along side of that of his grandfather, Judge Samuel Bayard—the burial service of the Episcopal Church was read by Rev. Mr. Norris, of Woodbury. The order was here given to the military to 'rest on arms,' and three rounds of small arms were fired by the escort. Any who are acquainted with Princeton Cemetery will feel that it is fitting that the remains of so brave an officer should find their resting-place in the midst of so many of the illustrious dead ! "

GEORGE DASHIELL BAYARD
SANS PEUR ET SANS REPROCHE.

APPENDIX.

"A people," says Macaulay, "which takes no pride in the noble achievements of remote ancestors, will never achieve any thing worthy to be remembered with pride by remote descendants." And Edmund Burke remarks, "that those who do not treasure up the memory of their ancestors, do not deserve to be remembered by posterity."

CONTENTS OF APPENDIX.

APPENDIX A.

THE parents of Gen. Bayard were Samuel J. Bayard and Jane Dashiell. His mother was a daughter of Rev. George Dashiell, a distinguished clergyman of the Episcopal Church, who, at the instance of his daughter, wrote, a few years before his death, in the family bible, the following recollections of his family history.

"My great-grandfather was a French Huguenot. After the revocation of the Edict of Nantes by Louis XIV, he fled to England to escape the bloody persecution that was then raging against the Huguenots, to compel them to submit to the fooleries and idolatries of Popery. What the family standing was in France, I know not. There has been a tradition in the family, that they were connected with the family of Henry IV But whether this tradition is founded on fact, or not, is of no consequence. The family must have been of high respectability or he could not have married into the Fairfax family.

"My grandfather emigrated to America, and settled on the eastern shore of Maryland, on the north side of Wicomico creek. He purchased all the land from the mouth to the head of the creek, on which he built a large brick house. My grandfather was probably the eldest son, as he inherited the family plate, marked with the name of Fairfax, which he brought with him from England. The plate and the home place, on which stood the family mansion, he left to my father, who was the youngest son, and but two years old when my grandfather died. In that family mansion I was born.

"GEORGE DASHIELL."

He died the fourth of March, 1852, in New York city, at the house of his son-in-law, William Bayard. The following is part of his obituary, published in the *Christian Observer*, Philadelphia, April seventeenth, 1852.

" The Rev. George Dashiell was born in Somerset county, Maryland, and received a classical education, and was graduated at Washington College, Chestertown, of the same state. Soon after he left college, he was converted to God, and in his nineteenth year commenced preaching. At the close of the revolution, the church was desolate, religion everywhere at a low ebb, ministers very few, and not evangelical—he saw the ruin, and his ardor hurried him to the work at once. In his twenty-first year, he was ordained at Philadelphia by Bishop White, for whom he ever entertained a profound and just esteem. On the eastern shore of Maryland, he passed the earlier years of his ministry—a most active and effective ministry—revivals constantly attending his preaching, until the whole peninsula seemed to glow with new life and power. At the commencement of the present century, he removed to Baltimore. He had visited that city upon invitation, and a wealthy merchant was so charmed with his eloquence and evangelical preaching, that he determined, if possible, to secure his services. Accordingly, pretty much at his own expense, he erected a spacious building, at that time the largest church in the city ; and Mr Dashiell, then a young man, in feeble health, a stranger, was invited by a few gentlemen to begin his ministry in Baltimore. Until the completion of the new building, by the christian courtesy of the German church, under the care of the venerable and apostolic Otterbien, Mr. Dashiell preached in their house on the morning of every Lord's day to crowds of people. God was with him. Sinners were converted, saints rejoiced, and by the time the edifice, prepared for him, was finished, a congregation filled it to overflowing. 'So mightily grew the word of God and prevailed.' For a long time he maintained a most prosperous course in the new church. Years passed—and with every year constant accessions of spiritual devoted christians. There seemed to be a perpetual revival. The prayer-meetings were always full, generally crowded. He had the happiest manner in engaging the co-operation of the church. The members were all active. They were enlivened by fervent exercises, and contributed to the growth of the church. Scarcely a male but led in prayer and gave a word of exhortation, as occasion offered. Of all the churches I have known, not one, to my apprehension, has approximated so near to the primitive model as this. And although it has long been sundered and scattered, as were the disciples at Jerusalem, upon the persecution, that arose about Stephen, I doubt not that its name is not only remembered, but its influence still felt. In the course of his long ministry at that place, hundreds professed the name of our Lord Jesus.

"Under his auspices, several young men entered the ministry—among them, Bishop Stone, late diocesan of Maryland. His house was the house of these young men, as long as they chose ; and his purse was open as their wants and necessities required.

"As a pastor, in dilligence, kindness and fidelity he was scarcely surpassèd. None escaped his attention ; but among the poor and destitute, the sick and the dying —not only of his own charge, but of the many, who in a large city may truly say—'no man careth for my soul,' his ministrations were constant and untiring.

"As a preacher, he was eminently *practical.*—He was not given to speculation. He had no taste for theories. He believed the word with the simplicity and confidence of a child. His constant theme was 'Jesus Christ and him crucified.' In the prayer-meeting, and the sick room, did he set Him forth most fervently and powerfully. In this lay whatever of strength he had. Though not a Calvinist in theory—he was, as the late Mr. Duncan of Baltimore, once said to him, the strongest Calvinistic preacher he knew.

"He was habitually *devotional.* He rose early in the morning, always, when in health, with or before the sun ; and his morning hymn was as regular and as punctual as the song of birds. Until breakfast, the time was devoted to prayer and the reading of the Bible. Though of fine literary taste, and fond of the poetry, philosophy, and eloquence of English literature ; of late years such works as 'Romaine's Life of Faith,' 'Walk of Faith,' etc., were his chief companions, the Bible ever constant and supreme. His devotional spirit was the secret of his

success. It kept his mind always ready ; and his sentiments always came fresh, warm and glowing.

"His was a most catholic spirit. He loved all men
that loved Christ. Orthodox in his own creed, he could
easily allow for diversities in things indifferent. Ever
treated by most of the orthodox churches as a brother,
he regarded them with sincere affection as brethren.
He preached for them, when invited, communed with
them, and labored with them, to build them up in their
most holy faith.

"He never ceased to preach. Though for thirty
years he had no stated charge, and was connected with
no particular denomination after his removal to the West,
whither the most of his children had preceded·him, he
never withheld his services where they were acceptable ;
and up to the last of his life he spoke with a fervor of
spirit, and strength of diction, a clearness of utterance,
a beauty of elocution, and a grace of manner, that won
admiration from polished auditors, and often reminded
his old friends of the strength and vivacity of his earlier
days."

APPENDIX B.

THE CHEVALIER BAYARD.

THE Memoirs of the Chevalier, written by his secretary* three years after his death, opens with the following account of his birthplace and parentage:

"The county of Dauphiny, which now forms part of the fair realm of France, abounds with good and gentle families which have sent forth so many visitors and noble knights, that their renown is bruited throughout christendom, and as scarlet surpasses all other dyes, the Dauphinese are called by all know them (without disparagement of other regions), the scarlet of the French nobility.

"One of these families of ancient and noble extraction, is that of Bayard, and well have those who have sprang from it maintained the honor of their house. For at the battle of Poictiers the great-great-grandfather of Pierre Bayard, the good knight without fear and without reproach, fell by the side of the French King John. At the battle of Agincourt, was slain his great-grandfather;

* The title of this work is :—" The *very joyous pleasant and refreshing history*, of the *feats, exploits, triumphs and achievements* of the GOOD KNIGHT, *without fear and without reproach, the gentle* LORD DE BAYARD."

his grandfather was left on the field of Montlhéry with six mortal wounds not to speak of lesser ones : and at the battle of Guignegaste, his father was so severely wounded, that he was never afterwards able to leave his house, where he died at the age of eighty."

Pierre du Terrail Seigneur de Bayard was born in 1476, at the Chateau de Bayard, in the valley of Graisivudun, a few leagues from Grenoble, the principal city of Dauphiny. For more than thirty years he served in the armies of France. For valor and skill as a leader he was unsurpassed, in an age when chivalry was still honored. At that time, none but princes of the blood or court-minions and favorites, were permitted to command the armies of France. But Bayard often directed the movements of her armies, and dictated the order of battle when others were in command and had the chief credit of success. He was brave, prudent and sagacious as a soldier ; a christian of unaffected piety, a courteous and generous gentleman, whose honor and virtue were proverbial in a wicked age. No vice, no act of cruelty or meanness ever sullied his fame. He was honored by his foes as well as by his friends, and his death equally lamented by both. He was killed by a gun-shot at the age of forty-eight. Russel the historian of modern Europe says : " Here (Biagrassa), fell the Chevalier Bayard, whose contempt of the arts of courts prevented him from ever rising to the chief command, but who was always called in times of real danger to the posts of difficulty and importance."

The age in which he lived, and all succeeding ages have with one accord bestowed upon him the appellation of "The good knight, without fear and without reproach."

There are many points of resemblance between the Chevalier's career and that of the Bayard who fell at Fredericksburg. The Chevalier always led the advance of the French armies ; so did General Bayard lead in the armies to which he was attached. The Chevalier was always in the rear protecting the army when retreating ; so also was General Bayard. Both were dexterous horsemen. Both were among the bravest of the brave. Both were remarkable for their courtesy and obedience to their superiors in command. Both died of gun-shots. And both in their last moments of life displayed that cool and calm composure with which the heroic soldier meets his death.

The papers of the Hon. Richard H. Bayard,* relating to the family history, have, through the kindness of his son, Richard Bassett Bayard, come into my hands. Among them, in the handwriting of the former, the following *memorandum* appears. A short time before his death, he showed the writer an extract from a French biographical dictionary, printed in the seventeenth century, which expressly refers to the Bayards of America as descendants from a branch of the Chevalier Bayard's family.

Notwithstanding the philosophic sentiment of Cicero, '*genus proceras et quæ non fecimus ipse, rex ea nostro voco,*' yet there is a natural desire and curiosity to know who were our predecessors, and to whom we owe our existence. Nor do the melancholy lines of Goldsmith weaken this desire :

---

* Hon. R. H. Bayard was twice elected to the Senate of U. S., and was afterward Minister-Resident at Berlin.

> " How loved, how honored one, avails thee not,
>   To whom related, or by whom begot,
>   A heap of dust alone remains of thee,
>   'Tis all thou art, and all the proud shall be."

Where there has been anything in qualities or actions to distinguish individuals, it is natural to desire to participate in the good-will and respect which they insure, and if not *ours*, in the sense in which the Roman orator uses the possessive pronoun, they are *more* ours than anybody else's.

" The BAYARD family, originally from France, derived their name from the chateau in Dauphiny, six leagues from Grenoble.

" The family name was Du Terrail, and the celebrated knight of that family, who was called ' *Le Chevalier sans peur et sans reproche*,' bore the name of Pierre du Terrail Seigneur de Bayard. He died on the thirtieth of April, 1524, at the age of forty-eight years, unmarried, and without issue. The members of the Terrail family, his collateral kinsmen, adopted his arms and being seigneurs de Bayard, bore that surname.

" During the religious troubles which distracted the kingdom of France in the sixteenth and seventeenth centuries, some of the family emigrated to Holland, and one of them married Anna Stuyvesant, sister of Peter Stuyvesant, the last Dutch governor of New York.

" Madame Anna Bayard, her husband being dead, accompanied her brother, Peter Stuyvesant, to New York, then called New Amsterdam, with her three sons, Balthazar, Peter, and Nicholas, where they landed on the fourteenth of May, 1647. From these three brothers, are descended all who bear that name in the United States. The Peter Bayard, above mentioned, is the person, who was one of the purchasers of the four necks of land on Bohemia Manor from Augustus Herman, which was afterwards called familiarly the Labbadee Fort.

"Bohemia Manor was patented to Augustus Herman in 1663 by Caecilius, first absolute Lord and Proprietor of Maryland, and confirmed by his son, Lord Baltimore, in 1682. It consisted of twenty thousand, seven hundred and sixty-nine acres, four thousand of which were in the state of Delaware."

APPENDIX C.

JOHN BAYARD.

COL. JOHN BAYARD, the great-grandfather of General Bayard, was born August eleventh, 1738, at the family mansion at Bohemia Manor, on a portion of which his great-grandfather settled in 1698. His father was James, youngest son of James Bayard and Mary Ashton. He was educated at Nottingham, Maryland, at an institution of high repute under the care of Rev. Samuel Finley, afterwards president of Princeton college, N. J. He and his brother James were twins, and married sisters, Misses Hodges of Philadelphia. He removed early in life to that city, and engaged in mercantile business. He became in Philadelphia a prominent man, and took an active part in the opposition to the attempt of Great Britain to tax and oppress the colonies. He joined the association called the Sons of Liberty, and John Adams in his Diary mentions him as one of a committee of that association, who, with Drs. Rush and Mifflin, at Frankfort intercepted the members of Congress of 1775 from the north, as they came, for the purpose of influencing them to choose Washington for Commander-in-Chief.

The Pennsylvania legislature in 1775–6 were not in

favor of independence, but a majority of the people were resolved upon it.   On the twenty-fourth of May 1776, a great public meeting took place in Independence square, the object of which was to compel the members of the legislature to declare in favor of independence, or resign. They resigned.   Bancroft, vol. viii., page 385, says : " On the twenty-fourth of May, a town-meeting of more than four thousand men was held in the State-house yard, to confront the instructions of the assembly against independence, with the vote of the Continental Congress, against ' oaths of allegiance, and the exercise of any kind of authority under the Crown.'   It was called to order by John Bayard, chairman of the inspection-committee for the county of Philadelphia; a patriot of singular purity of character and disinterestedness, personally brave, pensive, earnest and devout."

As soon as military preparation became necessary, a battalion of cavalry was organized, and John Bayard was elected and commissioned a colonel to command it.   He remained in command of this troop during the Revolutionary war.   He was in the battles of Brandywine, Germantown, and Trenton.

Late in the night preceding the battle of Princeton, Governor Joseph Reed and Col. Bayard crossed the Delaware, and arrived at the Coxe mansion (still standing near the old Trenton bridge).   Of course they supposed a battle at Trenton would take place in the morning, not aware that Washington had determined to surprise the British at Princeton in the morning.

Just before day, their servant roused them with the information that Washington had left for Princeton, and that the British were crossing the Assanpink.   They had only time to mount their horses, and pursuing the route taken by Washington, reached Princeton after the battle had been won.

When the war was over, Col. Bayard continued to take part in public affairs.   He was Speaker of the House of Assembly of Pennsylvania (the legislature then consisting of a single house), in 1784, and a member of the Continental Congress in 1785.

Col. Bayard's first wife was Miss Hodge of Philadelphia, whose brother Andrew was the father of Dr. Hugh L. Hodge, of the Medical College of that city, and of the Rev. Dr. Charles Hodge, professor in the Theological Seminary at Princeton, N. J.   The second wife of Col. Bayard was Miss Hodgden.   He soon lost her, and married Johanna White, sister of Gen. Anthony White, whose sister was the wife of Judge William Paterson, of New Jersey, of the Supreme Court of the United States.

After his third marriage, Col. Bayard removed to New Brunswick, New Jersey, and continued to reside there until his death in 1807.   He was several years presiding judge of the court of common pleas for Somerset county, New Jersey, and mayor of the city of New Brunswick.   He was trustee of the college of New Jersey at Princeton from 1778 to 1807, and for many years a delegate to the General Assembly of the Presbyterian Church.

CHILDREN OF COL. JOHN BAYARD.

Colonel Bayard had no issue by his second or third wife.   His children by the first wife, who attained maturity were James, Andrew, John M., Samuel, Nicholas, Jane, Margaret and Anna Maria.

APPENDIX D.

SAMUEL BAYARD.

SAMUEL, grandfather of General Bayard, was the fourth son of John Bayard.

He graduated at Princeton college in 1784, studied law with William Bradford, afterwards Attorney-general of the United States, and practiced law in Philadelphia, for seven years. In 1791, he was appointed clerk of the Supreme Court of the United States. After the ratification of the British Treaty, negotiated by Mr. Jay, he was appointed by General Washington, agent of the government to prosecute in the British admiralty courts, the claims of American citizens provided for by the treaty. He remained in London three or four years. On his return to the United States, he resided a few years with his father-in-law, Lewis Pintard, at New Rochelle. While there, Governor Jay appointed him president judge of the court of common pleas of Westchester county. He removed to New York city in 1803-4, and resumed the practice of law. He published about this time an edition with notes of Peake's Evidence, and an Abstract of the Laws of the United States, both works, useful at that time to the profession.

He was one of the founders of the New York Histori-

cal Society, now of established celebrity. Dr. John
W. Francis in his Discourse on the History of the Society,
delivered in 1858, thus refers to him, page 73: " The minutes of our first meeting notice the attendance of Samuel
Bayard. He was connected with the family of our
founder Pintard, and they were most intimate friends.
He was a gentleman of the old school, a scholar, a jurist,
a trustee of Princeton college, a public-spirited man,
and a hearty co-operator in establishing this association."

In 1806 he removed to Princeton, where he resided
until his death in 1840.

He was several years a member of the assembly of
the legislature of New Jersey, representing the county of
Somerset. He was presiding judge for many years of
the court of common pleas for that county. In 1814, he
was nominated and supported for Congress by the feder-
alists in his district, though not elected. He was always
a warm and decided federalist. But after the federal
party ceased to exist, he took no more interest in political affairs.

He was trustee of the College of New Jersey, and
treasurer of that institution for many years. He was also
a trustee of the Theological Seminary at Princeton. He
was for many years a delegate to the General Assembly
of the Presbyterian church. He was active in promot-
ing the course of religion, and with his relative, Elias
Boudinot was one of the founders of the American Bible
Society. He was a constant contributor to several religious publications.

Samuel Bayard married Martha Pintard, only daughter of Lewis Pintard (see notice of L. P. Appendix G).
His children were, Lewis, Susan, Samuel, William, Julia
and Caroline.

APPENDIX E.

THE BAYARDS IN AMERICA.

BALTHAZAR BAYARD, a Huguenot clergyman and professor of languages in a Paris institution, early in the seventeenth century left France to escape persecution on account of his religion. There is a tradition in the family that he was shipped from Rochelle in a hogshead. He soon rallied around him a congregation of Huguenot refugees, whose pastor he continued until his death.

He had three sons and a daughter. The daughter married Peter Stuyvesant, the last Dutch governor of New York. The widow of Balthazar accompanied Stuyvesant, and her sons and daughter to America, and arrived at New Amsterdam (now New York), May eleventh 1647.

The sons of Balthazar were named Peter, Balthazar and Nicholas.

Peter purchased lands on the Bohemia Manor, in 1684, a portion of which were in Delaware, and a portion in Cecil county, Maryland. He conveyed these lands to parties who reconveyed them to Samuel Bayard, Peter's son, who removed from New York, and settled there, and resided thereon until his death in 1789.

Peter married Blandina Conde. She was a lady of fine talents and great culture. She could write and speak the Latin, English, French and Low Dutch languages. She left very voluminous *MSS.*, which were lost during the revolutionary war. She was distinguished for her piety as well as learning. She was a lady of spirit and great influence in her neighborhood, and personally superintended and managed her plantation. At eighty years of age, she mounted her horse with agility, and controlled him with the dexterity of a skilful rider.

The issue of Peter and Blandina, were Peter, Samuel and James.

Peter (the second), married Susannah Richardson, whose issue was Elizabeth, who married the Rev. Dr. John Rodgers; Susannah, who married Jonathan Smith, whose sons were Jonathan Bayard Smith of Philadelphia, member of the old Congress, and Samuel Harrison Smith.

Samuel, second son of Peter and Blandina, had a son Stephen who went to Pittsburgh, from whom the Pittsburgh Bayards came.

James third son of Blandina and Peter, left two sons, John Bubenheim and James Ashton, so named after his mother's family. John Bubenheim dropped his middle name and always wrote his name John Bayard. In Appendix C., he is fully noticed. His twin brother James Ashton, was a surgeon in the revolutionary army, and died of the yellow fever in Charleston, S. C., while attached to the army in 1781. He left two sons, John Hodge and James Ashton. He married a Miss Hodge, sister of Colonel Bayard's wife. John Hodge left one daughter.

James Ashton graduated at Princeton college 1784, studied law in Philadelphia with James Ingersoll, and commenced practice in Wilmington, Delaware, in 1787. He was married to Anne Bassett, daughter of Governor

Bassett, of that state, who was also a senator in Congress, and judge of the Supreme Court of the United States, under the act passed at the close of John Adams' presidency.

James A., his son-in-law, was long distinguished as a politician and a statesman.

He was elected to the House of Representatives of Congress in 1796, and continued a member until 1803. Elected to the Senate of the United States in 1804, and remained in the Senate until 1813, when he was appointed commissioner to Ghent, to treat for peace with England. He was appointed Minister to Russia in 1815, but declined, and returning home, died July thirtieth, 1815. He took a prominent part in the election of president by the House of Representatives in 1801, as a leader of the Federal party, which after thirty-six ballots elected Mr. Jefferson. Having been appointed by Mr. Adams, Minister to France, and confirmed by the Senate on the nineteenth of Feb., 1801, he promptly declined, and, in a letter to his cousin, Samuel Bayard, of Princeton, said, that he could not consent to hold the office at the will of Mr. Jefferson. He and Gen. Pinckney, of South Carolina, and Morris, of New Hampshire, having terminated the contest by casting blank ballots, he said that he had ever made the motto of the Chevalier Bayard "without fear and without reproach," the rule of his conduct. His great speech, on the repeal of the Act respecting the organization of the Supreme Court, was long considered one of the ablest ever made in Congress.

He left four sons, and one daughter. The daughter never married. The sons were Richard H., James A., Edward, and Henry.

APPENDIX F.

THE NEW YORK BAYARDS.

BALTHAZAR BAYARD, who came over with Stuyvesant in 1647, married a Lockermans, and left a son and three daughters. The eldest daughter married Augustus Jay, grandfather of John Jay, Chief Justice of the United States. The second daughter married Samuel Verplanck. The son, Jacobus, married a Miss De Kay. His son married Mary Bowdoin, half-sister of Governor Bowdoin of Massachusetts.

Nicholas was the youngest of the three Bayards, who arrived in America in 1647. From him and Balthazar have descended the New York Bayards. He married a sister of Governor Stuyvesant, we think, before he left Holland. He was many years a member of the Council of State for the colonial Dutch government. He was eminent for his piety, as well as his political influence. In the turbulent period in which he lived, his integrity was esteemed by all parties. In the changes from Dutch to English, and from English to Dutch, and again to English supremacy, he maintained a high position. The demagogue Lester, during his usurped authority, found in Bayard a formidable impediment, and caused him to be indicted for high treason. The judge—Atwood—like another Jeffries, compelled the jury to find him guilty and sentenced him to be hung. He appealed to Queen Anne, and was pardoned (see Howell's State Trials, vol. xiv.). Lester was subsequently tried and convicted of high treason, and hung.*

Nicholas was several times mayor of New York, and when not mayor was generally an alderman. He died in 1711, leaving a son Samuel. His descendants intermarried with the Livingstons and Van Renssaelaers of Albany, and many of them, through the course of a hundred years, were often aldermen and sometimes mayors of New York city.† Samuel Bayard (a descendant of Nicholas), who was the owner of the land now covered by the city of Hoboken, took a military commission from the British. After the war of the Revolution commenced, his property was confiscated, and bought by Col. John Stevens, whose grandchildren (Samuel Bayard, late of Princeton, being their great-grandfather), will inherit it ; their father, a son of Col. John Stevens, having married Martha Dod, grand-daughter of Samuel Bayard.

The greater number of the Bayards of New York were Whigs, when the war of the Revolution commenced. A few were Tories, and emigrated to Nova Scotia, where their descendants are now living.

* See Brodhead's History of New York, vol. 2, and
            Smith's   do   do   do page 233.
* Valentine's History of New York.

APPENDIX G.

LEWIS PINTARD.

LEWIS PINTARD, great-grandfather of General Bayard, was born in New York, in 1732; his father a French Huguenot, having emigrated from France some years previous to the Revocation of the Edict of Nantes. When he was sixteen years old, his father died, and he immediately took charge of the business of his father, who was an importing merchant. Before the troubles which led to the Revolutionary war, he some years paid more than one third of the port charges of New York city. He was a cousin of Elias Boudinot, and they married the sisters of Richard Stockton, the signer of the Declaration of Independence. Captain Pintard, his brother, who, before the Revolutionary war, was an officer in the British army, married another sister. Captain Pintard was unwilling to fight for, or against the king, whose commission he held. He went, when the war commenced, to the island of Madeira, accompanied by the only son of his brother Lewis, Marsden Pintard. When the war was over, Marsden Pintard was appointed Consul of the United States for Madeira. He and his father then became the chief importers of Madeira wine into the United States. Lewis Pintard, after the war, was among the first who engaged in trade to the East Indies, then first opened to Americans. Lewis Pintard's only daughter, Martha, married Samuel Bayard.

Elias Boudinot was Commissary-general of the Revolutionary army, and Lewis Pintard acted for him as his deputy. Mr Pintard entrusted the bulk of his fortune to his son (he having retired from business), who was ruined by the French spoliations of 1797–8, for which his heirs have a valid claim on the government. His nephew John Pintard (who, left an orphan when a child, was brought up by him as an adopted son), was one of the the most eminent merchants of New York, and a great benefactor of that city.

Walter Barrett, in his " *Old Merchants of New York,*" page 217, speaks of " the proud old mercantile race of Pintards, that have flourished in this city almost two hundred years." Of John Pintard he says, " the word *illustrious* applies as well as to any man that ever lived."

The following letter of Gen. Washington to Lieut-general Howe, British Commander-in-Chief, is to be found in Sparks' "Writings of Washington," vol. iv. page 287.

" HEADQUARTERS MORRISTOWN,
January 20th, 1777.

" SIR :—I take the liberty to propose the establishment of an officer to reside at New York, under parole, to transmit no intelligence but what belongs to his office; whose business it shall be to provide necessaries for such prisoners as fall into your hands. Perhaps the establishment of such an officer with proper credits, may put a stop to the many complaints which I am daily under the necessity of hearing, some of them probably without foundation, and others from the want of many things which you are not obliged to furnish the prisoners. The gentleman whom I would beg leave to recommend as a proper agent is *Mr. Lewis Pintard*, the bearer, a person well-known in New York, and of long established reputation as a considerable merchant."

APPENDIX H.

CAPTAIN WILLIAM BAYARD.

WILLIAM BAYARD, late Captain United States Army, a double cousin of General Bayard, (their fathers being brothers, married sisters, daughters of the Rev. George Dashiell), was at San Antonio, Texas, when the war commenced on a visit to his uncle J. Yellot Dashiell, formerly surgeon in United States Army, more recently Adjutant-general of Texas during the rebellion. Having refused to stay in Texas, he was put under moderate restraint. Soon after, Charles Anderson, (brother of Gen. Anderson in command of Fort Sumter, and subsequently Lieutenant-governor of Ohio), was intercepted on his attempt to leave Texas, and placed with Bayard under the same restraint. They soon came to a common understanding to escape to the North. Through the aid of Union friends in San Antonio, Bayard and Anderson procured mules and started for the Mexican frontier, and after many narrow escapes in Mexico (where for safety they had separated), they arrived in New York in the winter of 1861. Mr. Anderson reached New York first, he immediately visited the father of young Bayard and expressed a high opinion of his gallantry and courage and his (Mr. A's) great obligation to him for his assistance in escaping from Texas. He said that as soon as William arrived, he must come to Washington, and every effort would be made by Mr. Anderson and his friends to procure him a commission in the army, which he was anxious to obtain.

Without delay after his arrival he proceeded to Washington, and was introduced by Mr. Anderson to the President and Secretary of War, and his merits properly represented. He was promised a commission as a second-lieutenant in the army, and in the meantime joined his cousin then Colonel of the First Pennsylvania cavalry, and was made by him battalion-adjutant. He was with General Bayard in the Falmouth night encounter, April eighteenth, 1862, and foremost in the fight. He was with his regiment throughout all the campaign of General Pope in Virginia. He participated in the battle of Cedar Mountain, and the second battle of Bull Run, and was with General Bayard in the valley of the Shenandoah in pursuit of Jackson. In September, the grade of battalion-adjutant having been abolished, he become volunteer-aide to his cousin. He was on leave of absence for a few days, when the battle of Fredericksburg took place. After that event, application was again made in his behalf for a commission. It was promised but not bestowed. But the whole heart of this noble young man was devoted to his country, and he determined to fight for her, with or without commission. He therefore, February 1863, enlisted as a private in the Fourth cavalry, (formerly the First), the regiment to which his cousin had belonged. He served in the ranks as a private with that regiment then in Tennessee, under Rosecrans in the campaign of Chickamauga. His gallantry and soldierly conduct were soon rewarded with promotion, and in October 1863, he was commissioned second-lieutenant; December 1864, brevet first-lieutenant for meritorious services in pursuit of Hood ; in April 1865, for gallantry in charging with his regiment the earthworks at Selma Alabama, brevet-captain and brevet-major ; and in July, 1866, was commissioned captain.

During his progress from a private to first-lieutenant, and brevet-major, he served in all the campaigns from Chickamauga, in the summer of 1863, to Chattanooga, Kenesaw Mountain, Atlanta, Nashville, and Selma.

After the war, at his own request, he was transferred to the Ninth Cavalry, then stationed on the western frontier of Texas.

In January 1871, by virtue of " General Order No. 1," Adjutant-general's Office, Washington, January second, 1871, he was placed on the list of supernumeraries, and dropped from the rolls : a case of flagrant and wanton injustice.

APPENDIX I.

REPORT OF MAJOR-GEN. W B. FRANKLIN.

(*Battle of Fredericksburg, Va.*)

" HEADQUARTERS LEFT GRAND DIVISION, }
    January 2d, 1863. }

" GENERAL :—I have the honor to make the following report of the operations of the Left Grand Division, from the eleventh to the fifteenth ult :

" On the tenth ult., I was directed to march to the bank of the Rappahannock, at the point determined for crossing, by means of two pontoon bridges below Fredericksburg, at a distance of about one and a quarter miles. At five o'clock A. M., on the eleventh ult., both corps started by separate roads, and arrived at the designated point about half-past seven A. M. The state of things at the bridges at this time was the following: Both bridges were in course of construction ; the lower about two-thirds finished, the upper about half finished. At nine o'clock, the lower bridge was entirely completed, at eleven o'clock, both were reported as completed, and passable for troops of all arms. The enemy made but feeble efforts to prevent the construction of the bridges.

The fact of the completion of the bridges having been reported to the Commanding-general, I was directed to keep
my position until further orders, taking care to prevent
any danger of their destruction by the enemy. At four
P. M., I was instructed to cross my whole command,
which order was shortly afterwards modified, so that my
orders were to cross about a brigade to ensure the safety
of the bridges. Davis' brigade of Newton's division,
Smith's corps, crossed with great enthusiasm, and took
position on the south bank about dark. Some of the
troops of Brook's division also crossed, but returned in
obedience to the orders as modified. Devins' brigade
drove away the enemy's pickets from the houses near the
crossing, threw out a line of pickets to the left and front,
and held the position during the night.

" At daylight on the morning of the twelfth, Smith's
corps began to cross. It was followed by Bayard's brigade of cavalry, which went immediately to the front to
make a reconnoissance. Reynolds' corps followed Bayard, and by one o'clock P. M., the whole of the grand
division was on the south bank of the river. The crossing was made in excellent order without the slightest
confusion or stoppage. Smith's corps had been previously ordered in compliance with the directions of the
Commanding-general, to form parallel to the old Richmond road with two divisions in front and one in reserve.
Reynolds' corps was to form at nearly right angles to
Smith's ; his right resting on Smith's, and his left on the
river. Two divisions were to be in line of battle and one
in reserve. The artillery was to be posted and used according to the direction of the Corps-commanders, as

the nature of the ground and position of the enemy might determine. .

" The dispositions indicated were made in the face of some slight opposition by the enemy's skirmishers, and a spiteful though nearly harmless fire from his artillery, and by four 'o clock the troops were in positions assigned to them. The ground on which the troops were disposed is in general a plain. It is cultivated and much cut up by hedges and ditches. The old Richmond road traverses the plain from right to left about one mile from the river, and nearly parallel to it. This road is bordered on both sides by an earthern parapet and ditch, and is an exceedingly strong feature in the defence of the ground, had the enemy chosen to hold it. On the right of my position is a deep run, and on the left about one mile in front of Reynolds' is Massaponax Creek. Both streams are tributaries of the Rappahannock. The plain is bordered by a range of high hills in front, which stretches from Fredericksburg to the Massaponax, nearly parallel to the old Richmond road, about five hundred or six hundred yards from it ; at the foot of the range of hills is the railroad. The ravine through which Deep Creek runs, passes through the hills near the centre of my front. Two brigades of Brook's division, Smith's corps, were in front of Deep Creek, forming the extreme right. The remainder of Smith's troops were in rear and to the left of Deep Creek, Reynolds' corps being about one mile from the Massaponax. The enemy had artillery on the hills and in the valley of Deep Creek, in the wood near Reynolds' right and on the Massaponax, so that the whole field was surrounded by it, except the right flank. His infantry appeared in all directions around the position. In front of Reynolds' right, the forest extends to the old Richmond road, coming nearer the river there, than at any other point in the vicinity of my position. The railroad traverses the forest.

" About a quarter to eight o'clock, on the morning of the thirteenth, Brigadier-general Hardie arrived from general headquarters, and informed me verbally of the designs of the Commanding-general in reference to the attack ; and that written orders would soon arrive by an aide-de-camp. These orders arrived soon after eight o'clock. In the meantime I had informed General Reynolds that his corps was to make the attack indicated by General Hardie ; and he ordered Meade's division to the point of attack to be supported by Gibbon's division. As Smith's corps was in position when the order of attack was received, and as a change of the line would have been attended with great risk at that time, and would have caused much delay, I considered it impracticable to add his force to that about to make the attack. I thought also that General Reynolds' force of three divisions would be sufficient to carry out the spirit of the order ; the words of it being, ' you will send out at once a division at least ————————taking care to keep it well supported and its line of retreat open.'

" At half-past eight o'clock, General Meade's division moved forward about five hundred yards, and turning to the right pushed towards the wood near the Bowling Green road. It was met by a severe fire of artillery. The fire was answered by the artillery of Reynolds' corps, which in the course of two hours or more silenced the enemy's batteries. The woods in which the enemy's infantry was posted, were then shelled for more than half-an-hour, and

Meade's division immediately afterwards moved on to the attack.

" In the meantime the two divisions of General Stoneman's corps which had been detailed as supports, and were then at the bridges, I ordered over to the support of General Reynolds. The advance of General Meade, was made under a general fire of the enemy's batteries, which was answered by all of Reynolds' and Smith's batteries, so that the artillery action became general along the whole line. Meade passed into the woods, carried them, crossed the railroad and gained the crest of the hill, capturing two flags, and about two hundred prisoners. At the crest of the hill the combat was kept up for some time. At the same time Gibbon's division advanced, crossed the railroad, entered the woods, took some prisoners, driving back the first line of the enemy. But the woods were so dense that the connection between Meade and his line could not be kept up.

" In consequence of this fact, Meade's line which was vigorously attacked by a large column of fresh troops, could not hold its ground and was repulsed, leaving the woods at a walk but not in order. Generals Reynolds and Meade rallied them beyond the Bowling Green road. Gibbon's division was also repulsed shortly afterwards. Just as Meade was repulsed, two regiments of Berry's brigade, Birney's division, Stoneman's corps, which had just arrived, were thrown into the woods on Gibbon's left. They also were soon driven out.

" While Meade's division was getting rallied, the remainder of Birney's division came up and drove the enemy from the front of the woods where he had appeared in strong force. This division with the aid of the artillery soon drove the enemy back to shelter, and he did not again appear. It also materially aided in saving Hall's battery, then seriously threatened. Gibbon's division then fell back in good order to its position of the morning and was relieved by General Sickles' division of Stoneman's corps, which took the position Gibbon had previously held. As the enemy made a serious demonstration on Reynolds' left, as soon as his disposition of Meade's division was discovered, he ordered General Doubleday's division to that part of the field. This division soon drove off the enemy's artillery forcing him to leave the river bank on this side of the Massaponax. Our troops advanced on the left and occupied the position held by the enemy in the morning.

" The operations on the left were materially aided by Captain De Russey, who brought his batteries opposite the mouth of Massaponax Creek, and drove the enemy from several artillery positions. But we were annoyed continually by firing from the other side of the Massaponax from long range guns. Little harm, however, was done by them. When Birney's and Sickles' divisions were placed in position, it had become too late to organize another attack before dark, and all of the troops under my command had either been engaged or were in line, except Newton's division, Smith's corps, which was held in reserve for both corps after the whole of Reynolds' corps had been engaged.

" Burn's division of Wilcox's corps was guarding the bridges, and on many accounts it would have been imprudent to have taken it away.

" While the engagement was progressing on the left, Smith's line of skirmishers was nearly constantly engaged, and his artillery did good service. An attempt was made to advance the skirmishers' line in front of Gen. Brook's division, which at first was unsuccessful as the supports of the skirmishers were falling back, they were attacked in heavy force and met with severe loss. The position of the enemy in this part of the field being exceedingly strong the attempt to advance here was abandoned. On Sunday the fourteenth, there was no change in the positions of the troops. A desultory cannonading, and a brisk skirmish fight along the whole line were carried on during the day with, I presume, about equal loss on both sides.

"On Monday the fifteenth, no change took place until about six 'o clock P. M. I was at that time at general headquarters, and was directed to recross my command during the night. The orders were at once telegraphed to General Smith, who was directed to make the preliminary arrangements, commencing the movement on the left. Upon my return to my headquarters about seven P. M., I found that the movement was just commencing. It was successfully completed during the night, so that at four A. M., of the sixteenth, all of the troops and material were on this side of the river and the men in camp.

"Our losses in killed and wounded on Saturday were heavy. The numerical list has already been transmitted to headquarters. The list of names has not yet been out, but will soon be finished and transmitted.

"*Brigadier-general Bayard, commanding cavalry division,* was killed by a piece of shell while at my headquarters, where he remained at my request to receive such orders as might be necessary for the cavalry. The loss of this gallant young general, is a severe blow to his arm of the service, and in him the country has lost one of its most dashing and gallant cavalry officers.

" Brigadier-general Jackson of Meade's division, was killed while leading his troops into action.   He had already shown distinguished gallantry on the day of his death, and his brigade under his command had defended the construction of the bridges on the previous day. Our losses in field officers is heavy, and I respectfully refer you to the accompanying report for their names.

" Nothing could be finer than the behaviour of the troops from the eleventh to the fifteenth ult., under fire, with little exception during the whole time, and exposed on a plain nearly surrounded with the enemy's artillery, they were steady and brave, and I never saw less straggling.

" I desire to express my thanks to Major-generals Reynolds and Smith, and Brigadier-general Stoneman, for their valuable assistance they rendered me in managing their commands.

" The Quartermaster and Commissary depots were well regulated by Lieutenant-colonel Tolles and Captain Sturdevant.   The men were rationed as regularly as though we had been in a permanent camp.

" The ambulance corps was well managed by Captain J. Howell Robinson.

" The remainder of my staff rendered efficient service, and I respectfully recommend them to the attention of the Commanding-general.   They are :

" Lieut.-Col. E. R. Platt, A. J. G.

" Maj. M. T. Mc Mahon, A. D. C.

" Capt. John T. Baker,   "

"   "   J. C. Jackson,   "

" Lieut. D. Lynn,   "

" Capt. James Starr and Lieut's. Albert E. Morrow

and E. N. Carpenter of the Lancer regiment, who were detailed as extra aides-de-camp, rendered very efficient services. Surgeons Chas. O'Leary and J. T. Heard, medical directors of the sixth and first Corps, in the absence of a medical director of the left grand division, were exceedingly efficient and energetic in the performance of their appropriate duties."

(signed)   " W. B. FRANKLIN.
" *Major-general Commanding left grand division.*"

To Major-general John G. Parke, Chief of staff.

APPENDIX J.

COLONEL A. V. COLBURN.

THE following letter from St. Louis, giving a rapid sketch of the military history of Col. Colburn will gratify those who loved and honored that noble soldier. No officer in the Union army was more universally loved and admired. Gentle, kind and affectionate to his friends, no braver man drew his sword in the late war. But he was not only among the " bravest of the brave," but he was a prudent discreet and sagacious officer and worthy of the post of confidential aide to the Commander-in chief. He survived his friend Bayard only about six months. Had he lived to the close of the war he would have risen to a very high rank.

ST. LOUIS, *June* 18*th*, 1863.

" Lieutenant-colonel Colburn, formerly Assistant-Adjutant-general on General McClellan's staff, who has been acting in the same capacity in this department for some time past, died last night after a few days illness.

SKETCH OF LIEUTENANT-COLONEL COLBURN.

" Lieutenant-colonel Albert V Colburn, formerly on he staff of Major-general McClellan, and recently Assistant-Adjutant-general to Major-general Schofield, commanding Department of the Missouri, was a native of Vermont, and entered the Military Academy at West Point as a cadet in 1851.   He graduated on the thirtieth of June 1855, in the same class with General Weitzel, General Averill, Adjutant-general Ruggles, Colonel Torbezt and other noted officers of the Union.   On the first of July 1855, he was brevetted second-lieutenant of the Second cavalry, and on the first of October of the same year was transferred to the First cavalry, with his full rank.

"When he entered the First cavalry the regiment was under charge of Colonel (afterwards Major-general) Sumner.   He went through the Kansas campaign, and during the time acted as quartermaster of the regiment, and acting-captain of Company B, at that time under command of Captain (now General) John Sedgwick.   In the winter of 1856, in the camp at Nebraska line, he had some hard words with Captain Walker, since an officer of rank in the rebel army.   Captain Walker abused every free State man, for which sentiment Lieutenant Colburn chased Captain Walker out of the tent.   From June, 1858, to 1861, he held the important position of regimental-adjutant.   He took part in the Cheyenne expedition, under Colonel Sumner.   The whole command during this expedition lived for twenty days on fresh beef alone.   He was next appointed aide to Colonel Sumner, who was placed in command of the Department of the West, with headquarters at St. Louis.

"At the commencement of the rebellion he brought eleven companies from the Western Department to Fort Leavenworth.   He was brevetted captain, dating from

July 1861, and was ordered to the command of two companies, which were sent forward from Washington, and led the same two companies, A and I, First cavalry—now known as the Fourth cavalry—during the whole day of the first battle of Bull Run. They were the last to leave the field of battle. For this act of gallantry he was, on the twenty-eighth of September 1861, appointed on the staff of General McClellan, with the rank of lieutenant-colonel—his full rank of captain of cavalry having been given him on August the third—and during every action he was generally among the most gallant. During the seven days' struggle he was about the last man to leave the field, and not then until the train and artillery had been secured. He was in every battle of the peninsula and in Maryland, and was highly respected by both officers and men. From the time he entered the service in 1855, he had been constantly on duty, not having once visited his family during the whole time. When General McClellan was, in November 1862, relieved by General Burnside, Colonel Colburn left the field with him as one of his personal staff; but the War Department disapproved of his leaving, and ordered his arrest. This summary action, without apparent cause, created a great deal of dissatisfaction among his personal friends and fellow officers. He was, however, shortly after released and ordered to the field with General Burnside.

"On the twenty-fourth of last May, when Major-general Schofield assumed command of the Department of the Missouri, he announced Lieutenant-colonel A. V Colburn as his Assistant-Adjutant-general in charge of the department office. Since that time he has ably administered the duties of his position until within a few days, when be was stricken down with a fatal illness. He died during the night of June seventeenth, much re-gretted."

APPENDIX K.

LETTER FROM GEN. McCLELLAN.

EXTRACT of a letter from General George B. McClellan, December twentieth, 1862:

"*To Samuel J. Bayard, Esq.,*

"MY DEAR SIR :—

"Allow me to offer you my most sincere and earnest sympathy in the great bereavement you have suffered ;— a loss shared by the army and the nation ; for in soldierly merit, devotion and courage, your son stood among the foremost and most gifted of our generals.

"It is gratifying in the extreme to me to know that, even in his last moments, he thought of his former commander ; and I shall ever remember that last tribute of his regard as one of the most sad and touching, yet gratifying incidents of my life."

THE LAST WORDS OF GENERAL BAYARD.

The correspondent of the Cincinnati Commercial, in describing the death of General Bayard, says :

"During the night he was in perfect possession of his faculties, and dictated several letters—one to his father, one to the young lady to whom he was engaged to be married, and one to Colonel Colburn, of General McClellan's staff. In the letter to the latter he said: 'Tell McClellan that my last regret, as a military man, is that I did not die serving under him.'"

14*

APPENDIX L.

MORTUARY TRIBUTES.

EXTRACT from a letter of Gen. William B. Franklin to S. J. Bayard. Dated Hartford, June thirtieth, 1873:

"Your son was assigned to my command. The day before he was killed he made an important reconnoissance with a part of his command on our right; was severely engaged, and discovered the strength and position of the enemy, gaining important information, which he reported to me.

"During the next morning he held his command in readiness for any orders he might receive; executed several orders as to cavalry duties, and was himself present at my headquarters from about noon until the time he was struck.

"His character as a soldier needs no eulogy. Among our cavalry generals he was, in my opinion, easily first; and, had he lived, his career would have been as brilliant and successful as that of any general officer. He would have won one of the prizes of the war.

" Unaccountable as it may be, there is a certain *glamour* about a name among soldiers; and much was expected of your son because his name was Bayard. In my recollection of him there is nothing that affects me so intimately as this—that among his comrades it was judged that he had come up to their expectations.

" The day of your son's death was, in many respects, the saddest day of the war to a true Union soldier. Inefficiency ruled the hour."

GEORGE DASHIELL BAYARD.

(From the *Press* of Philadelphia.)

" *To the Editor of the Press:*

"Sir: He is dead! Was it yesterday we saw him at the National Capital? lithe and graceful in figure, with an eye which lent brightness, and never yet knew shadow till he met Death on the field of battle. Alas! that laurels so green, worn so early, and won so bravely, should be wet with the tears of those who knew, and all who loved George Dashiell Bayard, the youthful soldier, now lost to his country, from his place among her noblest, her bravest and her best!

" When we last saw General Bayard, we were struck with the entire absence of ostentation in his bearing.

" It was in Washington, where he awaited orders, and, though rarely appearing in public, it was his custom to appear without any insignia of his rank.

" He was as modest as he was brave; yet he was conscious of his destiny. His face bore the impress of courage and determination. It is scarcely three years since he graduated with distinction at West Point. He then served for a time upon the Indian frontier, where he received a serious wound. When this 'rebellion of wicked weakness against righteous strength' startled the world, he hastened to stand in the front of battle and on the side of his country. Where danger was thickest General Bayard's sword flashed like the plume of Henry of Navarre. In the dissensions and jealousies which weaken the service and embitter the soldier's life, he took no part ; he knew and felt that for him the hour of danger was the hour for duty. Like the Chevalier Bayard of history, he was a knight ' *without fear and without reproach.*'

" In the bold, dashing, rapid raid of cavalry, General Bayard has been compared to Philip Kearny, 'the one-armed devil ' of infantry.

"With the same sweeping gallantry, he united, we are informed, more prudence, or, at least, greater evenness of temper. Had he lived another year he would have been major-general of cavalry.

" But he is gone ! The enemy will miss him. But none will mourn for him like the brave men he commanded, save the stricken hearts, so close to his own, to whom he leaves a deathless memory.

" As the soldiers of France answered for Latour D'Auvergne at roll-call, so will our heroic army in Virginia say of Dashiell Bayard, ' *He is dead on the field of honor.*' Let the young men who think it not 'graceful to enter this conflict on the side of a nation struggling for life bend low before the name of this youthful and heroic soldier, who has laid his life, dear to us all, upon the altar of his country.

" Let his sacrifice (alas ! that the rapacity of rebellion

demanded it), teach us to stand steadfastly beside the simple and glorious principles for which he has offered up his life!

"George Dashiell Bayard! with tenderness and reverence we leave thee.

" A grateful nation shall build a shrine for her *immortal dead*, and in the Westminster Abbey of America, we will pause before the names of Baker and Lyon, and Kearney and Bayard!   Again, farewell!

" ' We give thee to God ; to thy place in thy country's heart ; with tears, with affection, with gratitude and with prayer.'

"I am sir, with great respect, etc.,

"J. M S."

BAYARD.

(From the Philadelphia *Inquirer*.)

"This day, it is said, was appointed as the wedding-day of General Bayard.   But the terrible decrees of war have ordered otherwise.   Instead of leading a bride to the altar, his lifeless body is on its way to the tomb.   All the elements of romance are centered in his brief, brilliant and tragic career.   A soldier by nature, as well as by education, it was his day-dream while yet a subaltern, to command a regiment of cavalry.   But the object of his young ambition seemed to be far off until the outbreak of the rebellion, when it suddenly came within his reach.   Rapidly advancing by virtue of ' gallant and meritorious conduct in the field,' he not only achieved the command of a regiment of horse, thus realizing the dream of his youth, but won also the star of a general officer.   Throughout

come on and try again on the 1st of next September.
Unless he exerts himself very industriously he will fail
again.   I regret his failure, as I know you and his father
have been friends all your lives.   Mr. Brown, too, will
regret the failure of his appointee.*

"I am also sorry to say that Dickinson, of Iowa, is
also rejected.   I felt an interest in him because he was
from the Congressional District from which, if we had
remained in Iowa, I expected to come as a cadet.

"One named C., of Michigan ; another B., from Connec-
ticut ; J., from Alabama ; T., from Ohio ; G., from Pennsylvania ; H., from Virginia ; complete the unfortunate
eight.   G. was appointed at large.   Parents or guardians,
before they send their boys here, ought to be assured
that they are capable.   All that is required is, what
every boy of ten years of age can acquire at any common
school—provided they have any capacity for learning.
If they have it not, it is cruel to subject them to the
mortification of rejection, which if they have any sensi-
bility, must cloud all their future lives.

"As to Campbell, of Texas, of whom you spoke in one
of your letters, he assumes so many nativities that,
though he has been here a week, to-day is the first day
that I was aware of it.   Instead of being from Texas, he
was never there, though his father lives in that State.

"When I asked him where he was from, he replied

* Mr. Nevius, though he returned to West Point, did not continue there.   He subsequently became a Civil Engineer, and in that
capacity was in the service of the Camden and Amboy R. R. Company for many years, and highly esteemed.   He died while in the
employ of that Company.   He was a son of Judge Nevius, one of
the Judges of the Supreme Court of New Jersey.

from South Carolina. I made no further inquiry, and did not see him again until this morning. I find that he has generally lived in South Carolina, though he resided three years in Cuba. He is appointed from Alabama, and his father now lives in Texas. In consequence of all this, it was entirely owing to accident that I found him out—which I was desirous of doing, as his father is a friend of Uncle Dashiell.

"Campbell belongs to Company D., while I belong to Company A., so that our rooming together is out of the question. Gaston is a fine-looking fellow, but has engaged his room-mates.

"To-morrow, I will receive my musket, and after that will have to learn the musket drill. I expect I will receive an order in a few days to obtain my uniform. The whole of Company D. received orders for their uniforms to-day."

his service he was active, dashing, brilliant, successful ;
so that when he received his death-wound, at twenty-
eight years of age, his fame had spread over the whole
country as a noble gentleman and a chivalrous soldier.

" His death-scene is as worthy of admiration as his
career in life.   Calmly asking the surgeon who examined
his ghastly and gaping wound if there was ' any hope,'
and being told there was none, he turned with undis-
turbed composure, and without a murmur of pain, to ' set
his house in order ' both for this world and the next.
Everything was attended to with serene self-possession,
and having finished his work, he yielded up his life in
the service of his country.   In that fearful conflict at
Fredericksburg, where deadliest the death-bolts showered

> ' They met no nobler heart than thine,
> Young, gallant,' BAYARD."

EXTRACT FROM PYNE'S HISTORY.

PYNE, in his history of the First New Jersey cavalry,
thus refers to the death of General Bayard, page 135 :
" And then came to us with a shock, the intelligence
of the mortal wound received by our beloved brigade
commander.

" Rarely has there been a man who conciliated so perfectly, affection for the man and respect for the officer.
Every officer and man in the brigade, felt that he had
lost a personal friend, and the mourning of the troops
was sincere and enduring.   He met death calmly as he
had met every accident of life, and the day that was to
have united him to the woman of his love, closed upon
him in his coffin."

EXTRACT FROM A LETTER OF THE CHAPLAIN OF THE IRA HARRIS CAVALRY, (Second New York).

"A LITTLE after noon, we heard that General Bayard, our division commander was mortally wounded. At the hospital we found him. Of all the ghastly wounds I saw that day, his was the most awful. It needed but a glance to see, as he calmly stated to those who visited him, that 'his days on earth were numbered.' If his wound had been a mere scratch he could not have been more cool, quiet, and collected. He talked calmly of his death, as a settled thing and only inquired particularly, how much time he had left on earth. He was told perhaps forty-eight hours. He did not live twenty-four. My heart sank within me as he gave me his hand in farewell, and I almost murmured, ' Why are the best taken!'"

THE FIRST PENNSYLVANIA RESERVE CAVALRY.

Sketch of its history.

[From the Philadelphia *Inquirer*.]

"THE Reserve Corps kept together until the Spring campaign of 1862 opened, when it was deemed expedient to mass the cavalry. From that time on, the history of the corps and the regiment of cavalry has been different. The corps fought and won for themselves an undying reputation, and returned to the state in June. This regiment was absent from the army in one of Sheridan's raids, when the corps went away, and was left alone to serve out the extreme limit of its time in the field.

"As a synopsis of its operations individually, I will commence at its head. The first head of the regiment was Captain Hastings, of the regular army, who was made colonel of the regiment, August, 1861, but on account of unavoidable circumstances, he was not able to accept the proffered honor, and for a short time the organization was incomplete. But the material composing the regiment was such as would honor the state and its commander. It was not destined to remain long in this chaotic condition ; ' but as water seeks its own level,' so did this body of brave men find a commander in the gallant and lamented George D. Bayard, August the sixteenth, 1861, who was then made colonel of the First Pennsylvania Reserve Cavalry.

" The first victorious blood spilt was in participating with the Reserve Corps at the victory of Drainsville, December twenty-first, 1861. The winter was passed at Langley, five miles from Chain Bridge, in picketing and scouting. On one of these scouts the assistant-surgeon, Samuel L. Alexander, a young man of rare ability and promising usefulness, was killed by a party of the enemy in ambush. During the winter two more companies were added to the regiment making in all twelve companies, from as many different counties as there were companies.

" The spring campaign opened, and our young but experienced colonel was anxious to cross sabres with the foe. His first opportunity was at Falmouth, April eighteenth, 1862, where his officers to his satisfaction, displayed the true metal, and the men the proper courage to make soldiers. For this and many other brave and meritorious acts Colonel Bayard was promoted Brigadier-general. The First Pennsylvania Reserve Cavalry and the First New Jersey were placed under his command, thus forming the first brigade of cavalry in the Army of the Potomac. These two regiments, by the way, have fought side by side for three years, and been latterly called the ' twin regiments.'

" With these regiments, Hall's Maine battery and one battalion of the Bucktails, commanded by Lieut.-col. Kane, constituted Bayard's brigade. He is next heard from in the Shenandoah Valley, where he led the advance of General Fremont's army in hot pursuit after Jackson's retreating forces. The regiment participated in all the engagements of this campaign, among which those of Strasburg, Harrisonburg and Cross Keys were most prominent, commanded by Col. Owen Jones and Lieut. col. S. D. Barrows. Another turn of the kaleidoscope, and the regiment again appears before Jackson ; this time his advancing column on the Rapidan, south of Culpepper, skirmishing and fighting each day for a week, until it finally terminated in the pitched battle at Cedar Moun tain, August ninth, 1862, in which the first battalion of the regiment made the greatest sabre-charge of the war thus far, led by Major R. J. Falls. In the wake of this battle came Pope's famous retreat, in which it was not Brandy Station, Sulphur Springs and Bull Run alone, but daily fighting for the cavalry for two weeks, for Gen. Bay- ard covered the retreat.

" When the army again advanced, Bayard's brigade was in the advance, cleared the road of the enemy and surprised them at Rappahannock bridge. At the battle of Fredericksburg, it was the first to cross the river on the left wing, and had the honor of initiating the fight in which the loved, the lost, the longed-for Bayard, at that time considered the first cavalry officer in the Army of the Potomac, fought his last battle. After this battle, of December twelfth and thirteenth, 1862, the regiment went into winter-quarters at Belle Plains, (Camp Bayard, in honor of the lamented hero), under command of General Gregg, successor to General Bayard. In the meantime, Colonels Jones and Barrows resigned, and their places were filled by Lieut.-col. J. P. Taylor and Major David Gardiner, respectively promoted. The battles of Brandy Station, June ninth, 1863, followed by Aldie and Upperville, Gettysburg, Shepherdstown, Muddy Run, Culpepper, Sulphur Springs, Auburn and Bristow, closing with New Hope Chapel, November twenty-seventh, showed them to be commanders worthy of their predecessors, and emulated their example in shedding new laurels upon the regiment in every battle in which they led it.

" The winter of 1863–4, was spent in camp at Warrenton, but not a winter of ease. The picketing must needs be severe, when Moseby was making night hideous, and the passes of the Blue Ridge were open to the enemy on our right wing. During the greater part of the time in the last year Colonel Taylor was commanding the brigade, and Lieutenant-colonel Gardiner the regiment. The spring campaign opened about the first of May, the entire calvary corps under the command of General Sheridan, whose bold and skilful generalship made him a terror to his foes, and won for his command an enviable and lasting reputation. The First Pennsylvania Reserve Cavalry, was more particularly under the command of General Gregg, one of Pennsylvania's noble sons, who has won for himself undying laurels. During the campaign the regiment has added to its roll of honor the battles of Todd's Tavern, Childsburgh, Yellow Tavern, Richmond Heights, Hawe's Shop, Trevillian Station,

White House, St. Mary's Church, Gravel Hill, Nos. 1
and 2, and the series of late engagements along the Weldon railroad.   The regiment now leaves the field after
this three years of hard service spent at the front, with a
reputation second to no cavalry regiment in the service.
Their war path may be traced by the graves of fallen
comrades, and by the blood of hundreds who have fallen
in the shock of battle, but still live to emulate our just
cause by a living patriotism.   About two hundred remain
as veterans for three years more, and about four hundred
return to their native state and homes, bearing with
them the marks of their hard service.

" The Field and Staff, at the organization of the regiment, was as follows:—

" Colonel George D. Bayard,

" Lieutenant-colonel Jacob Higgins,

" Major Owen Jones,

" Surgeon David Stanton,

" Assistant-surgeon S. L. Alexander,

" Adjutant S. D. Barrows,

" Chaplain J. H. Beale,

" Quartermaster R. R. Corson,

" Present Field and Staff:—

" Colonel J. P. Taylor,

" Lieutenant-colonel David Gardiner,

" Major R. J. Falls.

" Major J. M. Gaston,

" Adjutant W P. Lloyd,

" Surgeon G. B. Hotchkins,

" Assistant-surgeon L. E. Atkinson,

" Assistant-surgeon R. H. Tuit,

" Chaplain J. H. Beale,

" Quartermaster G. H. Baker,

" Color-sergeant H. A. Wood.

" Colonel J. P Taylor, is the only one of the original captains now in the regiment, and Chaplain J. H. Beale, is the only one of the original staff.

" LIST OF OFFICERS KILLED IN FIRST PENNSYLVAVIA
RESERVE CAVALRY.

" Assistant-surgeon S. L. Alexander, Drainsville, November 27, 1861.

" First-lieut. A. Reed, G, St. Mary's Church, June 24, 1864.

" Second-lieut. W. H. Butcher, D, Cedar Mountain, August 9, 1862.

" Second-lieut. S. W. Greenlee, F, Hawe's Shop, May 28, 1864.

" Second-lieut. D. H. Wilson, A, Barker's Mill, June 2, 1864.

" Second-lieut. D. S. Buxton, L, White House, June 21, 1864.

" Second-lieut. J. S. Wright, M, St. Mary's Church, June 24, 1864.

" Second-lieut. G. W. Lyons, I, Carter's Mill, September 6, 1863.

" LIST OF WOUNDED IN ACTION.

" Colonel George D. Bayard, Drainsville, December 20, 1861.

" Captain J. P. Taylor, C, Cedar Mountain, August 9, 1862.

" Lieut-colonel D. Gardiner, St. Mary's Church, June 24, 1864.

" Major R. J. Falls, Gravel Hill, No. 1, July 28, 1864.
" Major N. I. McEwen, Brandy Station, June 9, 1863.
" Captain T. Streck, H, May 24, 1862.
" Captain H. A. McDonald, D, Cedar Mountain, August 9, 1862.
" Captain A. Davidson, F, St. Mary's Church, June 24, 1864, died July 31, 1864.
" Captain N. S. Craft, H, Hawe's Shop, May, 28, 1864.
" First-lieut. S. H. Mucilenathen, C, Shepherdstown, July 11, 1863.
" First-lieut. J. Kelly, A, Shepherdstown, July 16, 1863.
" First-lieut. T E. Lucas, F, Brandy Station, June 9, 1863.
" First-lieut. M Kennedy, K, Hawe's Shop, May 28, 1864.
" Second-lieut. S. W Grenler, F, Brandy Station June 9, 1863.
" Second-lieut. S. Morgan, K, Rapidan, September 15, 1863.
" Second- lieut. D. S. Buxton, L, New Hope Chapel, November 27, 1863.

"STILL PRISONERS OF WAR IN THE HANDS OF THE
ENEMY:

" Captain William Lands, L ; Captain R. J. McNitt, C ; First lieutenant J. R. Kelly, C.

" Before leaving the front the regiment was drawn up in line, and the following order was read :—

" ' *Headquarters, First Pennsylvania Reserve Cavalry near Petersburg, Va., Aug.—*, 1864.—General Orders, No. 18.—Officers and soldiers of the First Pennsylvania Reserve Cavalry :—You have now experienced three years of terrible devastating war. You are familiar with its toils, its hardships, and its scenes of bloodshed. During this time there has been no toil that your manly efforts have not overcome, no hardships that you have not courted for your country's sake, no field of strife too terrible to prevent you flaunting your banner in the face of your traitorous foes, and in every instance have you borne it off in triumph. Many have been the fields upon which you have distinguished yourselves by your personal valor, from your first victorious blood spilt at Drainsville, down to those greener in your memory, such as Todd's Tavern, Childsburgh, Hawe's Shop, Barker's Mill, White House, St Mary's Church, and last but not least, upon the bloody summit of Malvern Hill, and along the Weldon railroad, are still sounding in your ears, and eternally engraven in your hearts.

" 'But you have now reached the goal of your worthy ambition. You have won for yourselves, your regiment, and your State, an invidious reputation.

" ' Officers and soldiers of the First Pennsylvania Reserve Cavalry, allow me, on this the eve of our separation, to express to you my heartfelt thanks for your implicit confidence and ready compliance with every order, your noble courage and unflinching bravery upon every field I have had the honor to lead you ; your military career has been a brave and clear record, in which you have acquitted yourselves like men.

" ' But the war is not ended. There are more battles

yet to be fought, and more lives to be offered upon the altar of liberty. For this end some of you remain ; and many more of you will soon be back again to battle in this your just and holy cause. But wherever you may answer to the bugle call, and upon whatever field you may strike the black shield of rebeldom, let the memory of your fallen comrades strengthen your arms and encourage your hearts, ever mindful that you were once members of the First Pennsylvania Reserve Cavalry.

" ' May the god of battles and of mercy be your shield and protection !   By order of

"'JOHN P. TAYLOR,
" ' *Colonel Commanding regiment.*'
"'Lieut. W P. LLOYD, *Adjutant.*'

" After the order was read to the regiment, which had been formed by Lieutenant-colonel Gardiner, Col. Taylor made the following remarks.

COLONEL TAYLOR'S REMARKS.

" ' MY BRAVE COMRADES:—We stand to-day upon the threshold of an event which, when we left our homes three years ago, the most prophetic heart scarcely dared anticipate. The scenes then rife in our midst, such as the memory of an insulted flag upon Fort Sumter, which cast a gloom of shame over every true American heart, and the blood of brothers spilt upon the streets of Baltimore, sprinkled, as it were, over every loyal heart in the North, the rushing of men to arms, and our souls inspired by the spirits of our fathers, nerved us to action; and from homes of comfort, luxury and ease, we rallied in defence of our country.

" ' Another turn of the kaleidoscope found us marshalled beneath the proud ensign of our glorious republic, no longer separate and distinct in thought and action, but the firm resolve of the farmer, the willing hand of the mechanic and laborer, the shrewd energy of the merchant, the potent influence of the student, all suddenly converted into the trained and disciplined soldier, with hearts that beat as one. What you were then, and what you have since proven yourselves, you owe to the mighty impulses of your first brave and noble commander, Colonel George D. Bayard; imbued with the influence of his mighty genius you saw the star of his glory rising and shining brighter and brighter in the military sphere ; and alas, too, to set before it had reached its zenith. Following in his wake, ever ready to stand by you in the hour of danger, to share with you your toils and hardships, to cheer you in the hour of conflict, following strictly in the footsteps of his illustrious predecessor, the champion of your rights and reputation, came your second colonel, Owen Jones.

" ' Officers and soldiers :—Through your confidence and esteem, I had the honor to be your next commander, and as such I deem it a high honor, to-day, to stand before the shattered remnant of a once large regiment, to thank you for your esteem and the willingness with which you have acceded to my every request and complied with my every command, and for the manner you have so nobly and faithfully discharged your duties as soldiers. I believe I am the only officer now left in the regiment who was present with the Governor and his Staff, and heard him christen the regiment the First Pennsylvania Reserve Cavalry Regiment. And it gives me pleasure to think we can return to our native state those colors, then intrusted to our care, tattered and torn though they be, without a tarnish or a stain upon the reputation of the regiment.

" ' Officers and soldiers of the First Pennsylvania Reserve Cavalry, you are the veterans of more than thirty engagements; your banner has proudly floated over almost every field in which this historic Army of the Potomac has been engaged. The graves of your comrades are strewn from Gettysburg to the James River. Your war-path may be traced by the the blood of your fallen heroes, but by the strength of justice and the might of mercy you have plumed your arms with honor and victory.

" ' Enlisted veterans, when you were re-enlisting, my lips were sealed from encouraging you, because circumstances, unavoidable, rendered my remaining with you impossible. Let not our leaving discourage you. Be faithful, obedient, prompt and cheerful in duty as you have always been. A hopeful country waits to crown you. We shall not forget you. We shall continue to breathe the desired hope and christian prayer, that you may soon be permitted to return to your homes; that the red-handed monster war, whose pestiferous breath blasts with withering death everything lovely on earth may be banished from our distracted land, and peace, sweet peace, again returning, shed evermore her heaven-born blessing on our fair Columbia's soil ! ' "

THE END.